THE CASE ER

Author's Note

Just as Shakespeare in modern dress is still Shakespeare, so history in modern dress is still history. Despite the pizzas, guns, cars and telephones, this fictional detective story is based on real, historical events during the early years of the Christian church in the 1st Century AD. (Notes on the historical background can be found under *From Mystery to History* at the back of this book.)

For old friends who have read Ben Bartholomew's previous published adventures, the events of this story occur shortly after *The Case of the Vanishing Corpse* and more than twenty years before *The Case of the Secret Assassin*.

© Beacon Communications Pty Ltd. 1994

First published in the U.K. 1995
by arrangement with Hodder Headline (Australia) Pty Limited

01 00 99 98 97 96 95   7 6 5 4 3 2 1

OM Publishing is an imprint of Send the Light Ltd.,
P.O. Box 300, Carlisle, Cumbria CA3 0QS

The right of Kel Richards to be identified as
the Author of this Work has been asserted by him in accordance
with the Copyright, Designs and Patents Act 1988.

All biblical quotations in this book are taken from
The Living Bible: A Thought-for-Thought Paraphrase
by Kenneth N. Taylor. Used by permission.

British Library Cataloguing in Publication Data

Richards, Kel
  Case of the Damascus Dagger
  I. Title
  823.914 [F]

ISBN 1-85078-195-8

Typeset in Australia by DOCUPRO
and Printed in the U.K. by Cox and Wyman Ltd., Reading

THE CASE OF
THE
DAMASCUS DAGGER

KEL RICHARDS

M
publishing
CARLISLE, UK

CHAPTER 1

'Are you sure he wants to see me?'

'I want you to see him, and that's what matters.'

'But he hates me. He'll get angry. And for a man in his condition . . .'

'The fever has such a grip on him that he's delirious. He won't even know you're in the room.'

In the sunny courtyard of a hillside villa, in one of the upper-middle-class suburbs of Damascus, Tabitha Mason and Dr Tullus Matthias stood talking. Their mood was anything but sunny.

'Your father's been ill for what, three days?' asked Tullus.

'That's right. Three days now,' Tabitha replied. 'But you know how stubborn he is, and he's refused to see a doctor.'

'What were the first symptoms?'

'Stomach cramps, then muscular pains, vomiting and feeling very weak.'

'And with all that, he still won't see a doctor?'

'His regular doctor is out of town at a so-called medical conference in Cairo. In fact, he's probably lying by a hotel swimming pool, ogling belly dancers.'

'But isn't there a *locum* at the practice while he's away?'

'Of course. But Pappa doesn't like him.'

'There are a lot of people your father doesn't like,

including me,' said Tullus, shaking his head sadly. 'You know he hates me! So why do you insist that I examine him?'

'He's delirious—almost unconscious—so he won't know. And *I* think you're the best doctor in the world,' Tabitha replied, clasping her hands behind Tullus's neck, pulling his face towards her, and kissing him long and passionately.

'Ah, but you're biased,' said Tullus with a smile when he came up for air.

'Love is not blind, it is very clear-sighted. Now, will you please go and examine Pappa? I'm getting really worried about him.'

Tullus picked up his black doctor's bag, gave Tabitha another peck on the lips, and walked resolutely into the sick man's room.

Tabitha paced restlessly around the courtyard, scuffing up the dust with her sandals, then sitting on the stone wall around the well in the middle of the courtyard, then pacing again for a while.

She was standing in the shade cast by the lemon tree in the corner of the courtyard near her father's room when at last Tullus emerged.

'How is he?'

'He appears to have some sort of viral infection. I've given him an injection to reduce the fever, and a broad-spectrum antibiotic. He should sleep peacefully now for some time. And sleep is the great healer—not me.'

'Will he be all right?'

'Your father is normally as fit as a Minoan bull—it'll take more than a virus to knock him out.'

'He'll recover?'

'I'm certain of it.'

'I told you that you were wonderful!' she said, and kissed him again.

'I'd better get back to my own patients now,' said Tullus, closing the clasps on his bag. 'I'll come back later this afternoon and see how he's doing.'

'What should we do in the meantime?'

'Don't disturb him. Let him sleep—that's what he needs.'

Tullus hurried back to his surgery to see his morning patients. At lunchtime he had a quick sandwich and tried to read a medical journal. But the midday heat had risen to its usual oppressive level and after half an hour he gave up trying to concentrate and did what the rest of the city did at midday—lay down for a siesta.

A slightly cooler breeze had sprung up by the time Tullus awoke. He got up and hurried back to the Mason household, to take a quick look at Malachi Mason before his evening surgery.

When he arrived he found the villa hushed and still—most of the household had not yet arisen from their siesta. In the courtyard a young slave named Quaresimus was sitting on a small wooden bench in the shade of the lemon tree.

'Has the old man stirred?' asked Tullus.

'No, sir,' replied the slave. 'There hasn't been a peep out of him.'

'Have you taken a look at him since I left?'

'Miss Tabitha told me not to, sir. Just to sit here in case he woke up and called out.'

'Fine. You stay here while I go and find Miss Mason.'

'Yes, sir.'

Tabitha's bedroom was next to her father's. Tullus

knocked on the door, which swung open almost at once.

'I got up when I heard your voice,' said Tabitha. She was still tying a belt around her tunic as she stepped out into the sunlight of the courtyard and gave Tullus a peck on the lips.

'How's Pappa?' she asked.

'I haven't seen him yet,' Tullus replied. 'Let's go and see him together.'

Tullus and Tabitha entered her father's bedroom and moved quietly over to his bed by the windowsill. The old man lay on the bed, an unmoving shape half covered by a sheet.

'He's still sleeping,' whispered Tabitha.

But Tullus had swooped down next to the bed. 'No he's not,' he said urgently, 'he's not breathing.'

'Pappa!' screamed Tabitha, collapsing to her knees by the side of the bed. She pulled at her father's body, rolling him completely onto his back. A dark trickle of dried blood ran from the corner of his mouth, and the hilt of a large silver dagger protruded from his chest.

'Pappa!' screamed Tabitha again, in great distress.

Tullus knelt down and examined the body. 'He's been dead for a couple of hours at least,' he said, moving over to comfort Tabitha.

He put his arms around her, and she buried her head in his shoulder and sobbed uncontrollably.

'Quaresimus—come here!' called Tullus.

The slave appeared in the doorway.

'Fetch one of the women, quickly. One of Miss Mason's personal servants. Then come straight back!'

Quaresimus scuttled away, returning a moment later with a young woman beside him.

4

'Oh, Miss! Miss! What's happened?' wailed the young woman as she saw Tabitha.

'Take your mistress back to her room,' said Tullus, 'and look after her.'

When they had gone he turned to the slave.

'Quaresimus—I want you to run and fetch the City Watch, at once!'

'Yes, sir. What's . . .'

'Just run and get them! Now!'

Once Quaresimus had gone Tullus Matthias turned back towards the body and looked at it thoughtfully. Who had killed Malachi Mason? And why?

Being careful not to touch anything, he leaned over and took a close look at the wound and weapon. Suddenly he felt as if someone had poured ice water over his heart. He recognised the dagger—there could be no mistaking it. The ornamental hilt was a distinctive piece of ancient Damascan silver work. It was his. And it had been his father's, grandfather's, and great-grandfather's before him.

Why had it been used to murder Malachi Mason and how had the murderer got hold of it?

Tullus felt very frightened.

The clatter of sandals on stone nearby told him the authorities had arrived. A young officer in the distinctive leather tunic and red cloak of the City Watch (copied from the uniform of the Roman army) approached him.

Tullus explained in a few words what he and Tabitha had found.

'Who witnessed the murder, sir?' asked the young officer.

'No-one—as far as I know.'

'Who was the last person to see the victim alive?'

'Probably me.'

'A professional visit?'

'Yes. I gave him a couple of injections late this morning, he was suffering from a serious viral illness.'

'And then what?'

'I left him here sleeping, with a slave on guard at the door.'

'I see. Would you mind staying with the body doctor, while I summon the Crime Squad?'

Tullus waited, alone with the corpse, and too stunned for clear thought. Through the wall he could hear Tabitha's sobs and the soothing voice of her maid. Time passed, but in his befuddled state Tullus had no idea how much.

At last there was a clatter of feet and the sound of voices. Half a dozen people bustled into the room—some in the uniform of the City Watch, some in plain clothes.

The man who appeared to be in charge was short and solid, with hunched shoulders and a weather-beaten, deeply lined face. He took a cursory look at the body, muttered, 'So this is the victim, eh?', then turned and approached Tullus.

'Tragg is my name,' he said, 'Captain Tragg, of the City Watch Crime Squad. And you, doctor, are our prime suspect in the murder of Malachi Mason.'

CHAPTER 2

'We want you to do it, Ben. You're the right man for the job.'

'No. No. I've already failed once, and I don't want to let you down again. I don't want another death on my conscience!'

'You're being foolish,' said Parmenas, ignoring my pleas.

'I saw Stephen die,' I said levelly. 'Death by stoning is not a nice way to go. And it was my fault. You hired me as Stephen's lawyer. It was my job to prepare his defence. I helped him write the speech that got him convicted and killed.'

'The court was out for blood, Ben,' said Timon. 'No defence would have made any difference.'

'And this case in Damascus is not like that,' insisted Parmenas. 'One of our people is facing a criminal charge—a trumped-up charge!'

'A charge of murder,' added Timon. 'And he is a doctor, not a murderer.'

'Please, Ben—go to Damascus. Defend Dr Matthias. If anyone can save him, you can.'

We were in the front room of Timon's house, with the shutters closed and the blinds drawn. Even though it was nearly midnight, we had to be careful. We were a community under siege.

Most of our fellow believers had already left Jerusalem—only Peter and the leaders were intending to stay. And the half-packed boxes and chests in the room signalled the imminent departure of Timon and his wife Dorcas.

'I don't know, I really don't know,' I muttered, running my fingers through my hair. 'Damascus . . . what legal system operates in Damascus?'

'The Roman system,' explained Timon.

'I studied all that stuff in my law degree years ago. And I haven't used it for a long time. I've been working as a private detective, not a lawyer.'

The others watched me carefully, while I paced back and forth over the large Turkish carpet in the middle of the floor. The dim candlelight, that was all we dared use, cast flickering shadows on the walls.

'Rachel is expecting me back in Caesarea tomorrow,' I said, still resisting what I knew in my heart I should do.

'Use my phone,' said Timon. 'Call her. Tell her what's come up. Tell her what her fellow believers are asking you to do.'

'All right, I'll call her. But I won't tell her, I'll ask her.'

'The phone's in the hallway,' said Timon, leading the way.

As I dialled the number of my home in Caesarea I glanced at my watch. Almost twelve. Rachel would be asleep. A telephone call this late at night would make her think the worst, especially with the savagery of the current persecutions.

'Hello?' Rachel's sleepy voice at the other end of the line.

'Rachel? It's me—Ben.'

'Ben? What are you doing ringing at this time of night? What's wrong?' a note of rising panic in her voice.

'Nothing's wrong, honey,' I reassured her, 'everything's fine.'

'Then why . . .?'

'There's a job that's come up. Not here, but in Damascus.'

'Damascus?'

'Apparently the persecution has already spread that far. And one of the believers has been arrested on a false charge of murder. The deacons want me to go to Damascus to defend him.'

'Then you must go,' said Rachel, without a moment's hesitation.

'But, honey, we've already been apart for a week.'

'Yes, I know, sweetheart, and it's felt like a month. This shouldn't happen to newly-weds. But there are some duties that are higher than what you and I feel for each other.'

'Yes . . . I suppose you're right,' I muttered glumly.

'You know I'm right—in your heart of hearts.'

'I guess . . .'

'So you go to Damascus—my brave defender of the faith. And remember that I love you.'

'I love you too . . .'

There was some more mushy stuff that you won't want to hear, and a few minutes later I walked back into the front room.

'What did she say?' asked Timon.

Before I could answer there was a heavy pounding on the front door.

'Open up in there,' bellowed a voice from the street, 'this is the Temple Police! We have this house surrounded.'

Timon, Parmenas and I exchanged glances. Part of me was angry and made me want to fight my way out, but another part of me thought of Rachel, and didn't want her to have to identify my corpse. These persecutors were serious. They had dungeons into which people just 'disappeared', and torturers who knew their business.

'You are surrounded. There is no escape. Come out with your hands up.'

'Quick!' whispered Timon. 'They may not know you two are here. Hide, while I go out and talk to them.'

'Where?'

'In those two chests.'

At either end of the room were two large, matching chests made of Lebanese cedar, and decoratively carved with pictures of camels and palm trees.

Parmenas and I needed no further encouragement, especially as the pounding on the front door had resumed. I ran to one of the chests and flung it open. Inside it was stacked high with folded linen and blankets.

'What will I do with this?' I whispered.

'Give it to me, I'll stack it under the beds.' Timon's wife, Dorcas had appeared. She was in her night-dress, having been roused by the racket. Parmenas and I stuffed bundles of linen into her arms and she hurried upstairs while we leapt into our respective chests and lowered the lids.

'You have one minute to open this door, or we'll break it down!' It was a new voice—quieter but infinitely more threatening. I thought I recognised it and, if I was right, it was the most dangerous man in Jerusalem!

Inside the total darkness of the chest I could hear Timon sliding back the bolts of the front door, and heard him call, 'I'm coming.'

'Where's your wife?'

'She's upstairs,' replied Timon.

As he spoke I heard Dorcas's footsteps come down the stairs, cross the room, and go out the front door.

Shortly afterwards Timon's voice could be heard protesting, 'There's no need for handcuffs—we'll come quietly. We're not resisting arrest.'

'Search the house,' snarled one of the voices, 'and be quick about it!'

Then the slap of sandals on stone floors as officers of the Temple Guard hurried from room to room. In my hiding place I froze, barely breathing.

Feet approached our end of the room. A curtain was swished to one side. Small pieces of furniture were scraped aside.

I held my breath.

Someone was standing right next to the lid of the chest I was hiding in. But instead of opening it, he sat on it, and barked out more orders.

'You two—check upstairs!'

I couldn't hold my breath any longer and slowly released it through my nostrils. When I breathed in again some dust got up my nose, and I thought I was going to sneeze. But the moment passed.

The search was quick and perfunctory. Obviously it was Timon and Dorcas they had come for, and they didn't care—for the time being—about anyone else.

'That'll do lads, move out,' said the officer sitting above me. I heard him get up and move away, then the others followed, and within moments the house was quiet again.

I was about to raise the lid of the chest and look out, when I heard the front door slowly opening. This time it sounded like only one person had entered the room.

Curiosity overcame my fear, and very, very slowly I eased the lid open a crack, and put my eye to it. At first I could see nothing—the narrow strip of the room within my field of vision was empty. Then, stepping softly, a man walked halfway across the room and paused.

He was short and dark. His hair was thinning, on the crown of his head even though he was a young man, but around the sides it was long and black. He had a thick, black beard, a hooked nose, and deep-set dark eyes, above which thick, black eyebrows met in the middle.

This was the man whose voice I had heard earlier—the man I, and all the Christians living in Jerusalem, feared the most. His name was Paul Benson*, and he came from the Cilician city of Tarsus. He was well-connected, and moved in the top circles in Jerusalem. And he used his family connections, and his contacts in the Pharisees party, for one purpose only—to persecute the followers of Jesus. Driven by a burning hatred, he was trying to wipe the name of Jesus off the face of the earth.

His eyes raked the room. Then he walked over to the candles burning on the coffee-table and, one by one, blew them out. As he lowered his face close to the candles I could see his expression—it was pure, unadulterated hatred, a hatred so strong he could barely contain it.

With all the lights extinguished he walked from the room, pulling the door closed behind him. Only after the silence had continued uninterrupted for

* Of the tribe of Benjamin, therefore a 'son' of 'Ben'.

several minutes did I dare to push the lid of my chest fully open.

My eyes had adjusted to the darkness, and a thin ray of moonlight creeping between the curtains showed me that the room was deserted. I eased my cramped limbs, and climbed out of the chest.

'They're gone, Parmenas,' I said quietly. 'You can come out now.'

The lid of the chest at the far end of the room opened, and Parmenas emerged.

'Why didn't they find us?' he asked.

'They weren't really looking. It was Timon and Dorcas they were after.'

'What will you do now?' he asked.

'From here,' I replied, 'my road leads to Damascus.'

CHAPTER 3

Parmenas and I left Timon's house by the back door, just to be on the safe side. As we hurried through the darkened streets of Jerusalem doubts began to form in my mind.

'I wonder if I should?' I said aloud.

'Should what?' said Parmenas.

'Should still go to Damascus,' I explained.

'You're not getting cold feet are you?'

'No! Certainly not! I'm wondering if I wouldn't be more use here in Jerusalem, defending Timon and Dorcas.'

'You go to Damascus, Ben. That's where you're needed. Timon and Dorcas will be charged with heresy like the others. Peter and James will take care of them. And so far Stephen is the only one who has actually been executed.'

'The one I defended!' I said bitterly.

'It was Stephen's choice to run his defence the way he did. He made that clear to everyone. He walked into it with his eyes open. We know the path that we walk is dangerous. These people killed The Master and they won't hesitate to kill any of us they can get their hands on.'

'Then, Timon and Dorcas . . .? I should stay!'

'Let Nicodemus look after their defence. Peter and the others will instruct him. In Damascus there is a follower facing a murder charge, and only you have the experience to handle that.'

He was right. I knew he was right.

We parted company in Absalom Street, just past the Hippodrome, and I hurried back to my parent's house—the only place in Jerusalem that offered me free overnight accommodation.

I eased myself in through the front door, took off my shoes, and began to tip-toe up the stairs. It was no use.

'Benjamin, my son—is that you?'

My Mamma doesn't have ears, she has a radar!

'No, Mamma,' I replied, 'it's the High Priest just dropping in on the way home from the Temple to discuss a little theology.'

'Oh, my boy, you are such a wag!' said Mamma, as she flip-flopped to the head of the stairs in large, fur-covered slippers and a pink quilted nightgown.

'Did you have a nice meeting with your friends?'

'Two of them were arrested. Aside from that, it was very nice.'

'Arrested! Benjamin, what are you doing hanging around with such people?'

'Mamma, they're not bankrobbers. They were arrested for being *Christians*.'

'That's enough! You think the bank robbers and the Christians go in different cells? Let me tell you, my son, they eat the same bread and water and share the same slop bucket.'

'Yes, I know. What's happened to Timon and Dorcas is terrible.'

'That's not what I meant. It's what might happen to you that is terrible. You might be arrested for being a Christian, and get locked up with some mass murderer. Oh, Benjamin, your throat might be slit in the middle of the ear, from night to night!'

'Calm down, Mamma. Don't get hysterical. You're working yourself up into a state. If you're not careful you'll have to take one of your pills in a minute.'

'I'll have to take a whole bottle of pills. And lay down in a warm bath. And slash my wrists. That's the only way to stop worrying about my son.'

'There's nothing I can do about it, Mamma. It's the authorities. They're the ones who are persecuting the Christians. What can I do? Tell them to stop?'

'You can stop being a Christian! That's what you can do!'

'Mamma, be reasonable. Now that I have discovered the truth, you expect me to pretend to believe in a lie?'

'What's all that racket down there?' came Pappa's voice from the upstairs bedroom.

'Oh, it's you, Benjamin,' he said, emerging from the bedroom and tying a cord around his dressing gown. 'What are you doing out of bed, Mamma? It's one o'clock in the morning already.'

'Keep your pants on, Pappa,' said Mamma, 'I'm just trying to talk some sense into this boy of ours. Two more of his friends were arrested tonight, but he won't listen to me!'

'Mamma,' said Pappa, stifling a yawn, 'in the first place, I have my pants on already. And in the second place, our Benjamin is 37 years old and a married man. I think he can make up his own mind.'

'A mother knows best! And I know it's just not safe for him here in Jerusalem.'

'Well, tomorrow morning I leave Jerusalem, Mamma,' I said, 'so you can stop worrying.'

'Leave? Why didn't you tell me earlier?'

'Because I didn't have a . . .'

'Now I can stop worrying a little. You're going back to join Rachel down at Caesarea? How very sensible!'

'Actually, Mamma I'm . . .'

'But look at the time! It's one a.m. already! We should all be in bed. Would you like I should make you some hot cocoa Benjamin?'

'No thank you, Mamma. But it's not . . .'

'In that case we should be going up to bed. Come along you two men. Shoo! Shoo! It's upstairs and back to sleep for this family.'

Mamma led the way upstairs. As she did so Pappa turned to me and quietly asked, 'So, if it's not Caesarea, where are you going tomorrow, my son?'

'Damascus.'

'Damascus, eh? On business?'

'I'm defending a man charged with murder.'

'Murder, eh? How are you travelling there?'

'I thought I'd go by train.'

'Train, eh? What time does it leave in the morning?'

'I don't know yet, I'll check the timetable before I go to bed.'

'Stop dawdling, you two,' Mamma called. 'It's way past bedtime.'

When I got into my old room I checked the train timetable I still kept in the drawer of the bedside table. The Damascus train left at 7.00 a.m. I set my alarm and tried to sleep.

A quarter to seven the next morning found me standing at the North Gate, travelling bag slung over my shoulder, feeling more like a mummy halfway through the embalming process than a living human being.

The early morning sun caught the motes of dust that drifted lazily in the gentle currents of air floating across from the Kidron Valley. To my left was Wood Market, still quiet at this time of the morning. To my right, stamping on the dry ground and raising clouds of dust, was the train I was taking to Damascus—a camel train.

A short, fat, bald man, carrying a roll of tickets and wearing a money pouch on his belt, approached.

'You here for the morning train?' he asked.

'Yes,' I stifled a yawn, scratched my unshaven chin.

'Destination?'

'Damascus.'

'That'll be ten denarii.'

'Ten? But last time I was on this train, Damascus was only eight denarii.'

'Yeah. And now it's ten. If you're unhappy, take another train.'

'There is no other train.'

'In that case it's ten denarii.'

I paid the man.

'Many passengers on this trip?' I asked as he tore my ticket off the roll.

'Not a lot. Mainly cargo—sacks of grain, rolls of cloth, and cartons of ornamental terracotta from the Cleopas Pottery Works at Emmaus. And we're due to pick up some barrels of pickled fish on our way through Galilee.'

'I see. How safe is the road these days?'

'What do you want from me? Insurance? I'm not going with you, I just run the Jerusalem office. You want to travel these roads, you take the risks.'

'In other words, there are still terrorists about.'

'In other words, it's your neck, not mine.'

'Do the Romans provide a guard for the train?'

'Four men. But only to just over the hills. After that, you're on your own. Mind you, some of our camel drivers would frighten their own mothers. I think you're pretty safe.'

'Better than being a private traveller.'

'You're telling me, buster! Just last week they brought in a guy from the Jericho Road. Beaten nearly to a pulp he was. The road bandits had attacked him and stolen everything he had. I felt sorry for the poor guy.'

'Why do they do it?' I said, more to myself than to the little ticket seller. 'Why do human beings behave so viciously towards each other. Why do people have this desire to *hurt* other people? Why is there suffering and evil in the world?'

'Listen, buster,' said the little ticket seller, 'I don't know how to work the controls on my VCR, how should I know why there's suffering and evil!'

Shortly afterwards, the camel that was to be 'mine' for the journey was ordered by its driver to kneel, and I climbed into the passenger's saddle on its back.

The camel driver, an ugly customer with greasy hair, a moustache like an Australian fast bowler, and black stubble on his chin, climbed into the front part of the saddle, and pulled on the rope fastened to a hole near the camel's nose. At this signal it lurched to its feet and, following a few more tugs on the rope, lurched off to join the other camels in a long, straggling line.

We waited for nearly half an hour before the rest of the camel train was assembled. Then someone near the head of the line roared out an unintelligible command, and we were off.

'How far will we get today?' I asked, addressing my question to the back of the driver's head. He appeared not to hear me, so I asked him again, louder.

He turned around and scowled over his shoulder: 'Sychar, if we're lucky—and make enough speed.'

As if on cue, the leader of the camel train roared out another command, and the camel drivers whipped their animals to a faster speed. The camels began 'pacing'—a medium-speed movement in which both legs on the same side rise and fall together.

As the animal swayed from side to side, mile after mile, on and on, I began to feel that bilious dizzy feeling of seasickness and finally understood why camels are called 'ships of the desert'!

CHAPTER 4

That night we stayed at the Well View Motel in Sychar. When I laid my weary bones down onto the lumpy motel mattress I thought I would never get to sleep. But I crashed into oblivion almost at once.

My tired mind was soon dragged into a nightmare in which, once again, I was back at Stephen's trial and helpless to prevent its horrible and murderous outcome.

The trial had been held before the High Council, and the council chambers were packed for the dramatic event. Lying witnesses testified against Stephen, saying that he had constantly spoken against the Temple and against the laws of Moses.

'We have heard him say that this fellow Jesus of Nazareth will destroy the Temple, and throw out all of Moses' laws,' they declared. At this, everyone in the council chamber saw Stephen's face become as radiant as an angel's!

Then the High Priest asked Stephen, 'Are these accusations true?'

Stephen rose to his feet, and delivered the speech that we had prepared together—a speech he insisted he wanted to give.

The High Council listened in silence while Stephen gave a lengthy summary of the history of God's dealings with the Israeli nation. They can't have missed the point he was making—that again and again throughout history, the nation had turned its back on God and killed God's messengers.

Finally he came to the subject of the Temple. 'God doesn't live in temples made by human hands. "The heavens are my throne," says the Lord through his prophets, "and earth is my footstool. What kind of home could you build?" asks the Lord. "Would I stay in it? Didn't I *make* both heaven and earth?"

'You stiff-necked heathens!' Stephen continued, 'Must you forever resist the Holy Spirit? But your fathers did and so do you! Name one prophet your ancestors didn't persecute! They even killed the ones who predicted the coming of the Righteous One—the Messiah whom you betrayed and murdered. Yes, and you deliberately destroyed God's Laws, though you received them from the hands of angels.'

The Jewish leaders were stung by Stephen's accusations, and ground their teeth in rage. But Stephen, gazing steadily upward, cried out to them, 'Look, I see the heavens open and Jesus the Messiah standing beside God, at his right hand!'

At that there was a riot. The crowd mobbed him, putting their hands over their ears, drowning out his voice with their shouts, and dragging him out of the city to stone him to death.

The rules of the High Council were that the official witnesses had to be the executioners. I was there and saw these men take off their coats and pick up stones the size of house bricks with which to kill Stephen. And the man who held their coats for them was Paul Benson!

As the murderous stones came hurtling at him Stephen prayed, 'Lord Jesus, receive my spirit.' And he fell to his knees shouting over the din, 'Lord, don't charge them with this sin!' With that, he died.

I woke up in a cold sweat, shaken once again by the fury of those people who had rejected, or ignored, God's intervention in this world through Jesus.

It took a while to calm down and then I let my head sink back into the pillow. I must have fallen back to sleep, because the next thing I was aware of was one of the camel drivers hammering on my door.

'Mr Bartholomew,' he yelled, 'we leave in twenty minutes.'

I spent ten minutes having a hot, refreshing shower. Then I quickly consumed some coffee and bread rolls, and mounted my camel for the next stage of the journey.

We followed the road through the khaki-coloured hills into the broad plain of Esdraelon, with the heights of Nazareth rising up before us to the north. As the morning progressed we climbed into those hills, and then down again to the plain of Ahma.

Early in the afternoon we reached a point where I could see, a thousand feet below, a splash of bright blue water cupped in the curve of a hill. We then descended into the heat of the lakeside of Galilee.

Passing the city of Tiberias we continued north around the edge of the lake. At Magdala some of the camels were loaded with barrels of pickled fish, bound for the markets of Damascus. Later, as the sun was setting we arrived at Capernaum at the northern end of the Sea of Galilee. We were to spend our second night on the road here.

After a much-needed meal, I walked through the moonlit streets of Capernaum. The paving stones beneath my feet were the very ones over which Jesus had walked. Many of those crowding the streets earlier as our camel train had arrived would have been men and women who had seen and heard Jesus.

The synagogue by the water's edge was the one in which Jesus had preached.

As I walked I wondered whether these sights would have any effect on Paul Benson? If he could see these places and people would it mitigate his burning rage against the followers of Jesus? Somehow I doubted it.

The next day we continued our journey, with the road to Damascus leaving the northern end of the Sea of Galilee, and climbing steadily into the southern slopes of the Lebanon mountains. I lost sight of the lake as we moved upwards through the hills—some brown and stony, others aflame with the flowers of spring.

Late in the morning we reached the ford across the River Jordan known as 'The Ford of the Daughters of Jacob'. Here the river was about eighty feet wide. The ice-green water from the melting snows of Mount Hermon flowed rapidly between banks lined with oleanders, papyrus and the box-like tree called 'The Balm of Gilead'.

The camels splashed across the ford, as unheeding of the cold water as they would be of burning sands. On the other side we continued, up a tremendous hill road.

At last, reaching the top, I turned to look back at Galilee. Lying far below was one of the most beautiful, exquisite sights in the world. The whole lakeside was clearly visible, with Tiberias and Capernaum on the west bank and the wild mountains of Moab lying folded together on the east. Beyond that, the Jordan Valley disappeared into a quivering heat mist.

The camel train moved steadily onwards. The road now ran across a sand-coloured upland almost straight to Damascus, with Mount Hermon towering to the left, its snow-capped summit blazing in the early afternoon sun.

About twenty miles out of Damascus I caught sight of the city lying low on the horizon. It looked like an oasis of feathery green, with white domes rising out of the greenery.

It would be at about this point on the Damascus Road that an event of stupendous importance would occur in just a few days' time. However, that was something that I could not know as my camel train carried me swiftly towards my destination.

We approached Damascus through miles of apricot trees, entering the city through the Gate of the East late in the afternoon. We arrived as the local citizens, at the end of a hot day, were drinking sweet coffee in the many coffee shops built on piers over the river Barada.

Our camel train came to a halt in the centre of Damascus's main street—*Vicus Rectus*, or Straight Street. Running as straight as an arrow from one end of the city to the other, it was a mile long, a hundred feet wide, and divided into three sections: a central track for chariots and horsemen, and a path on each side for pedestrians.

I dismounted, shouldered my travelling bag, and walked down the street, carefully avoiding the horse-drawn carts, the flocks of sheep, and the strings of camels bumping over the cobbles.

The whole of Straight Street was one long bazaar, or marketplace, lined on each side with hundreds of little shops fitted with pull-down shutters. At each doorway traders tried to lure passers-by into shops stacked with brassware and pottery. Greek and Armenian merchants stood chatting on the footpaths, and carpet sellers wandered past, holding up their wares.

Opening off the main bazaar were dozens of smaller side streets, each with its own speciality. I walked past streets filled with shops selling the crystallised fruits for which Damascus has always been famous. Then there were streets hung with red, yellow and blue slippers, and cobblers sitting under these decorations swiftly adding to the collection. I saw the gold and silver street where the jewellers worked; though Damascus jewellery, I knew, was not very good. There was a famous saying that the art of jewellery was born in Egypt, grew up in Aleppo, and came to Damascus to die.

I pulled out of my top pocket the scrap of paper with the address that Parmenas had given me. My contact was a man named Joe Barnabas, and the address was not far from where I was on Straight Street.

I branched off and walked down quiet lanes lined with blank walls. I was thinking what a dull and grimy city Damascus was when I came to the place I was looking for.

It was a plain wooden door, set into a wall that had once been white stone, but had been stained by time a dull brown. I knocked and eventually the door was opened by a child, a little girl, who looked up at me with wary eyes.

'Hello,' I said, looking down at the child. 'Is your mamma or poppa about?'

She didn't reply, but holding tight to a kitten in her arms, ran inside the house. Looking around, I got a pleasant surprise; there was a whitewashed courtyard, dazzling in the late afternoon sunshine, with a splashing fountain, a well, and a shady sycamore tree.

A moment later a young man in a pale blue robe, somewhat grubby after a day's work, stepped out into the courtyard.

'Can I help you?' he asked.

'The name is Bartholomew—Ben Bartholomew . . .' I started to explain, but before I could continue he interrupted me.

'Ben! We've been expecting you. Welcome to Damascus. Come inside, have a drink and freshen up after your long journey. You must be feeling pretty hot and tired. How was the trip? By the way, my name is David Gideon—everyone calls me Dave.'

The babble of information continued as he led me into the pleasant coolness of the house. In the front room was a small group of people, apparently awaiting my arrival. Dave introduced them and I shook hands with them in turn.

'Folks, this is Ben Bartholomew. Ben, this is Joe Barnabas, beside him are Ananias and Nicolaus. This is my wife, Miriam, and you've met our daughter Phoebe. The large, silent man over here is George— he's from Abyssinia'

The introductions were followed by a babble of greetings from the group. I was offered a cup of the sweet coffee they drink in Damascus, and offered a large, comfortable cushion on which to sit.

'How much do you know about this case?' asked Joe Barnabas, once we were settled.

'Very little,' I replied, 'I know that the charge is murder . . .'

'A trumped-up charge!' snorted Ananias.

'So unfair!' added Miriam.

'. . . and that the accused is a certain Dr Matthias,' I continued, 'but that's about all I do know.'

'Then let me fill you in,' said Joe. The others fell silent, and left it to Joe to brief me on the case.

'Tullus Matthias is a Christian, a member of our group. He is around 25 years old and a Greek-trained physician. A few months ago he became engaged to be married to another member of our group—a 19-year-old named Tabitha Mason. Unfortunately Tabitha's father did not approve. Malachi Mason is—or rather, was—a member of the synagogue council and a wealthy businessman. He strongly disapproved of his daughter's Christian faith, and forbad the match—a true love match—between her and Tullus. He was so upset that he became one of the moving forces in the persecution of Christians here in Damascus.'

'By "he" you mean this Malachi Mason?' I asked.

'That's right,' said Joe. 'So Malachi was putting his money and his influence behind the persecution. His chief ally in this was a man you'll meet in court—an odious worm named Aaron Burger, the District Attorney of Damascus.'

'Why would the D.A. want to get involved?'

'For a number of reasons. To advance his own career for a start. The authorities tend to smile on people who persecute Christians. And he seems to hate Christians anyway. He has also been encouraged by his cousin, who you will have heard of.'

'Heard of who?'

'Aaron Burger's cousin. His name is Paul Benson.'

'Him! He's looming as the most dangerous man in the Roman Empire, as far as we are concerned.'

'You'll understand then why this Aaron Burger has been giving us such a hard time.'

'How does he come into the story of Tullus Matthias, and Tabitha and Malachi Mason?'

'He's part of the background that you need to understand.'

'All right,' I said 'go on.'

'Malachi Mason was stabbed to death. The murder weapon was an antique dagger owned by Tullus and the last person to see him alive was Tullus. After Tullus saw him the room he was murdered in was put under guard.'

'It looks bad for him,' I said.

'It couldn't possibly look worse.'

CHAPTER 5

There was a long silence in the room. In the end it was Dave who spoke.

'Where do you want to begin, Ben?' he asked.

'With a hot shower, a hot meal and a change of clothes,' I replied. 'Then I want to talk to Dr Matthias, and visit the scene of the crime.'

It was early the next morning before I set off for the Damascus jail to see Tullus. Joe Barnabas escorted me there, having arranged visitors passes in anticipation of my arrival.

The prison was a square, stone fortress on the eastern edge of the city. As we approached the grim, forbidding building, all I could see beyond the prison was a flat, clay-pan desert stretching to the horizon. The red-brown clay was cracked and dry, and dotted here and there with stunted desert plants.

Joe knocked on the huge, double wooden doors. After a long wait one of the doors creaked open on its heavy brass hinges.

'Yes?' said the jailer, his head appearing around the door.

'We've come to see one of the prisoners,' said Joe, producing the two visitors passes.

'This early?' complained the jailer.

'Is that a problem?' I asked.

'It might be,' sneered the jailer, wiping a dribble

of fat from his breakfast sausage off the stubble on his chin.

'The passes say anytime between 7.00 a.m. and 7.00 p.m.,' I said. 'It's after 7.00 a.m. . . .'

'Only just,' grumbled the jailer.

'Do you want me to go to the magistrate and tell him the jailers refuse to honour passes he has issued?' I asked.

'All right, come in,' muttered the jailer, pulling the door open.

We crossed a small courtyard, and went through an open doorway opened into a dark tunnel. The tunnel twisted left, right, then left again, and we finally came to a small, heavy wooden door. Sitting in front of the door, on an upturned barrel, his head resting against a stone pillar, sound asleep and snoring noisily, was a fat turnkey.

The jailer kicked the turnkey in the ankle, and he woke with a start, grunted with surprise, and waddled to his feet.

'Let these two in,' snapped the jailer. Then he turned and asked, 'Which of my little flowers do you want to see? I have a choice selection here—rapists, assassins, burglars, arsonists . . . take your pick.'

'It's Dr Matthias we've come to see,' said Joe.

'Ah, the good doctor. That murdering swine is likely to slip his scalpel in between your ribs and straight into your heart. Dangerous habit for a surgeon.'

Joe and I ignored this sneering remark.

After much clumsy fumbling with keys, the turnkey opened the door.

'Take them to cell 13,' snarled the jailer, 'and wait for them.'

'Yes, sir,' the turnkey mumbled, still not fully woken up.

The jailer turned on his heels and disappeared.

'Follow me,' said the turnkey, waddling through the doorway and down an even narrower and darker corridor which, at intervals, had heavy wooden doors, set deeply into the stone.

'This is the one,' said the turnkey, coming to a halt.

He fumbled with his keys and then the lock for an eternity, but at last managed to push the door open, and Joe and I stepped inside.

'I'll wait out here. Knock when you want to come out,' he said, as the door swung closed behind us, and the key clicked ominously in the lock.

My eyes were still adjusting to the darkness, but I could make out the dim figure who had risen from the mattress in the corner as we entered. By the pale light from a single, high, heavily barred window he looked young, but nothing at all like a respectable doctor.

'Joe!' he said, with a cry of delight, stepping forward. The two men hugged each other warmly.

'Tullus,' said Joe, 'meet your defence attorney—Ben Bartholomew.'

At closer range I could see that Tullus was unshaven, untidy and unwashed. It was hard to imagine what he would look like scrubbed up and in his proper setting. He offered his hand and I shook it.

'I'm glad to see you,' he said. 'I'd offer you a seat, but there's only this small wooden stool.'

'We can stand,' I said.

'What can you do for me? Can you get me out of here?' he said.

'I'll try,' I said. 'That'll be my first priority. I'll

call into the court this morning and arrange for a bail application hearing, and see if I can get you released on bail pending the trial.'

'Do you think you can?'

'On a murder charge it's never easy. But with enough character witnesses we might pull it off.' Turning to where Barnabas was standing quietly in the corner, I said, 'We'll have to get Tullus cleaned up for the bail hearing. Shaved, washed, dressed. He has to look like a respectable citizen.'

'I can organise that,' replied Joe.

'Now the important thing,' I continued, turning back to Tullus, 'is to get you out of here permanently. And to do that I need to learn more about the facts of the case. I need to know what the evidence against you is, what issues the District Attorney will be piling up to point to your guilt, and how we can respond.'

'Where do you want to begin?' Tullus asked, suddenly more hopeful.

'How long had you known the victim?'

'Malachi? No more than a year. About as long as I've known Tabitha, his daughter. I met him through her.'

'And how did you meet her?'

'At the believers' meetings.'

'She introduced you to her father?'

'Yes.'

'When?'

'After we'd known each other for a few weeks. When we both realised that we . . . liked each other.'

'And how did her father react when you met him?'

'When Tabitha first introduced us I don't think he realised that I was a Christian. All he could see was the prospect of his daughter marrying a doctor—and he was pleased about that.'

'Why?'

'He himself is a merchant, or *was* a merchant—quite a wealthy one, but definitely a member of the merchant class. He had ambitions for his daughter. He wanted to see her marry into the professional class. But only within the Jewish community of Damascus, of course. As a member of the ruling council of the synagogue he was strict about that.'

'So at first your interest in his daughter pleased him?'

'That's right.'

'When did it go sour?'

'After a few weeks—when he finally tumbled to the fact that I was a Christian.'

'And that made him angry?'

'Furious. His daughter being a Christian was a great embarrassment to him. He hoped that her Christianity was just a phase that she was going through, that she would grow out of it. The prospect of her marrying a Christian horrified him.'

'So how did he react?'

'He threw me out of his house. Ordered me never to come back.'

'And did you? Come back, that is?'

'No. Not until the day he died, at least.'

'What about your relationship with Tabitha?'

'Malachi realised that Tabitha has a mind of her own, and he didn't want to lose her completely. So he didn't forbid her to see me.'

'Just to marry you?'

'Yes.'

'So you and Tabitha kept seeing each other?'

'Yes. And she was working on changing her father's mind.'

'With any success?'

'None at all.'

'Do you have a rival? Was there someone else Malachi Mason wanted his daughter to marry?'

'Yes. Before I came on the scene there was a lawyer he kept trying to match her up with. After he gave me the shove he went back to inviting this lawyer to his house for dinners, and pushing Tabitha at him.'

'Ask him which lawyer, Ben,' said Joe's voice, from over my shoulder.

'All right, which lawyer?'

'The District Attorney of Damascus—Aaron H. Burger!'

'This is getting complicated,' I said, after a pause, 'very complicated. Was Tabitha interested in Burger?'

'Not in the least,' replied Tullus.

'What about Burger—was he interested in her? Or was it all Malachi's idea?'

'He was interested all right. He was obsessed with her. Still is. And furious with me for having "stolen" her from him.'

'So, Tabitha was in the middle, you on one side, and Malachi and Burger on the other?'

'That's about the shape of it.'

'And now Malachi's dead?'

'Yes.'

'Tell me about it.'

'He became ill with a fever, probably caused by a virus. His own regular doctor was out of town, and he was a cantankerous character and wouldn't see anyone else. He got worse. Was slipping in and out of consciousness. Finally, Tabitha got so worried she called me in.'

'How did Malachi feel about being treated by a doctor he hated?'

'He didn't know. He was delirious with the fever.'

'Why did Tabitha call you, rather than some other doctor?'

'She thought that if I treated him successfully it might mend the relationship. Besides which, she was very worried about him and she . . . well . . . she has inflated ideas about my medical skills.'

'When did you see him?'

'A week ago today. In the middle of the morning.'

'What condition was he in?'

'Feverish. Delirious.'

'What treatment did you give him?'

'Two injections. A strong pain-killer to ease his discomfort and let him sleep. And a broad-spectrum antibiotic to fight the infection.'

'How did he respond?'

'I waited by his bedside until the pain-killer had started to work. When I left him he was sleeping peacefully.'

'And just a few hours later he was sleeping permanently?'

'He was dead, yes.'

'With your knife sticking out of his chest?'

'That part I can't understand, I just can't understand it at all.'

'Slopping out time! Everyone out of their cells!'

It was the voice of the jailer, echoing harshly up and down the corridor, and bringing our interview to an abrupt end.

'We'll be back,' I assured Tullus, as the fat turnkey came in and hustled us out the door.

CHAPTER 6

'What do you think, Ben?' Joe asked once we were walking back into the city.

'The outlook is bleak so far. But I don't even know the full story yet, so let's not get ahead of ourselves.'

'Where to now, then?'

'It's too early to go to the courthouse for the bail application, so why don't you take me to the scene of the crime?'

On the northern side of Damascus, on a hillside backing onto the river, was a 'garden suburb' of villas. It was here that Joe took me. The Mason villa was typical of the area—square, white, substantial, and built around an inner courtyard.

We knocked at the front door and were admitted by a young male servant Joe introduced as Quaresimus.

'You'll want to talk to him,' said Joe, 'he's an eyewitness.'

'Later,' I said. 'Let's see the lady of the house first.'

Although it was still early, Tabitha Mason was up and dressed and supervising the work of servants in the kitchen.

'Please accept my sympathy on the death of your father, Miss Mason,' I said when Joe introduced us.

'Thank you, Mr Bartholomew. Call me Tabitha.'

'I will, if you'll call me Ben. I take it you're in charge here now. Your mother . . .?'

'My mother died when I was eight years old. Running the household is good for me—at the moment it's keeping my mind off what's happening to Tullus. Have you seen him? How is he?'

As we spoke Tabitha led the way into a large, sunny courtyard, with a stone-walled well in the centre and lemon tree in one corner. We sat at a table under the lemon tree, and Tabitha instructed a servant girl to bring us coffee.

'We saw him this morning,' I explained.

'He was in good spirits,' added Joe, 'and Ben is going to try to get him out on bail.'

'Do you think you can?' Tabitha brightened. 'Oh, that would be wonderful! I can't bear to think of him in those horrid cells.'

I could see why Tullus Matthias and Aaron Burger had both fallen in love with her. She was a very beautiful woman—soft pale skin, flaming red hair, and eyes a luminescent green.

'I'll do my best about release on bail, but I'm not promising anything.'

'Doing your best is all we can ask,' she said softly. 'It looks bad for him, doesn't it?'

'So far. But I've hardly begun my investigation yet.'

'What can I tell you? What can I do to help?'

'For a start, you can show me where it all happened.'

'Right here. Behind us. This is . . . was . . . my father's bedroom—the one closest to the lemon tree. Like all the rooms it opens onto the courtyard.'

'Only one door?'

'Yes.'

'So there is no other way into or out of the room other than this door that we can see?'

'Well, there are two small windows which open into an alleyway outside. But no-one could get through them—they have iron security bars across them.'

'It happened a week ago?'

'Yes, exactly one week ago today. I was becoming more and more worried about Pappa, so I called Tullus and asked him to come over.'

'When did you call him?'

'At breakfast time.'

'And when did he arrive?'

'The middle of the morning. I don't know the exact time.'

'Was it wise to call in Dr Matthias—knowing how much your father disliked him?'

'Oh, how I wish I never had! Then none of this would have happened!'

'But why did you call him, and not some other doctor?'

'I was so worried. And Tullus is such a wonderful doctor. I knew if anyone could do something, he could.'

'Weren't you worried that your father might complain? Or refuse to see him?'

'Pappa was drifting in and out of consciousness with the fever. He was delirious.'

'And what he didn't know wouldn't hurt him, eh?'

'Tullus didn't hurt him, he wouldn't hurt a fly. You must believe me!'

'I believe you, Tabitha, but there's a judge and jury we have to convince. Tullus arrived about the middle of the morning?'

'That's right.'

'And your father was in his room the whole time?'

'Yes. He'd hardly been out of bed for two days.'

'When did Tullus go in to see him?'

'Almost at once. He spoke to me for a few minutes, then he went in.'

'And how long was he in there?'

'I don't know. Ten minutes, perhaps. That's all.'

'What did he say when he came out.'

'That Pappa was sleeping peacefully. And that we should let him sleep.'

'Did he promise to come back?'

'Yes, in the afternoon, he said.'

'Then he left?'

'Yes.'

'What did you do?'

'I did the shopping list. Gave instructions to the maidservants. That sort of thing.'

'Did you go in and see your father?'

'No.'

'Who did?' I asked

'No-one. Tullus said to let him rest, so I put one of the servants outside the door to see that he wasn't disturbed.'

'Which servant?'

'Quaresimus.'

'I better talk to him. Now, can you show me the room?'

Tabitha stood up and led the way over to the nearest door. She pushed it open, then stood back. Clearly she didn't relish walking into the room in which her father had so recently been murdered.

I stepped inside, Joe following me.

It was an ordinary bedroom, roughly square. The walls were whitewashed and undecorated. On my right, as I stood in the doorway, was a small coffee-table with a few books piled on it. I took a quick look. There was nothing interesting, just a paperback thriller (*Sylvester Versus Arnold: Battle of the Gladiators*) and a recent copy of *The Midas & Croesus Investment Newsletter*.

In the corner to my left was a chest. I walked over and opened it up. It contained nothing but clothes.

In the middle of the far wall, between two small windows was a single bed. Each of the windows was barred, as Tabitha had said, and the bars were only about four inches apart. I shook each bar. They were solid, no-one had got in or out that way. The sliding glass windows inside the bars were open.

'Were these windows open on the day of the murder?' I asked Joe.

'I don't know,' he replied, 'I'll find out.'

He ducked out the door and I continued my search of the room. The only piece of furniture left to look at was a small, round table with a ceramic jug and washbasin on it. It held no clues.

'The windows were open halfway,' said Joe, coming back in. 'Is it significant?'

'Probably not. But I like to check.'

I looked around the room one more time. It was so bare and empty—it could tell me nothing.

Back in the courtyard Tabitha was once again sitting under the lemon tree. The coffee had arrived, and she was pouring it into three cups.

'Was the room always so plain and bare?' I asked.

'Always,' she replied, 'Pappa liked it like that. He made a lot of money, but he didn't spend it on himself. In fact, I think he made money for the sheer pleasure of making it. "The thrill of the hunt" he once called it.'

'Exactly what pleasure did he derive from making money?'

'I feel ashamed to admit it, but he loved to do deals that outsmarted other people. If he could get one up on someone he would come home chuckling with pleasure.'

'He liked to cheat people in other words?'

Tabitha didn't reply, sipping her coffee instead.

'Look, Tabitha, somebody murdered your father. If it wasn't Tullus it was somebody else. If I can find out who, Tullus will go free. If I don't, he might hang. If your father cheated people, then there must be someone somewhere—maybe more than one—with a motive for murder. Can you see what I'm getting at?'

'Yes, of course. And it's foolish of me to try to protect Pappa's reputation now that he's gone. Everyone knew what he was like anyway. He boasted about it.'

'So what was he like? What did he boast about?'

Tabitha took a deep breath and swallowed hard before she replied, 'He tricked people. He bribed officials. He did deals. Being "clever" was what he boasted about.'

'I see,' I said, then sipped my coffee in thoughtful silence.

'So who did your father trick, Tabitha?' I asked. 'Who might have a motive for murder?'

'I don't really know, Ben. Honestly, I don't. Pappa never told me any of the details of his business activities, just came home laughing and joking on his 'good days' . . . when he had pulled off another deal.'

'Did he have any business partners or friends who would know?'

'One—Seth Yentob.'

'Who's he?'

'Pappa's partner. The name of the firm is Mason and Yentob.'

'I take it that you now own your father's half of the business?'

'Oh, no. On the death of one partner, ownership reverted to the other partner. But Pappa has left me well provided for. He had his own real estate investments that were not part of the company.'

'I see, and this Seth Yentob—what's he like? What sort of a man is he.'

'A thoroughly odious snake of a man! I wouldn't trust him an inch!' snapped Tabitha with sudden, and surprising, fire in her voice.

'So . . . a snake. And a snake with a good motive to murder your father!'

CHAPTER 7

'Now, I'd like to talk to Quaresimus, if I may?'

'Yes, of course. I'll go and fetch him for you,' said Tabitha.

'Joe, I need to find out more about this Seth Yentob. And about Malachi Mason's business dealings. Who could help me with that?'

'Hhmm. Let me think,' said Barnabas. 'There is one member of our Christian group here in Damascus who might know. Or might be able to find out.'

'Who?'

'A man named Eli Samuelson. He's in the import–export business. He probably hears all the gossip that runs around the merchants of the city.'

'Arrange a meeting, I'd like to talk to him.'

I finished drinking my coffee, and the servant named Quaresimus walked up.

'You wanted to see me, sir?'

'Correct,' I replied. 'Take a seat.'

'I'd prefer to stand, sir.'

'I like eyes on a level. Sit down.'

He did what he was told.

'Cast your mind back to one week ago. I want you to picture exactly what happened that day—in detail.'

'I'll never forget it, sir,' said Quaresimus.

'You can cut all the "sir" stuff, just answer the questions.'

'Yes, s— Ah, yes.'

'How long were you stationed out here in the courtyard that day.'

'Hours and hours,' he replied, a bitter note in his voice.

'A hot day, was it?'

'Blazing hot. And dusty with it.'

'So what time did you start guarding Mr Mason's door?'

'The middle of the morning it would have been. I'd already been working in the courtyard for more than an hour, drawing the household's daily water supply from the well.'

'And you were hoping for some nice, cool, indoor duties?'

'I always do exactly what I'm told, sir,' said Quaresimus, sitting up very stiffly. 'Excuse me, sir. I apologise for the "sir". I get flustered sometimes, s—'

'Never mind. You saw Dr Matthias arrive?'

'I did.'

'When?'

'While I was drawing the water.'

'Were you surprised to see him?'

'Astonished. You could have knocked me over with a feather. He'd been banned from the house. I had heard the master shouting at him, telling him never to come back.'

'What did he do when he arrived?'

'He talked to the mistress. He didn't seem to want to treat the master—with the bad feelings between them and all—but the mistress persuaded him. She can sweet talk anyone into anything, can the mistress.'

'And then what happened?'

'Well, then the doctor went in to see the master, didn't he?'

'How long was he in there?'

'About two shakes of a camel's tail. Not long at all.'

'And then?' I prompted.

'And then when he came out he talked to Miss Tabitha, who then gave me my orders. "Do not disturb Mr Mason", she said, "and stop anyone else from going in and disturbing him". Those were my orders, and that's what I did.'

'Did anyone try to go into Mr Mason's room.'

'One of the young maids came to change the water in his wash jug. "No you can't!" I said. "You can't go in there—doctor's orders" I said.'

'And she didn't go in?'

'Of course not! I wouldn't have allowed it. She gave me a bit of lip—she's a cheeky lass—and then she went away.'

'No-one else tried to go into Mr Mason's room?'

'No-one.'

'No-one at all?'

'Not a blessed soul. Well, it was siesta time by then, wasn't it? So the rest of the household lay down for an afternoon nap.'

'Everyone except you?'

'I had been told to stay on guard, and on guard I stayed.'

'But you didn't like it, did you?' I said.

'Eh?'

'Sitting out here in the heat of the day while everyone else lay down in the cool shade indoors—not much fun.'

'I don't know anything about "fun". I do my duty. And I knew what my duty was that day, and I did it.'

46

'Did anyone see you doing it?'

'Eh?'

'Did anyone see you sitting here, without a break, throughout the heat of the day?'

'Well . . . they couldn't, could they? They were all having their siestas. No sir, it was just me, all on my lonesome, sitting here on guard duty all afternoon without a break.'

'That will do for the time being, Quaresimus,' I said, 'but I may want to talk to you again later.'

'Very good, sir,' he replied, rising stiffly to his feet, and walking away.

'I don't believe he told me the truth—or at least not all of it.'

'What will you do about him?' asked Joe Barnabas.

'Nail him,' I said, 'in my own good time!'

'So, what next?'

'Can you take me to the Damascus District Court. It's time to file that application for a bail hearing.'

The clerk's office at the courthouse was the usual disorganised bun rush that such places always are. A sign said to take a numbered ticket and wait. It was going to be a long wait—the number on the ticket I held in my hand said XXXV and the clerks were only up to serving number XIV.

I told Barnabas not to bother waiting. So, after making arrangements to meet me for lunch at the Gideons' house, he left.

Every ten minutes or so the clerks would call out another number.

'XV . . . XVI . . . XVII . . . XVIII . . .' and so on.

Each time, someone would shuffle up to the counter, present their ticket, and conduct their business—lodging documents, filling in forms, or whatever.

The morning slowly dragged by, until finally, the clerk's voice roused me from the drowsy half-sleep I had fallen into . . . 'XXXV'.

'Does anyone have XXXV?'

I hurried to the counter and showed my ticket. 'I want to apply for a bail hearing.'

The sullen clerk pushed a form across the bench top. When I had completed the form I pushed it back again. The clerk ran a tired eye over the page to make sure every blank had been filled in. Then he banged a rubber stamp on it fiercely, as if trying to cure his boredom by assaulting the paper.

Without looking up he muttered, 'His Honour Judge Hezion will hear the application tomorrow morning. Court begins at 10.00 a.m. Next, XXXVI.'

Over lunch Joe Barnabas brought the others up to date on what was happening.

'A bail hearing? Tomorrow morning?' said Miriam. 'Do you really think you can get Tullus released, Ben?'

'Quite possibly,' I replied, 'But I'm promising nothing. With the help of everyone here we can turn on an impressive array of character witnesses, and that should help. Nevertheless, it is a murder case, and judges are notoriously nervous about granting bail in murder cases.'

'But it's a trumped-up charge!' snorted David Gideon derisively.

'The judge has to treat it like any other murder case,' I explained patiently, then remembered, 'Joe, did you contact Eli Samuelson?'

'Yes I did,' replied Barnabas. 'Called in on him as soon as I left you at the court. He'll see us first thing after siesta.'

The siesta again! We were all supposed to be frozen into immobility during the siesta, and I didn't like it. But that afternoon I discovered that 'frozen' was not exactly the right word. 'Cooked' was more like it.

At about the lunch hour the breeze dropped, and any moisture in the ground began to steam up into the still, hot air. You could feel the humidity rising. By the time lunch was over there was only one thing you were able to do—sweat!

Working in these conditions felt impossible. All you wanted to do was retire to a cool, dark bedroom, and lie down under a slowly revolving ceiling fan—which is what we did, me along with the rest since I make a point of respecting local customs.

About the middle of the afternoon a cooling breeze sprang up—the 'desert doctor' the locals called it—and suddenly I felt human again.

After an afternoon cup of sweet, strong Damascus coffee, Barnabas and I set out for Eli Samuelson's house, located on the banks of the river, in the 'old money' part of the town. We rang the bell and a servant admitted us into a large courtyard garden—with fruit trees, flower beds and trickling fountains.

Eli Samuelson was seated in a comfortable garden chair reading a book. He was white-haired, with a ruddy complexion, a broad smile, and sparkling white teeth.

'Joe Barnabas, my old friend! It is lovely to see you again, dear brother. And this, I take it, is the famous Ben Bartholomew. Your exploits in out-witting the Caiaphas Gang are well known in these parts, Brother Ben.'*

* See *The Case of the Vanishing Corpse*

I stammered an embarrassed reply, and we were waved into seats by Samuelson's side.

'Bring some drinks for my guests. Something cold, I think,' said our host to one of the servants.

'At once, Eli,' replied the servant.

'You let your servants address you by your first name?' I asked in surprise.

'This is a slightly unusual household,' Eli admitted.

'A very unusual household!' commented Barnabas, 'Tell him about it, Eli.'

'Really Joe, you make too much fuss about what I do,' said Eli, flapping his hands with embarrassment.

'Then I'll tell him,' said Barnabas.

'Tell me what?' I asked.

'All of the servants in this house are slaves purchased by Eli,' explained Barnabas.

'Well, that's not unusual,' I said.

'Let me finish. All of them were purchased from cruel or harsh masters. All of them were rescued from dreadful situations and given their freedom by Eli.'

'Their freedom? That *is* unusual!'

'They stay here as salaried servants. They have good living quarters, are well clothed, well paid, and eat as well as Eli and his family.'

'That's very generous of you, Mr Samuelson,' I said.

'Well,' said Eli, still looking a little embarrassed, 'It was not something I planned. But whenever I travel around Damascus and see a slave being cruelly or savagely treated I just can't abide it, I really can't. So I buy the slave from their harsh master and bring them here.'

'And how many of your present staff would be people you have rescued in this way?' I asked.

'By now, just about all of them,' said Eli, 'I've been in the "rescue" business—as you call it—for many years now.'

Our drinks arrived, and I turned the conversation towards the purpose of the visit. 'What can you tell me about the late Malachi Mason and his business dealings?'

'Quite a lot,' replied Eli. 'Quite a lot indeed.'

CHAPTER 8

'For a start,' I said, 'was he the cheat I have heard he was?'

'Oh, absolutely!' said Eli, 'A most dreadful cheat, I'm afraid I have to say. Mind you, he would have said it himself if he was here. He never hid the nature of his dealings. Being open about his dishonesty was all part of the game for Malachi. He was a charming rogue.'

'If he was that open about it,' I asked, 'why did anyone have dealings with him?'

'Because, dear brother, lots of businessmen like to play the same game. They were prepared to do deals with Mason, knowing that they would have to watch his every move, but also knowing that many of the deals he engineered were highly profitable for all concerned.'

'I see. Or at least, I think I see. But some people must have felt cheated by such a wheeler-dealer. Can you suggest any?'

'A few. Most merchants regarded Mason as an "honest thief" if I may use that expression, and many of the people he cheated were traders in other ports around the Mediterranean. The people for whom he often pulled off windfall profits were merchants here in Damascus.'

'So most of his enemies were not in this city?'

'Precisely.'

'Most, you say. But that doesn't mean all. Who, in Damascus, had a score to settle with Mason?'

'I can give you a few names to start with.'

'Right,' I said, pulling out my pocket notebook, 'shoot.'

'Firstly—Seth Yentob.'

'His partner?'

'Well, think about it for a moment. If there was one man in this city who had to keep a constant, non-stop eye on Mason's sharp practices it was his partner. If Mason could pull off a swift one that delivered profit to himself but not his partner he would do it. And Seth Yentob knew that. So check him out.'

'I will. Who else?'

'There's a man named Silas Levi—another merchant. Or, rather, he *was* a merchant. Nowadays he's a clerk in a shipping firm. Malachi Mason drove him into bankruptcy and out of business. At least that's what Silas says.'

'Okay, I'll talk to him as well.'

'Then there's a ship's captain named Ahab Ishmael. He was master of a trading vessel named *The Jonah*, owned by Mason–Yentob Enterprises. When the ship sank in a storm at sea he lost his family, his crew, his cargo, his life savings, and his left leg. He blamed Mason for cutting corners on the ship's maintenance and repair work.'

'Was he right? Did the complaint have any basis?'

'I don't know, but it's worth checking out. Oh, and there is one other person I heard about recently, a former secretary employed by Mason. Her name is Della Rhodes. He sacked her, and she protested about unfair dismissal.'

'Della Rhodes,' I repeated as I wrote down the

name, 'I'll have a word with her as well. That the lot?'

'For the time being. I'll ask around. If I hear any other rumours, I'll pass them on. We must all do what we can to help our dear brother Tullus.'

I snapped my notebook shut, Barnabas and I said our farewells, and we stood up to leave. Eli walked us as far as the front gate. As we were leaving, a young servant arrived—from the markets, judging by the parcels he was carrying.

'Good afternoon, Eli,' he said as he entered.

'Good afternoon, young Abner,' said Eli, smiling broadly as he spoke.

As we walked back towards the centre of town I remarked, 'That is a most remarkable household.'

'Eli Samuelson is a most remarkable man—a man of enormous generosity and compassion. And his wife is just as warm and kind as he is,' Joe said, as we walked back towards the heart of Damascus.

Meanwhile, a scene was occurring in Jerusalem that I wasn't to hear about until much later—a scene that was to have a profound effect on those of us in Damascus.

That day, in Jerusalem, in the religious court called the Sanhedrin, Paul Benson stood before a panel of judges.

'Exactly what is it you are asking us for, Mr Benson?' said the Chief Justice, who was also the High Priest.

'A letter,' replied Paul, 'addressed to synagogues in Damascus, requiring their co-operation in the prosecution of any followers of Jesus I find there, both men and women, so that I can bring them in chains back to Jerusalem.'

'An extradition order, in other words?'

'Precisely!' Paul snapped, his face flushed with emotion, the pupils of his eyes dark points of hatred.

'Just exactly what do you want to do with these so-called "Christians"?'

'Wipe them out!' Paul hissed with quiet fury, 'Destroy them! See every last one of them killed as the evil heretics they are!'

'An admirable aim indeed,' said one of the junior judges, the other judges on the bench nodding in solemn agreement.

'But we already have an agent operating in Damascus. A man named . . . ah, what is his name again?' murmured the Chief Justice.

'Mr Aaron Burger, your honour,' replied the clerk of the court, 'the District Attorney of Damascus.'

'Well, there you are then,' said the Chief Justice, shrugging his shoulders. 'If we have no less a person than the District Attorney in that city prosecuting Christians at every opportunity, surely your presence there will be extraneous?'

'Not so, your honour,' replied Paul swiftly, 'Mr Burger—who is my cousin, and whose excellent work I know well—is only prosecuting local Christians, citizens of Damascus. But my spies tell me that there are Christians from here in Jerusalem who are now fleeing to Damascus to escape my operations. I want to go after them.'

'I see,' muttered the Chief Justice.

'My work, your honour,' continued Paul, 'will not duplicate that done by Mr Burger, but will complement it.'

'And what is your plan, or policy, once you reach Damascus, Mr Benson?'

'My policy is slaughter, your honour,' said Paul,

breathing hard, 'imprisonment and slaughter. I intend to break their spirits, and then break their necks!'

'An excellent policy. And you will target those Christians who have fled to Damascus from Jerusalem leaving the local Christians to Mr Burger?'

'I will, your honour.'

'In that case I propose that we issue the extradition order that you request,' said the Chief Justice, looking up and down the bench. The other judges nodded in agreement.

'You will want it to be an open order, I assume?' he continued.

'Precisely, your honour. Unrestricted with respect to both numbers and names. And may I have a set of blank arrest warrants as well?'

'So ordered,' said the judge, banging his gavel. 'If you call into the office of the clerk of the court this afternoon the necessary documentation will be available for you to collect.'

'Thank you, your honour,' said Paul, 'And I have one other request to make, if I may?'

'Yes, of course. What is your request?'

'That I be granted a platoon of Temple Guards to accompany me to Damascus.'

'That seems reasonable enough. If we are to authorise your activities then we should give you the resources to carry them out.'

'I would like to hand-pick the officers myself, your honour. I need some big, tough lads for this operation.'

'Indeed. So ordered.' Again the gavel banged.

Barnabas and I had reached Straight Street, and were heading for the alley that would take us back to the house when he heard a sudden commotion further up the street. There was a loud crash, and the sound of men shouting and women screaming.

We hurried towards the spot where a crowd was already gathering.

'What happened?' I asked one of the men on the edge of the crowd.

'An accident of some sort,' he replied.

'A horse pulling a heavy cart suddenly bolted,' said the man standing beside him, 'and plunged into a shopfront.'

'Is there anything we can do to help?' asked Joe with deep concern written all over his face. He then started pushing his way through the crowd, asking, 'Has anyone been hurt?'

As we got closer to the front of the crowd we could see the damage. A horse was lying on its side, whinnying. The cart it had been pulling was smashed to matchwood, and the blocks of dressed stone that had been loaded on the cart were spilled over the footpath and into the shop that the cart had crashed against.

'Is there anything we can do to help?' asked Barnabas again. 'I have first-aid training, if that's of any assistance.'

A man who had been kneeling on the pavement stood up and shook his head sadly. 'It's too late, they all appear to be dead—the driver of the cart, and the three people who were in the shop at the time. All dead.'

'Are you sure?' said Joe. 'Let me check.'

I stood back and watched Joe move around amongst the bodies checking for a pulse, or some sign of breathing. When he came back to where I stood, his face told the story.

'All dead?'

He nodded. 'Died instantly by the look of it.'

We turned and began to walk back slowly back the way we had come.

'Why?' I asked, as we walked on with heavy hearts, and with that sense of shock, of numbness, that seeing an accident always gives you. 'Why must there be so much suffering in this world? There is suffering caused by evil human beings—people like Paul Benson and the terrorists who attack lone travellers on deserted roads—and there is this other suffering, caused by accidents. Why does it happen? It shouldn't be like this!'

Barnabas stopped and looked me straight in the eye, 'This is something you and I should talk about, Ben,' he said. 'Later. Not now, later.'

CHAPTER 9

Early the next morning Barnabas set off for the prison with a change of clothes and shaving tackle so that Dr Tullus would be able to cut a respectable figure in court.

I arrived at the District Court shortly before ten o'clock, knowing I had a battle on my hands.

The courtroom was crowded—largely with lawyers, their clerks, and, occasionally, their clients. At a few minutes past ten Judge Hezion entered, and the clerk of the court called out, 'All rise.'

The judge took his seat.

'This court is now in session—Judge Hezion presiding,' chanted the clerk. We all resumed our seats.

'I'll begin by reading through the list,' said the judge, and then read through the list of matters scheduled for the day. Our matter was near the top of list.

'Matter number VII,' said the judge, 'Bail application hearing in the matter of *The Empire versus Matthias*—the charge being murder.'

'Ben Bartholomew, your honour. I appear for the defendant,' I said, leaping to my feet.

'And I appear for the prosecution, your honour,' said a voice from the other side of the courtroom.

'Ah, the District Attorney in person. Good morning, Mr Burger,' said the judge.

'Good morning, your honour.'

I looked across the room at the man who was to be my opponent in this legal battle. Aaron Burger, I had been told, was only in his early thirties, but he looked at least ten years older. He had bags under his eyes that you could pack for a weekend away, and deep lines around the corners of his mouth. His black hair clung to his skull in closely clipped curls. His shallow eye sockets gave him an almost popeyed appearance.

'How long do you imagine this matter will take, gentlemen?' asked the judge.

'It can be disposed of fairly quickly, your honour,' said Burger. 'A bail application on a capital charge is merely a formality. I'm sure my learned friend would agree?'

'No, I don't agree at all,' I said. 'My client will be pleading not guilty, and will be vigorously defending this charge, your honour. He is a professional man with no previous convictions of any kind, and of impeccable standing in the community. The defence takes this bail application very seriously indeed.'

'Then how long do you think you will want to argue the matter?'

I glanced over at Burger and said, 'Half an hour should be sufficient.'

Burger nodded, 'If my friend wants to take this application seriously, then half an hour should deal with it.'

'Very well,' said the judge, 'I'll hear the application as soon as I've finished reading through the list.'

Judge Hezion proceeded to call matter number VIII, and to work his way steadily through all twenty matters on his list for the day. Some of them were bail continuations, some to record consent agreements, and a few required the hearing of arguments. These were scheduled to be heard after our bail application.

At about eleven o'clock Judge Hezion said, 'Mr Burger and Mr Bartholomew, we can now proceed with your bail application matter.'

'We're ready, your honour,' I replied, walking to the bar table.

'So is the prosecution, your honour,' said Burger, joining me.

'Is the prisoner available?' asked the judge.

'He's down in the holding cells, your honour,' said the sergeant-at-arms.

'Bring the prisoner up,' ordered the judge.

There was a delay of a few minutes, and then Tullus was brought into the court—in chains and between two armed officers.

'I would ask your honour to have the chains removed during the course of the hearing,' I said, knowing the psychological difference it can make seeing a man heavily chained in the dock.

'Objection your honour,' cried Burger leaping to his feet.

'On what grounds?'

'The charge is murder, your honour, and it is customary for persons accused of murder to remain shackled.'

'Mr Bartholomew?'

'My client is not a waterfront thug, your honour, but a highly qualified professional man and a respected citizen. He has no history of violence, and in the presence of prison guards and the sergeant-at-arms it is surely possible for him to have a few moments comfort while his matter is heard.'

'I'm inclined to agree with Mr Bartholomew,' said the judge, 'Mr Burger?'

'As your honour pleases.'

'Remove the prisoner's shackles.'

After a moment of clanking keys and chains Tullus was able to stand in the dock, clean-shaven and neatly dressed, looking like a responsible, upright citizen—exactly the impression I was hoping to create.

'Proceed, Mr Bartholomew,' instructed Judge Hezion.

'The court already has the formal application for bail?' I asked.

The judged rummaged around amongst his papers and found the correct document.

'In support of the application I draw your honour's attention to my client's lack of any previous convictions of any sort, and to his good standing in the community as a medical practitioner. I shall be calling several witnesses to attest to my client's good character and reliability, your honour.'

'Go ahead and call your first witness, Mr Bartholomew.'

'I call David Gideon.'

David made his way to the witness box and was sworn in.

'Please tell the court your full name and occupation.'

'David Elias Gideon—I own and operate a building materials supply company.'

'Are you acquainted with Dr Tullus Matthias?' I asked.

'I am.'

'In what capacity?'

'In several capacities.'

'Please tell the court of the ways in which you know him.'

'Well, in first place, he is my doctor. He looks after myself, my wife and our daughter.'

'And what sort of a family doctor have you found him to be?'

'Excellent. Diligent, concerned, supportive, compassionate. I can't speak highly enough of his skills as a healer and his concern for his patients.'

'Has he ever let you down?' intervened the judge.

'Never, your honour,' replied Gideon. 'He's always turned up punctually when he's said he would, and always provided exactly the care he's promised. If anything, he's delivered more than he promised.'

'Very good,' said the judge. 'Carry on, Mr Bartholomew.'

'And in what other capacity do you know Dr Matthias, Mr Gideon?' I asked.

'As a fellow member of the family of Christian believers here in Damascus.'

'Have you known him long in that capacity?'

'Several years.'

'And what impression have you formed of his character in that time?'

'The highest possible impression. I have found him to be loyal, honest, supportive and gentle.'

'And truthful?' asked the judge.

'Strictly truthful. Absolutely a man of his word, your honour.'

'Thank you, Mr Gideon.'

'I have no further questions, your honour,' I said, and resumed my seat at the bar table.

'Mr Burger—do you have any questions for this witness?'

'Just a few, your honour,' said Burger, rising to his

feet. 'Mr Gideon, this circle of 'Christian believers' that you mentioned—this is well known as a heretical sect is it not?'

'I wouldn't put it like that . . .'

'No, I'm sure you wouldn't, Mr Gideon. But that's the truth, isn't it?'

'No, that's not fair!'

'This sect—the followers of Jesus—has been banned by the Temple authorities in Jerusalem, hasn't it?'

'Yes, but . . .'

'Hasn't it?'

'Yes, but . . .'

'On the grounds of blasphemy and heresy?'

'Yes, but . . .'

'Just answer my questions, Mr Gideon.'

'Perhaps you should allow the witness to complete his answer, Mr Burger,' commented the judge.

'As your honour pleases,' murmured Burger.

'What did you want to add, Mr Gideon?' asked Judge Hezion.

'Only that there are large numbers of faithful, orthodox Jews who believe, as I do, that our faith is completed and fulfilled in Jesus, the one and only son of God. Believing that, we seek to live as good Jews, and as faithful followers of the very high moral standards that he taught. There is nothing subversive or improper in our beliefs, your honour.'

'And you are telling the court,' continued the judge, 'that the defendant shares your views?'

'That is correct, your honour.'

'Thank you, Mr Gideon. You may resume your cross-examination, Mr Burger.'

'I have no further questions of this witness, your

honour,' Burger sneered, a tone of disgust in his voice.

'Mr Bartholomew, call your next witness.'

'I call—Tabitha Mason.'

A shocked murmur ran around the courtroom, and then a hush fell as the door opened and Tabitha entered.

She was dressed demurely in a plain, black dress, which had the effect of making her Titian hair, pale skin, and green eyes look even lovelier. She entered the witness box and was sworn in. Everyone in the courtroom could see that the whole time she was taking the oath she couldn't keep her eyes off Tullus. And his eyes were glued to her.

'Miss Mason, how long have you known my client?' I asked.

'About twelve months,' she replied, in a quiet voice.

'And what is your relationship to him?'

'I love him enough to marry him,' she said firmly and defiantly.

A murmur of consternation ran around the courtroom. The judge banged his gavel several times, and an expectant silence returned.

'You understand that he is charged with murder?' I continued.

'Yes.'

'Specifically, with the murder of your father?'

'Yes.'

'And yet you appear today as a character witness for Dr Matthias?'

'I do.'

'Please tell the court why.'

'Because I not only love him, I know him. I know

him to be a kind and gentle man incapable of violence of any sort.'

'Miss Mason,' I asked, 'were you fond of your father?'

'Yes . . .' she said with a sob, her striking green eyes glistening with tears, '. . . very much. My mother died when I was only a child, and my father and I were . . . were . . . very close.'

Tabitha buried her head in her hands and began to sob quietly.

'Would the sergeant-at-arms please fetch a glass of water for the witness,' said the judge.

A moment later the sergeant-at-arms offered Tabitha a glass of water, which she refused. She dabbed at her eyes with a damp handkerchief, and pulled herself together.

'Are you fully recovered, Miss Mason?' asked Judge Hezion.

'Yes,' she answered, her voice little more than a whisper.

'Are you prepared to answer further questions?'

'Yes, I am.'

While this exchange was going on I noticed, out of the corner of my eye, Burger scribbling a hasty note, and his clerk rushing out of the court, note in hand. Now, what trouble was Burger cooking up, I wondered?

'You may resume, Mr Bartholomew.'

'Thank you, your honour.'

'Miss Mason,' I continued, 'have you found my client to be a truthful and reliable man?'

'Yes.'

'In all the time you have known him, has he ever lied to you?'

'No.'

'Has he ever let your down?'

'No, never.'

'No further questions, your honour.'

'Mr Burger, have you any questions for this witness?'

'Yes, I have, your honour.'

Burger rose ponderously to his feet and turned to face Tabitha.

'What are your feelings towards the accused, Miss Mason?'

'I've already told the court,' protested Tabitha, 'I love him, and will marry him.'

'Did your late father approve of your relationship?'

'No.'

'What did he say about it?'

'He said he didn't want me to marry Tullus.'

'Come now, Miss Mason. He expressed himself a little more strongly than that, didn't he? I put it to your that he forbad the match—is that true?'

'Y . . . yes . . .'

'*Strictly* forbad the match?'

'Yes.'

'And banned Dr Matthias from visiting your home, is that correct?'

'Yes.'

'Thus giving Dr Matthias a strong motive for murdering your father!'

'No! No!'

'Objection, your honour,' I said, leaping to my feet. 'This is a bail application, not a murder trial. As such these questions are immaterial.'

'Objection sustained. If you wish to take your questioning in some other direction, you may continue, Mr Burger.'

'I have no further questions, your honour.'

'Have you any further witnesses, Mr Bartholomew?'

'No, your honour.'

'Do you wish to introduce any witnesses, Mr Burger.'

'No, your honour, no witnesses.'

'In that case, I will listen to your arguments and then make my ruling.'

CHAPTER 10

'Mr Bartholomew—the court is ready to hear your closing arguments.'

'Thank you, your honour. The main thrust of what I am saying to the court today is, I am sure, already apparent. Namely that my client is not a criminal but a respectable and responsible citizen. I understand the ordinary reluctance of the court to grant bail in murder cases, but this case, I suggest, is out of the ordinary. We are dealing here with a man widely recognised as truthful and reliable. We have solid citizens prepared to lodge bail for him, and to undertake that he will appear in court to answer the charge against him. I put it to you strongly that Dr Tullus Matthias should not be treated like a sailor who has killed a man in a drunken fight, and that he should be released on bail until the date set for the hearing.'

'Thank you, Mr Bartholomew. Mr Burger?'

'Your honour, the prosecution's argument is a simple one. A murder charge is a murder charge, regardless of who the accused happens to be. Whether he's a doctor, or a dock worker, it should make no difference. A man who has killed before could easily kill again. And a man with the financial resources of a doctor could easily flee from the jurisdiction of this court. On those grounds, your honour, we most vigorously oppose bail.'

'Thank you, Mr Burger. Dr Matthias, please stand

and face the court. I am inclined to accept the testimony of the character witnesses I have heard, and to release you under the recognisance of your lawyer, Mr Bartholomew. Do you understand that if I do so, you will be giving this court a most solemn undertaking to appear here on the date set for your trial?'

'I most certainly do, your honour.'

'In that case, I set bail in the sum of—'

The double doors at the back of the court suddenly burst open and a striking figure strode into the courtroom. He was, I think, the biggest man I had ever seen—tall, broad-shouldered and dressed in the uniform of a general with gold and silver medals scattered across his chest.

'Your honour,' he boomed in a parade-ground voice, 'The state seeks leave to intervene in this matter.'

'The court recognises General Pol,' said Judge Hezion.

So, this was the famous General Pol—commander-in-chief of the armed forces of King Aretas IV, King of Syria. Pol had great authority in Damascus, and was answerable only to the King's representative—Lord Hazael, Ethnarch of Damascus.

General Pol strode towards the bar table, his leather riding boots clumping loudly across the stone floor. 'I am under instructions from Lord Hazael to officially and formally oppose bail in this matter.'

'I see,' said the judge, who then held a whispered consultation with his associate, who produced a law book which the judge also consulted.

'If the Ethnarch chooses to officially and formally object to the granting of bail—' began the judge.

'He does!' boomed General Pol.

'—then my hands are tied, and I am required to

accede to his objection. The application is refused, and the prisoner remanded in custody. Next matter.'

Tullus looked desperately at Tabitha as his shackles were refastened and he was led away by his jailers. I too turned to look at Tabitha, and found her face—just a moment before full of hope—now a picture of tragedy, with silent tears trickling down her cheeks.

David and Miriam Gideon gathered around to comfort her. Joe Barnabas hurried to my side, just as Aaron Burger walked past on his way out of the courtroom.

'Bad luck, counsellor,' Burger said with a sneer.

'I don't think luck came into it,' I snapped back.

'If you want to know what you're up against, call in to my office, and I'll show you the evidence—it's foolproof.'

'But is it jury-proof?' I cracked, then turned my back on him.

'What did you mean about luck not coming into it?' asked Barnabas.

'General Pol's appearance was not a coincidence. Burger summonsed him. When he realised that Tabitha's testimony had tipped the hearing against him, he sent out a note calling for assistance.'

'If General Pol will respond to a summons from Burger, then we're up against some powerful players.'

'That we are, Joe my brother, that we are.'

'So what next, Ben?'

'I need to hire a local private eye, a good one—someone who knows Damascus as well as I know Jerusalem. Any suggestions?'

'Mallard is the man you need.'

'Mallard?'

'Paul Mallard is the best private investigator in the city. '

'If he's the best, he's what I want. Lead me to him.'

We left the court precincts and walked back towards the centre of the city. About halfway down Straight Street we turned sharp right into the business district.

Mallard's office was in a modern, glass-fronted high-rise building. It looked like a corporation's headquarters, and was a far cry from the dingy office I had operated from when I was a P.I. in Jerusalem.

As the elevator whizzed us upwards Barnabas said, 'Mallard's office is on the eighth floor.'

In fact, the Mallard Detective Agency offices—crammed with operatives and office workers—occupied almost half of the eighth floor.

We were seated in a reception area surrounded by potted palms and piped music until a cool blonde secretary whisked us into the presence of the man himself.

Mallard was dressed in pale-grey slacks and a check sports coat, and looked more like a golfer than a gumshoe. Tall and solid, his athletic build running a little towards fat, he had thick blond hair swept straight back, a chiselled chin suggesting determination, and a flashing smile and blue eyes signalling warmth and an easygoing friendliness.

'Welcome, gentlemen, what can I do for you?' he said after the introductions had been made.

'It's the Malachi Mason murder case that we're interested in,' I explained.

'Phew, you only pick the big ones don't you!' whistled Mallard.

'What do you mean?'

'My sources at City Hall tell me that the powers that be want a quick, clean conviction.'

'Well, I'm leading the defence, so any sort of conviction is the last thing I want.'

'Naturally. Where do I come in?'

'If my client, Dr Tullus Matthias, is not guilty— then someone else is.'

'Stands to reason.'

'With a strong case against Tullus, my best move is to identify the real killer.'

'And you think I can help?'

'I hope you can help, Mr Mallard, I certainly hope you can.'

'Call me Paul everyone does—or "PM" for short. Now—what's my assignment?'

'Malachi Mason's background, and any of his known associates who might have borne him a grudge, or wanted him dead.'

'I'll get right onto it,' said Mallard, scribbling in a notebook. 'Any specific names you want me to start with?'

'Four to begin with. Silas Levi—claims he was driven out of business by Mason. Captain Ahab Ishmael—blames Mason for the loss of his ship. Miss Della Rhodes, a former secretary—sacked by Mason. And Seth Yentob—'

'Mason's partner?'

'Right.'

'I'll put an operative onto each of those people, and, with a bit of luck, we should have some results within 48 hours.'

We shook hands on that and then signed a contract! It was all very different from the sort of 'shake-hands-on-a-deal' one-man detective business I was used to.

After lunch I decided to take up Aaron Burger's offer of a meeting—'know your enemy' is always a good tactic.

The D.A.'s office was in City Hall, an imposing sandstone building fronted by Corinthian columns. Inside the vast entrance lobby I found the building directory, a crowded wall sign peppered with arrows and room numbers indicating where to find the various government departments.

On the second floor I pushed open the frosted glass door marked 'District Attorney' and found myself in a cramped and dingy reception room. The place was deserted so I tapped the bell on the reception desk. Several minutes later I tapped it again—harder.

Eventually a tired-looking public servant arrived and asked my business.

I asked to see Burger and gave my name. The public servant yawned an incomprehensible reply and disappeared again. I took a seat in a straight-backed wooden chair, the only kind in the room, and waited . . . and waited.

Eventually the public servant slouched back and made an unappetising offer: 'Follow me,' he said.

He led me down a narrow corridor, past the sound of distant typing, to a second frosted door. This one had the words 'Aaron H. Burger, District Attorney' painted on them in gold leaf.

'Mr Burger will be with you shortly,' said the sullen servant, then slouched off back down the corridor. Was I supposed to wait outside the door, or what?

I went inside.

It was clearly Burger's private office, and it was empty. There was a vast desk in the middle of the room, ancient walnut in colour. The carpet was a dingy grey and the padded leather chairs a dark green.

I was beginning to understand the lines on Burger's face. This decor alone could achieve that!

On three sides the walls were lined with floor-to-ceiling bookshelves. I walked over for a closer look: legal textbooks and bound copies of law reports.

The fourth wall had plain timber panelling decorated with primitive African weapons of war: shields covered in leopard skins, razor-sharp knives, and wicked-looking spears with long, straight wooden shafts that ended in gleaming metal points. The arrangement was nicely symmetrical except for the middle group of spears. I was rearranging them a little more neatly when a voice spoke from behind me.

'Good afternoon, Mr Bartholomew.'

I turned around. It was Burger.

'I was just . . . admiring your collection,' I muttered, to cover my embarrassment.

'My brother is in the Roman Army—he brought these souvenirs back from a campaign in North Africa. Please take a seat.'

CHAPTER 11

'I take it you're here to discover just how hopeless is your attempt to defend Matthias?' Burger said, as I lowered myself into one of the dark green, leather-covered chairs.

'I've come to discuss the case, if that's what you mean,' I replied.

'There's little to discuss,' said Burger in his strangely nasal, whining voice, ambling around his large desk and adding, 'Matthias is guilty for sure, guilty as hell.'

I was surprised at the venom in his voice.

'Where's your objectivity?' I challenged. 'You sound very personally involved.'

He looked daggers at me for a moment, then lowered himself slowly into the chair behind his desk.

'The facts are very simple,' he said, staring down at his blotting paper, 'and beyond dispute.'

'Remind me,' I said.

'It all hinges on access to the murder room. There was only one door leading to the bedroom in which Malachi Mason died—the door to the courtyard. There were two small windows, but both are heavily barred, and even a monkey couldn't get in through those, let alone a murderer. You agree?'

'I agree.'

'Good. So the whole matter ends up revolving

around that one door. And that door was under observation for the whole of the afternoon. There was no way anyone could have got into, or out of, Mason's room without being seen by the servant on duty. And he saw no-one!'

'Perhaps he's been bribed by the murderer to keep quiet? Or threatened with death if he speaks?'

'If you try to shake his testimony you'll fail!' snarled Burger. 'He is an ideal witness—an honest, upright citizen, confident, clear, and unshakable.'

'We'll see about that.'

'I've already had him checked out thoroughly. I am convinced that he has not been bribed, or threatened, or . . . whatever other fantasy you try to concoct. I've had a lot of experience with witnesses over the years—and this man is as good as a witness gets! If you attack him, you'll only make your own case look weaker.'

'Okay, so there was only one door, and there was a servant watching the door. If I grant that, what next?'

'Next is the fact that your client was the last person to see Mason alive . . . that your client is the only person—the *only* person—who could have killed Mason. Opportunity, Bartholomew, that's what it all hinges on, opportunity. And only one person had the opportunity to commit the crime—your client!'

'I see,' I rubbed my chin thoughtfully.

'That Mason was killed with a distinctive dagger owned by your client is mere icing on the cake. We don't even have to establish that to prove Matthias *must* have been the murderer, because no-one else could be.'

'It's a good thing you're not relying on the evidence of the dagger, because there isn't any.'

'What do you mean?'

'The dagger doesn't prove a single thing. It could have been stolen at any time by anyone. My client once owned the murder weapon, that's true. But owning it is not the same as using it.'

Burger dismissed all this with a wave of his hand.

'Irrelevant,' he snapped. 'We don't need the weapon for our case. As I said before, this trial is going to revolve around opportunity. And on that matter my case against your client is fireproof.'

He had me worried. The prosecution's case was going to be a hard one to shake.

'This is a classic murder case,' continued Burger. 'Motive, means, and opportunity are the three keys in every murder—and Matthias had all three. Motive—because he wanted to marry Tabitha. Means—the dagger was his,' he ticked them off on his fingers as he spoke, 'and opportunity—because no-one else was able to get at the victim during the period when the murder occurred.'

Burger stood up, indicating that the interview was over. I had heard his case, there was nothing more I needed to know for the time being, so I took the hint and headed for the door.

As I turned the doorknob Burger spoke again, 'By the way, there's one other thing that you might like to know.'

'What's that?' I turned and asked.

'My cousin is on his way to Damascus.'

'Your cousin?'

'Paul Benson. You've heard of him, surely?'

Paul Benson! On his way to Damascus! This was bad news on top of bad news.

'Why is he coming?' I asked.

'On business,' Burger sneered. 'He is bringing

arrest warrants and extradition orders for the Christians of Damascus. Perhaps you'd like to warn your friends that the storm is about to hit!'

'When will he be here?'

'This fax,' said Burger, waving a sheet of paper, 'was sent when he left Jerusalem several days ago. He should arrive in the city later today.'

I stood, stunned by the news I had just heard.

'You can go now,' snarled Burger, with a dismissive wave of his hand. 'I have work to do.'

I snapped out of my coma, and left the office.

As I trudged across the city, back to the Gideons' house where I was staying, my heart was in my boots. Paul Benson! Bringing his savage persecution of Christians to Damascus! The news could hardly be worse.

When I pushed open the door and stepped into the courtyard I found everyone there, sitting in the afternoon sunshine: David and Miriam, Joe Barnabas, Ananias, Nicolaus, George the big Abyssinian, and little Phoebe and her cat.

They were looking very glum and depressed.

'We have some dreadful news,' said Barnabas in response to my greeting.

'You've heard then?' I said.

'The news reached us just after you left,' said Miriam, as she dabbed her eyes with a damp handkerchief. 'Poor Eli.'

'Poor Eli? Poor everyone, I would have thought.'

'What do you mean, poor everyone?' asked Ananias, looking puzzled.

'Well, he'll persecute anyone he can get his hands on,' I said. 'I've seen him operate, and it's not a pretty sight.'

'Who are you talking about?' asked George.

'Why Paul Benson, of course!'

'What about Paul Benson?'

'What about him? He's coming *here*—that's what about him! I thought you all knew. I thought that was why you were looking so sad.'

'No, this is news to us,' said Ananias.

'Where did you hear this?' asked Barnabas. 'How do you know?'

'Burger told me,' I explained. 'He's Paul Benson's cousin, and ally in persecution. And he received a fax notifying him of the imminent arrival of the great persecutor himself.'

'When?' asked David quietly, 'When will he arrive?'

'It could be tonight,' I said.

'Oh, no!' sobbed Miriam, 'It's too much. On top of everything else, it's just too much!'

'On top of what else?' I asked.

'It's Eli Samuelson,' said Barnabas, 'he's been killed—he and his wife and children.'

'That's dreadful! What happened?' I said, horror-struck.

'It was the servants,' said David, 'they rose up in rebellion, killed Eli and his family, looted his house, and set fire to the buildings.'

'That's appalling! Why? Why would they do that? After all he has done for them?'

'That's what we've been asking ourselves all afternoon,' said Miriam tearfully. 'Eli and his family were so good to them—rescued them from slavery, and treated them like members of the family. Why would they do it?'

'Because,' said Barnabas, 'They didn't care about what Eli had done for them, they didn't care what he had rescued them from, or how well he cared for them. They only cared about the fact that he didn't keep his firearms under lock and key. They only cared about the fact that they were not locked up in barracks overnight. So they seized what they took to be a golden opportunity. They decided it was easier to steal than to work, and so they seized what they thought was their own advantage.'

'That's horrible!' I said. 'Simply horrible. When did it happen?'

'Last night,' said Nicolaus. 'It was discovered early this morning when neighbours saw smoke rising from the buildings. An officer from the City Watch came and told us the news just after you left to go to the District Attorney's office.'

'What's being done about it?'

'Well, Eli's former servants have fled the city, but an army patrol is being sent out after them.'

'Good!' I said. 'I hope they feel the full weight of the law upon them!'

'Talking about the full weight of the law,' said Ananias, 'tell us more about Paul Benson. Did Burger tell you why he is coming to Damascus?'

'I asked that, and he said "On business". And that's not good news for us,' I said, 'since we all know what business Paul Benson is in.'

'The persecution business!' muttered Ananias.

'Precisely! And Burger told me that he is bringing arrest warrants and extradition orders with him.'

'It gets worse and worse!' moaned Ananias. 'I think I might leave town for a while. It's the only way any of us will be safe!'

The evening meal that night was a quiet and gloomy affair.

I retired to my room early to do some serious thinking. The arrival of Paul Benson would make my task harder, but I still had to focus on the main game: getting Tullus Matthias off the murder rap. And that was not just looking hard, it was looking impossible!

CHAPTER 12

Next morning I put all thoughts of Paul Benson out of my mind, and concentrated on the case against my client.

I decided that the key witness was Quaresimus. It was his testimony I had to either break or find some way around.

Quaresimus had not told me the truth—at least, not the whole truth. That's what my instinct told me, but I needed evidence, not instinct. And how could I test the point at which he was lying?

As I paced around the Gideons' courtyard after breakfast I concocted a plan. Then I rang Tabitha and told her what I wanted her to do. That done, I walked down to Straight Street and bought myself a loose-fitting robe called a *galabiyah* at one of the clothing stalls in the bazaar. Most of the men of Damascus wore these. I then added a *keffiyeh* to wind around my head.

With shopping bags loaded with my disguise I walked back home, then spent the rest of the morning working on the legal documents I had to complete for Tullus's murder trial.

After an early lunch the city of Damascus settled into its usual siesta. The streets were emptied and the noise of the city hushed. But instead of resting along with everyone else, I dressed myself in my disguise and stepped out into the street.

The air was hot, humid, and still as death as I walked across town to the Mason villa. Once there I positioned myself in a shaded doorway diagonally across the street from where I could keep the villa under observation.

After twenty minutes my patience was rewarded when I saw Quaresimus slip surreptitiously into the roadway, and hurry off down the street.

When the people of Damascus have their siesta there is always one servant in every household who is told to stay on duty. This so-called 'siesta duty' is unpopular, and avoided by most servants as much as possible. From my phone call to Tabitha I had learned that Quaresimus never objected to siesta duty.

I had asked Tabitha to roster Quaresimus on siesta duty for the day. Now my instincts were paying off.

Keeping at a careful distance, and hugging the walls of the buildings, I shadowed him halfway across town. He didn't stop until he came to a tall apartment block, where he knocked quietly on the front door. The door opened instantly and Quaresimus stepped inside.

I settled down to wait opposite, hidden in the shade of a stone pillar. The heat of the day passed slowly, and I found myself yawning and wanting to nod off to sleep.

At length, the front door opposite opened again, and Quaresimus stepped back out into the street. This time he was not alone—a young servant girl was beside him. They stood in front of the apartment block and kissed passionately. Then Quaresimus hurried down the street, with the girl waving him goodbye.

Once he was out of sight, she turned to go back inside. I ran across the street, and before the girl could pull the door closed, jammed the door with my foot and grabbed her elbow.

Her mouth was wide open and ready to scream. I clapped my hand across her mouth and said, 'Promise me that you won't scream, and I'll take my hand away. If you do scream you'll probably lose your job—and Quaresimus will lose his too.'

A light of understanding flashed in her eyes. She nodded and I removed my hand.

'What's your name?' I asked.

'Dinah,' she replied in a nervous whisper.

'And I take it, Dinah, that you work in this building as a maid?'

'Yes. My mistress has the top-floor apartment.'

'Quaresimus is, of course, your boyfriend.'

'We're going to get married,' she said, with a pout of her lips.

'Congratulations. But until that happy day, you two meet while everyone else is having their siesta—right?'

'Well . . .'

'Right?' I repeated, grabbing her arm.

'Stop it, you're hurting me!'

'Tell me the truth, then.'

'Yes, all right. He gets away whenever he can during siesta. It's the only way we can have any time to ourselves.'

'Now listen—this is very important. Was Quaresimus here a week ago yesterday?'

'No . . . he couldn't have been, she said, thinking back.'

'What do you mean?'

'I wasn't here. Last week my mistress and I were away for the whole week. We went to visit her sister in Jericho who's just had a baby.'

'Last week?'

'Yes.'

'The whole of last week?'

'Yes! I'm telling the truth.'

'Yes, I think you are telling the truth,' I said. 'It would be too easy to check up on.'

'Do you have any other questions?'

'No, you can go now.'

'You won't tell anyone about us, will you?'

'No,' I said with weary sigh. 'Your sordid little secret is safe with me.'

As soon as I released her arm, she closed the door.

I walked slowly back to the Gideons' house, annoyed that my plan had only uncovered a red herring. I had had hopes of proving that Quaresimus had not been on duty as he claimed to be when Malachi Mason was murdered. If I could show that I would blow Burger's 'opportunity' case out of the water. But my hopes had turned to dust.

Back in my room I discarded my *galabiyah* and *keffiyeh*, then called a taxi and rode across town to the Mason villa.

Tabitha greeted me and showed me into a private sitting room where we could talk without being overheard.

'Well?' she asked eagerly, as soon as the door closed behind us, 'Did it work?'

'Yes and no,' I replied. 'Yes, Quaresimus does have a girlfriend, and he does slip out during siesta to visit her.'

'Well then . . .?'

'But, no, he didn't visit her on the day of the murder.'

'Are you sure?'

'The girlfriend wasn't even in town on that day.'

'Oh,' said Tabitha quietly, her face falling. 'Well, thanks for trying anyway, Ben. It was a good idea, it's just a pity it didn't come off.'

'Hang on, Tabitha, don't get discouraged yet. I'll have more than one good idea, you know.'

'I'm sure you will,' she replied with a sad smile.

'While I'm here, let me take you back to the day your father died, and go over the details again,' I said.

'If you think it will help.'

'I have to keep going over the ground until I find a crack.'

'Yes, of course.'

Tabitha clapped her hands and a servant came running. She ordered cups of the strong, sweet coffee. After the coffee was served I began my questions again.

'How long had your father been sick when you called in Tullus?'

'Three days,' she said wearily.

'When your father first became sick did you suggest calling in the doctor?'

'Of course. I pleaded with him to let me call for medical help. But his own doctor was away and he wouldn't hear of it.'

'Did he have any visitors during those three days?'

'On the first day his partner, Seth Yentob, called in.'

'Did he seem worried by your father's illness?'

'Not especially.'

'Who else?'

'On the day before . . . before father died . . . that man came. He was always calling in to see father.'

'What man?'

'Aaron Burger.'

'Really? So Burger was here the day before the murder?'

'Yes. But it doesn't mean anything. As I said, he was always dropping in. He was my father's friend, not mine.'

'Did he express any concern about the state of your father's health?'

'He seemed a lot more worried than Yentob had been. Of course, father had got a lot worse since Yentob's visit, so that probably explains why.'

'Probably. You say that Burger was worried. How did he express this?'

'He told me to get Tullus in to take a look at father.'

'He did what? That's extraordinary! Surely he hated Tullus as much as your father did.'

'It sounds strange when I say it, but if you'd heard him, you would have realised how nasty and sarcastic he was being when he said it.'

'What do you mean?' I asked.

'Well, he walked out of father's room and asked if a doctor had seen him. I explained about father's stubbornness. A sly smile came over Burger's face and he said something like "That boyfriend of yours is supposed to be a wonderful doctor. Why don't you get him in?". But he said it with such malice that I knew he didn't mean it.'

'All the same . . .'

'He was just being nasty, Ben,' insisted Tabitha, 'I could tell that.'

'Nevertheless, you took his advice.'

'No I didn't. Well, not really. I thought about it for myself. And when it was clear that father was getting worse, and he was so delirious that he wouldn't know who was treating him anyway—well, then I decided to call in Tullus, regardless of what father would say about it afterwards.'

'But it was Burger who planted the idea in your head, wasn't it?'

'Not really,' snorted Tabitha, with a toss of her hair, 'I would have thought of it myself if he hadn't said anything.'

'But by saying it,' I insisted, 'he made sure you thought of it.'

Tabitha didn't reply, but sipped her coffee instead.

'I think Mr Burger's personal interest in this case is worth a little more investigation,' I muttered to myself, draining my coffee cup.

CHAPTER 13

Leaving the Mason villa, I took a taxi back to the Gideons', where I had the cabbie wait while I changed back into my disguise of *galabiyah* and *keffiyeh*. Then I had him drop me opposite City Hall.

Thinking I might have a long wait, I stopped a passer-by, 'Scisne ubi pocillum coffeae apud hanc locum possim capere?'

'Eh?' he replied.

'I said: know where I can get a cup of coffee around here?'

'Well, why didn't you say so! There's a nice little coffee shop just over there.'

'Thank you,' I said, thinking what an ignoramus, doesn't anyone speak Latin anymore?

The coffee shop faced the front steps of City Hall, so I took a seat, ordered coffee, picked up a copy of *Tempus* news magazine someone had left lying on the table, and settled down to watch for Aaron Burger.

After the office workers had left, and the sun was setting over Mount Hermon, Burger emerged from City Hall and hailed a cab. I hailed another and stayed close behind him.

It turned out that Burger lived in the penthouse of a very new, very expensive-looking apartment block. Definitely not a place for the hoi polloi! They must be paying district attorneys well these days, if he could afford to live there.

I paid off my cab, and took up a position in the shadows on the footpath opposite Burger's apartment. He emerged in a tuxedo an hour later and stood on the footpath, not hailing a cab, but watching the passing traffic.

Waiting for someone, I thought, so I hailed a passing cab.

'Where to?' asked the cabbie.

'Just drive me a block down the street, and then pull over.'

'And for this you hailed a cab?'

'Just turn on the meter and drive.'

'If you say so, buster—it's your denarius!'

A block down the street the taxi pulled in between two parked cars and came to a halt.

'Now what?' asked the driver.

'Just wait,' I said.

'Until when? Until you get some of idea of where you want to go?'

I could see Burger clearly in the cab's rear-view mirror, so I sat, watched and waited.

We didn't have to wait long. A limousine pulled up carrying another man in a tuxedo and two young women in evening dress. Burger joined them in the limo, and it sped off.

'Now,' I snapped to the cabbie, 'follow that limo.'

'This is more like it,' he said, engaging the gears and taking off, 'I've been a cabbie for fifteen years, and all that time I've been waiting for someone to say "Follow that car".'

We stayed behind the limo all the way through the city, and out to a spot south of the city walls on the banks of the Barada river.

They eventually pulled up in front of a flashing neon sign saying Caesar's Palace—Casino and Nite Club. I had my taxi stop on the opposite side of the road, paid off the cabbie, and stood, obscured by a palm tree, watching Burger's party pile out of the limo amidst much laughter. The second man in the group I now got a good look at for the first time—extremely thin with a face like a weasel. Burger and Weasel Face entered the nightclub with the girls clinging onto their arms.

I prowled around the exterior of Caesar's Palace. It was a mammoth building, almost the size of a real palace. At the back of the casino I tiptoed around garbage bins, looking through windows for some way to get in and see what Burger and his friends were up to.

The first window looked into a cloakroom, the next a bar, the next a kitchen. Finally, I peered through a small, high window, and found myself looking into the waiters' change room. There was a row of lockers, and a number of freshly pressed tuxedos draped over hangers.

Not far from the window was a locked door. After a minute's work with my penknife, I stepped into a short corridor, then turned to the left, and found myself in the change room.

'Who are you,' snapped a voice behind me, as I searched through the rack of tuxedos for one my size.

'Ah . . . I'm . . .' I stuttered, turning around to face a dark-haired man in a tuxedo, '. . . I'm . . . Kaleed's cousin.'

'Kaleed's cousin?'

'Yeah, that's right, Kaleed's sick tonight, and he asked me to come in and do his shift for him.'

'I don't know any Kaleed.'

'Sure you do,' I insisted. 'He's the good-looking one.'

'Oh, him. I guess I just never knew his name. That's the trouble with working in a place with such a big staff. You know what to do?'

'Yeah. Sure. Kaleed explained everything to me.'

'Okay then, get on with it.'

He left, and I breathed a sigh of relief. I found a tuxedo my size—it's handy being a standard size— and slipped back out into the dark at the back of the building.

There in the shadows behind the back wall of Caesar's Palace I changed from *galabiyah* and *keffiyeh* into tuxedo. I hid my things under a bush, combed my hair, and made my way back to the street.

I approached the front door of Caesar's Palace with my shoulders back and what I imagined to be a confident and sophisticated smile on my face. It worked.

'Good evening, sir,' said the commissionaire, holding open the front door for me.

The interior was even more palace-like than the exterior—assuming that the palace belonged to a ruler with extremely bad taste. It was all gilt, dark red velvet, and marble, with leather lounges, polished timber, chandeliers, and ivory-coloured deep pile carpet. These ingredients had been mixed together the way a child mixes up coloured blocks—in a haphazard jumble.

I prowled through the bars and the nightclub area without catching a glimpse of either Burger or Weasel Face. Then I tried the casino lounge. They were not at any of the rows of brightly coloured poker machines, nor the roulette table or any of the card tables. Where could they have got to?

At a blackjack table they were changing croupiers. As he walked across the room, I grabbed the arm of the croupier who was going off duty.

'Excuse me,' I said.

He turned and glared at me.

'I'm on a break,' he snarled.

'One quick question. Have you seen Burger tonight?'

'Who wants to know?'

'Me. I'm a friend of his. He told me to meet him here tonight. But I can't see him anywhere.'

'He'll be in the high rollers' room, of course.'

The croupier nodded towards a door at the back of the casino lounge, with a gorilla in a tuxedo standing guard, and occasionally letting someone in or out.

'You're a friend of Mr Burger?' asked the croupier.

'Sure. Aaron and I are old friends,' I replied. 'Legal colleagues.'

'Come with me then.'

The croupier led me to the door, and said to the gorilla on guard duty, 'This gentleman is a friend of Mr Burger's.'

The gorilla's ugly face creased into what he imagined was a smile as he said, 'Good evening, sir,' and opened the door for me.

I thanked the croupier for his assistance, nodded politely to the gorilla, and stepped into the high rollers' room.

Inside, the lights were dim, and the chatter subdued. There was serious gambling going on here.

I soon spotted Burger and Weasel Face at the roulette table—their girls at the bar hitting the booze. Burger was watching the wheel intently, looking every inch a serious gambler.

Weasel Face was standing one pace behind him, not gambling, just watching the action.

It was a very boring evening. For the next three hours I watched Burger gamble and lose. Then gamble some more and lose some more. And then up the stakes, and lose even more. By the end of the night I was wondering where he got his bottomless pockets from.

Eventually he and Weasel Face grabbed their drunken girlfriends from the bar and headed off. I followed at a discreet distance as they waded through the well-heeled crowd, climbed back into their limousine at the front door, and disappeared into the night.

Well, well, interesting behaviour for a District Attorney, I thought, as I followed them into the night, saluted by the commissionaire as I went.

Back in the shadows behind the back wall I changed back into *galabiyah* and *keffiyeh*, pushed the now-crumpled tuxedo in through the window of the waiters' room, and headed for home.

The next morning over breakfast I described what I had seen to David Gideon.

'This weasel-faced character,' I said, 'do you know who he might be? Does my description ring any bells for you?'

'As a matter of fact, it does,' replied David. 'I'm sure I've seen his picture in the social pages. It sounds very much like a man named Judas Justus.'

'Who's he when he's at home?'

'He is, or rather was, Burger's partner in the private law practice he had before he became District Attorney. In fact, the firm is still called Justus and Burger.'

'I see,' I muttered. 'Very interesting. And Caesar's Palace—have you heard of the place?'

'Everyone has.'

'What can you tell me about it?'

'Only the gossip.'

'Which is?'

'The rumour is that it's owned by a bookmaker and gangster named Joel Tree.'

'And he's a big wheel in Damascus?'

'If crime ever got organised in this town, he'd be the organiser,' said David.

I helped myself to a second cup of coffee, then asked, 'Is there any word on those servants who killed Eli Samuelson and his family?'

'According to the radio this morning they've all been rounded up. They were found in the desert not far north of the city. Or, at least, what was left of them.'

'What was *left* of them?'

'Yeah, there had been some falling out between them, so it seems, and half of them were dead—killed by the others.'

'A kind of rough justice, I suppose,' I remarked.

David stood up, pulled on his cloak, and started for the door, munching on a last piece of toast as he went.

Turning around with one hand on the doorknob, he said, 'It's odd that we haven't heard anything from Paul Benson yet.'

'Yes . . . I suppose it is,' I replied.

'He should have been in town for a day or two by now—and still no word of beginning his operations against the believers. For such a passionate persecutor I would have expected him to be hotter off the mark than this.'

'Yes, you're right.'

'Next time you're talking to Aaron Burger, Ben, ask him if Paul Benson has, in fact, arrived in Damascus.'

CHAPTER 14

No sooner had the door closed behind David, than the phone began to ring.

'Hello?' I said, picking up the receiver.

'Hi. Is that Ben Bartholomew?'

'Speaking.'

'It's Paul Mallard here, Ben. I have reports available for you on those four people you wanted checked out.'

'Very efficient. Why don't I call in to your office some time this morning?'

'I'll be expecting you.'

I was gulping down the last of my coffee and reaching for my cloak when there was a knock at the door, and Joe Barnabas walked in.

'Morning, Ben. Anything I can do to help you today?'

'I don't think so. I'm on my way down to Mallard's office to hear his preliminary report into possible enemies of Malachi Mason. Then I need to contact Burger about the date for the committal hearing for Tullus.'

'Well, if there's anything I can do, don't hesitate to ask. Any information, any question, anything.'

'The only question I have, Barnabas old friend, is one that you can't answer—that I suspect no-one can answer.'

'Oh? What might that question be?'

'The big one: why? Why does all this happen? Why are people hurting and suffering in this world? Why are Tullus and Tabitha, for example, suffering right now? Why does Paul Benson behave the way he does? Why—if God is all-powerful and all-loving—is there suffering and evil in the world?'

'Hhmm . . . yes, that certainly is a big question.'

'And you have no answer, right?'

'Well . . . at the risk of sounding glib and superficial,' murmured Barnabas, 'there *is* an answer.'

'Tell me then.'

'In short, the answer is—us!'

'I don't follow . . .' I muttered, puzzled.

'What I mean is that this is a world of suffering and evil because of us—because of the human race.'

'Oh, sure, there are some bad people.'

'Not *some* bad people, Ben. We are *all* part of the problem, not part of the solution.'

'That's pretty sweeping.'

'The fact of the matter, the grim reality, is that every human being—every man, woman and child—knows, really knows in their heart of hearts, that God is the maker and ruler of the world. And, yet, everyone has rejected the ruler by running their lives their own way without God.'

'Everyone?'

'Everyone!'

'And that's what you mean by saying that everyone is part of the problem, not part of the solution?'

'Yes. You see, everyone is guilty of ignoring God. That's the big issue, ignoring God. People don't usually make a big song and dance about it, they just leave God out. They just make their plans and get on with their lives, ignoring God. They turn their backs on God. And that means they are cut off from God—separated from him.'

'When you put it like that it sounds like such a little thing,' I said, 'such an ordinary thing.'

'I don't know about ordinary,' said Barnabas. 'It certainly is common. But it's not a "little thing". It's a big thing—the biggest possible thing. The underlying cause of all the suffering in the world.'

'Now that's something I don't figure!' I complained. 'I can't see the connection.'

'How can I explain this?' murmured Barnabas, running his fingers through his hair. 'Look, what we human beings have done to God is exactly like what Eli's servants did to Eli!'

'Eh? I don't follow?'

'Well, Eli had rescued those people, looked after them, given them their freedom, and treated them well. Right?'

'Right.'

'God has done the same for us. We did not make ourselves—we are made. And it is God who made us. And God provides all the good things in this world for us. Every square meal we eat, every good night's sleep we get, every good friend we have, every beautiful sunset we see is a gift from God. Every morning when we wake up, God has given us another 24 hours.'

'So, God is like Eli, and we are like the servants?'

'Up to a point, Ben! Don't press my comparison too far! But, yes, God gives us so much—life, and, energy, and strength, and time. And just like Eli's servants we so often misuse and abuse those gifts— we use our time, and strength and energy doing things that dismay and disgust God.'

'You're saying that the human race is in rebellion against God?'

'Precisely.'

'Okay. If I accept that, I still don't see how that explains suffering.'

'Once Eli's servants rebelled and ran off, they quickly fell out among themselves and turned on each other. Without Eli's management and direction they fell apart.'

'And we do the same?'

'Yes. Look at it like this. If I am ignoring God, then God has no place in my life. After all, the only place that God can have in my life is to be in charge—and I've taken his place, I've taken charge of my life. Okay?'

'I'm with you so far.'

'So, without God in my life, what is the biggest thing in my life?'

'I'm not sure that I . . .' I hesitated.

'Me!' said Barnabas, thumping his chest. 'Without God in my life, the biggest thing in my life is ME! And that's where all the selfishness and hurt and suffering in this world spring from.'

'Look, I'll talk to you about this again later, all right?'

'If you wish.'

'But right now I should be getting over to Mallard's office.'

'I'm sorry if I've been holding you up,' said Barnabas with a grin. 'I can get a bit carried away sometimes.'

I left the house, walked down the alley outside the front gate, and made my way to Straight Street.

It was midmorning and already the day was hot. Weaving my way around the camels and donkeys, bustling through crowds of pedestrians, dodging the pavement pedlars, I was soon dripping with sweat. It was a relief to leave the noise and bustle of Straight Street behind and enter the quieter streets of the business district.

Within a few minutes I could see the glass tower that contained the office of Mallard Detective Agency looming up ahead of me.

'Excuse me,' said a voice at my elbow.

'I'm in a hurry,' I said, not looking around, assuming it was another pedlar.

'Just a minute of your time, Mr Bartholomew,' said the voice.

At the sound of my name, I stopped, turned and found myself facing a man almost as wide as he was tall—with broad shoulders, a barrel chest, and bulging muscles under his grey business suit.

'Yes?' I inquired.

'If I could have just a minute, Mr Bartholomew,' he said, 'I have a message for you.'

The man had a completely bald, bullet-shaped head.

'What sort of message?'

'If we could just step out of the traffic for a moment—to somewhere quiet?'

'I guess so,' I followed Bullet Head into one of the narrow alleys opening off the main boulevard, and he moved into the shadows at the mouth of the alley, motioning me to follow.

'Now what's this message?' I asked, stepping towards him.

'It's this,' he said, and as he spoke his fist plunged into my stomach like a bulldozer into soft sand. I wasn't expecting the blow, and crumpled up like a paper bag.

As I hit the ground I saw his foot swinging towards my ribs, rolled to one side, grabbed the foot as it flashed past, and pulled hard.

Bullet Head came crashing down—right on top of me! It felt as though the Great Pyramid had collapsed on my rib cage. Then a fist crashed into the side of my head. For a while all I could see were stars, and all I could hear was a sort of whistling noise inside my brain.

I managed to force one eyelid open. Bullet Head was standing over me, prodding me in the ribs with his foot.

'You hear me okay, Bartholomew?' grunted a voice from a million miles away. Prod, prod. Right into the bruised ribs.

'Ouch! Yeah . . . I hear you,' I wheezed.

'That's the message I was asked to deliver,' prod, prod. 'You understand what it means, don't you? Go back to Jerusalem! You're not welcome in Damascus!'

Then he was gone, and I was alone in the alley.

I pushed myself painfully to my feet, leaning heavily on the brick wall next to me. As my head became clearer, the pain felt worse. I mopped some blood off the side of my head, and dusted down my clothes. There was a barrel of rainwater not far away, and I splashed cool water over my face, and over my cuts.

I cursed myself for being all kinds of a fool and walking into the attack. Then I began wondering who wanted me out of town? What made it worthwhile sending a goon like Bullet Head after me?

As soon as I was breathing normally again, and feeling at least halfway human, I made my way to Paul Mallard's office, just around the corner from where I was attacked.

As I staggered into the reception area, the cool blonde behind the reception desk gasped, 'Oh! Good grief! What's happened to you? Mr Mallard! Mr Mallard, come here, quickly!'

A moment later Mallard was at my side. 'Looks like you've had a little fun, Mr Bartholomew. You'd better step into our infirmary, and we'll see what sort of damage has been done.'

'Infirmary?' I asked.

'This sort of thing happens to our operatives from time to time, so we have a trained first-aid attendant on staff, and a room that we have converted into a sick-bay.'

He led me through the general office, and into a small room fitted out with a bed, several chairs, and a large first-aid cabinet.

'This is Gertie,' said Mallard, as a middle-aged woman stepped into the room, 'or "Matron" as we sometimes call her. She'll patch you up.'

'Lie down on the couch, Mr Benson,' commanded Gertie, in a firm not-to-be-ignored voice. I did as I was told, then she stripped off my shirt and with expert fingers checked out my bones while I described to Mallard what had happened.

'Fortunately, nothing is broken, said Gertie, 'I'll just clean and patch up your cuts and bruises.'

'Do you recognise my description of Bullet Head?' I asked Mallard.

'I sure do,' he replied. 'The man you've described could only be Otto Strong.'

'Who's Otto Strong when he's at home?'

'He's a thug and standover man employed by the top gangster in Damascus—a little charmer named Joel Tree.'

CHAPTER 15

When Gertie had patched me up, and I was decently
dressed again, I followed Mallard to his private
office.

'Why do you think Otto Strong attacked you?'
asked Mallard, after ordering coffee for both of us.
'Who wants you out of town?'

'Presumably, Joel Tree,' I replied, 'since Strong
works for Tree. But why? That's what I can't even
begin to understand.'

'Perhaps Tree is involved in this Tullus case?'

'Perhaps, but I can't see how.'

'On the other hand,' said Mallard, thoughtfully,
'perhaps Joel Tree was doing someone a favour.'

'What do you mean?'

'Perhaps he got his private thug, Otto Strong, to
beat you up on behalf of someone else.'

'Who would Tree do favours for? Who has done
something for Tree that created a debt?'

'That I don't know. But would you like me to ask
around town?'

'Yes please.'

His secretary soon arrived with coffee. While she
poured and we milked and sugared I continued puzzling over the reason for the attack on me.

'What about Aaron Burger?' I said. 'It's just possible that the District Attorney wants me out of town
because I'm defending Tullus Matthias. I saw him

gambling heavily at Tree's casino last night. Gambling and losing, I might add.'

'But that doesn't make any sense,' protested Mallard. 'If Burger owes gambling debts to Tree, that would mean that Burger owes Tree favours—not the other way around.'

'Yes, of course—you're right,' I said, sipping my coffee. 'At any rate, leaving the gangster element to one side for the time being, what have you discovered about those four names I gave you?'

'I have it all here,' replied Mallard, pulling a file out of his desk drawer. 'You can take this report with you, but let me summarise it.'

'Fine.'

'Firstly, then, Seth Yentob—business partner of the late, and, I might add, unlamented, Malachi Mason.'

'Yentob wasn't sorry to see Mason go?'

'You got it. Under the terms of their partnership, on the death of one partner the entire ownership of the firm reverted to the surviving partner. So Seth Yentob, a rich man, has become even richer as a result of Mason's murder.'

'Anything else?'

'Just this: neither partner kept the other fully informed of what they were doing. They both played their cards pretty close to their chest. My man got the impression that Yentob was probably cheating Mason, and Yentob has certainly complained that Mason was cheating him.'

'An unusual partnership, I would have thought.'

'That's it in a nutshell, Ben—couple of sharp, wheeler-dealers, yoked together by joint investments, but neither trusting, or even liking, each other.'

'Would Yentob have murdered Mason?'

'Probably not in person. That's beneath the dignity

of a business executive like Seth Yentob. But he'd be perfectly happy to hire someone else to do it for him.'

'Did he?'

'That I don't know.'

'Okay, who's next?'

'Silas Levi.'

'What's his story?' I asked.

'Only a few years ago he was running his own wine-importing business in competition with Mason and Yentob.'

'And nowadays he's not?'

'Nowadays he's a clerk, pushing a pen for a denarius a day in the offices of a transport company on Straight Street.'

'What brought about his downfall?'

'To hear him tell it, it was Malachi Mason single-handed,' explained Mallard. 'Silas Levi claims that Mason decided to deliberately put him out of business. Not because of any special malice, but just as part of the wheeler-dealer game that Mason liked to play. And he played very rough: bribed government officials to win contracts, falsified accounts, paid thugs to rough up Levi's employees. Every dirty trick in the book.'

'Do you think it's true?'

'My guess is that it's about half true. Maybe Mason targeted Levi's business, or then again maybe he didn't. Either way, in the end Levi went bankrupt because he wasn't a smart-enough businessman. But he can't face that fact, so he has to find a scapegoat to blame for his own failure.'

'And he found his scapegoat in Mason?'

'Right on the button!'

'Did he hate Mason enough to kill him?' I asked.

'No doubt about it,' snapped Mallard. 'Pure hatred—that's our Mr Silas Levi. But did he actually do it? That's another question. And my feeling is: I doubt it. I think Silas is a wimp. I think he's all talk and wouldn't have the nerve to murder anyone.'

'Okay then, number three—Ahab Ishmael.'

'Now Captain Ishmael is another kettle of fish entirely. He reportedly has a violent temper and would murder you as soon as look at you, although recently he's hit the bottle.'

'And he hated Malachi Mason?'

'Yes, and unlike Levi, my contacts suggest that Captain Ishmael's complaint is probably justified. Mason and Yentob owned a fleet of ships operating out of the port city of Sidon. Mason was notoriously tight with money. When it came to repairs for one of his ships he would give the job to the shipyard with the lowest quote even if he knew the result would be sloppy work.'

'And that's what happened to *The Jonah*?'

'Spot on. On her last voyage, not long after leaving for Crete, *The Jonah* ran into a major storm. Captain Ishmael claimed that if the ship had been in good repair they would have been able to ride out the storm and made it to a safe haven. As it was, the ship started breaking up almost at once. In less than half an hour the vessel had virtually disintegrated. Ishmael told my man that in thirty years at sea he had never seen anything sink so fast. All of the cargo and many of the crew were lost. On top of which Ismael had his life savings tied up in that cargo. And it gets worse.'

'How?'

'Captain Ishmael's wife and two daughters were on board with him. All three were drowned. The mast collapsed on Ishmael's leg, crushing it, and preventing him from going to their rescue. He watched helplessly, clinging to a piece of wreckage, in enormous pain, while his family was dragged under. He vowed to take his revenge on Malachi Mason.'

'And did he? In your view, is Ahab Ishmael the killer?'

'Unlikely. Despite his violent temper, for Ishmael to murder Mason he would have had to sober up first, and he's rarely sober these days.'

'I see. And the fourth name on your list was a young woman.'

'That's right—Della Rhodes, Mason's former secretary. Apparently Mason likes his secretaries warm and cuddly. Rhodes was cool and efficient, so he sacked her. She's a strong-minded young woman, and took him to court claiming unfair dismissal. He responded by producing fabricated evidence that supposedly demonstrated her incompetence. She lost the case, and became deeply embittered against Mason.'

'Understandably.'

'The details are all here in this report, including addresses, in case you'd like to check any of them out for yourself.'

'Thanks,' I said, accepting the file he handed over, 'I'll have a careful read of this, and in the meantime, will you make some discreet enquiries into just who a gangster like Joel Tree might be doing favours for?'

'I certainly will.'

Leaving Mallard's office I made my way back to City Hall, and the office of Aaron Burger.

When I asked to see the District Attorney I was admitted almost at once, finding Burger surrounded by an ocean of paper.

'Bartholomew!' he said, looking up from his work. 'What a surprise—not necessarily a pleasant one.

What can I do for you? Have you persuaded Dr Tullus Matthias to plead guilty yet?'

'No I haven't, and I won't be trying to.'

'A pity. What can I do for you then?'

'The committal hearing—when will you be ready to proceed, and when can we get a court date?'

'I'm ready to proceed immediately if you are.'

'The defence is ready, be assured of that,' I replied. I was lying through my teeth, but the committal hearing was something that I wanted to get over, so that I could put my energy into the trial itself.

'Let me make a phone call to the chief clerk of the District Court,' said Burger, 'and see if we can set a date on the spot.'

It turned out to be not quite as simple as that, but after fifteen minutes of phone calls and negotiations, the committal hearing was set for the day after next.

Once that was settled I rose to leave.

Halfway to the door I turned and asked, 'By the way, this cousin of yours, Paul Benson, has he arrived in Damascus yet?'

'Yes, he's here,' snapped Burger, flustered, 'he's . . . staying with a friend, he's . . . well . . . he's not well at the moment. But he'll be recovered soon, and then you Christians won't know what's hit you!'

I was tempted to ask how he'd enjoyed his time at the casino the previous night, but I didn't. What I knew about his gambling habits I thought it wise to keep to myself for the time being. Perhaps it would prove to be useful knowledge at some time in the future.

I arrived back at the Gideons' house in time for a late lunch and a steamy siesta.

I woke up with a start at the end of my snooze, and looked at my bedside clock with alarm. Time was ticking away and I had a client to defend on a murder charge, so far with nothing that even looked like a strong defence.

Then an idea fell into my mind. As so often happens, my unconscious had solved a problem for me while I was asleep. The idea was so exciting that I decided to act on it at once.

CHAPTER 16

I set off to visit Tabitha at the Mason villa, and was admitted by a doddery old servant named Septimus.

'Step this way, sir,' he said, 'the mistress is already entertaining another guest in the courtyard.'

'Perhaps I shouldn't disturb them,' I said. 'I can wait here, in the sitting room, until Miss Mason's guest is gone.'

'As you wish, sir,' quavered Septimus, and tottered off.

I was glad I had suggested waiting when I glanced through the window that looked onto the courtyard and saw that Tabitha's guest was Aaron Burger! For a minute I stood, still as a stone statue, watching them. Burger was standing very close to Tabitha, and as I watched he reached out to stroke her hair.

Very gently and quietly I slid the window open, trying to overhear what was being said.

'We used to be friends,' Burger's voice came drifting in softly from the courtyard, 'and we can be again.'

'No,' replied Tabitha, 'No. That's not possible. You know how I feel about Tullus.'

'I understand, believe me I understand. It's a young girl's fascination. And he is a very charming and good-looking young man. But you have to face reality, Tabitha. He wanted you so desperately that he murdered your father.'

'No,' she protested very quietly—almost a whispered protest.

'The evidence is incontrovertible. Dr Matthias's guilt is beyond doubt. It will be proved in court very shortly. And when that happens—well, the death penalty is mandatory. He will be executed.'

Tabitha's head sank down onto her chest, and she began sobbing quietly.

'I know how heartbreaking this must be for you,' said the slimy Burger, turning on more charm than I would ever have believed him capable of, 'but life must go on. Your life must go on, Tabitha.'

Burger reached out and gently stroked Tabitha's hair again. 'Perhaps I can help,' he continued. 'You and I were once very close. Your father wanted us to be. He's gone now, but surely his wishes mean something to you. In fact, I'm sure they mean even more to you. So, when this is all over—why don't you and I get back together again. We could . . .'

Tabitha angrily brushed away his hand. 'No!' she shouted, 'Never! You and I will never get together! Never!'

'You're upset at the moment—I understand that.'

'You understand nothing!' yelled Tabitha, 'If you want to understand something, understand this: I find you utterly loathsome. Your touch feels to me like the touch of a reptile!'

Good on you, Tabitha! I said to myself. Go for it!

'Spending time with you,' she continued with quiet intensity, 'feels like time spent wallowing in a sewer. And now, if you don't mind, this conversation is at an end. Please leave.'

Burger's face went red with anger. His features were seized by a violent hatred. The poisonous expression on his face reminded me for a moment of his cousin, Paul Benson.

'Yes, I'll leave,' he said, with that quiet intensity that is more dangerous than shouted anger, 'but I'll make you sorry that you ever rejected me.'

He walked towards the exit, then stopped and turned back to face her. 'If I can't have you, no-one will.'

And with that he left.

Tabitha broke down, weeping loudly, all the emotional strain of the past week and a half coming out in her tears. I left the small sitting room and hurried to her side in the courtyard.

When she saw me she buried her head in my shoulder and wept uncontrollably. I could do nothing, except pat her shoulder and murmur comforting words.

'I heard what Burger said,' I told her, 'and you're not to worry about him. He's all boasting and hot air. Tullus is innocent, and we are going to prove that. Tullus will not be convicted. Within a short time he'll be back in your arms again.'

Tabitha finally began to quiet down and wipe her eyes.

'Oh, Ben,' she said with a sniffle, 'do you really believe that?'

'Of course I do.'

'You'll look after Tullus, won't you? You'll get him off this horrible murder charge?'

'Yes I will. In fact, I came here today because an idea has occurred to me.'

'Yes?'

'Is Quaresimus around?'

'Not at the moment. I sent him down to the markets.'

'Good! While he's out I want your permission to search his room.'

'But why? I thought you'd abandoned that line of inquiry?'

'So did I, until this idea occurred to me. Now, where is his room?'

'This way, I'll show you.'

'And you can help me in the search as well,' I said, following Tabitha to the servants' quarters.

Quaresimus's room was small and sparsely furnished, like most servants' rooms. I looked around and decided that the chest of drawers and the small bedside table were the most likely places.

'Let's start searching,' I said.

'What are we looking for?' asked Tabitha.

'A small book, probably a notebook, or something of that sort.'

Tabitha looked puzzled, but set to work helping me search the room.

Neither the bedside table nor the chest of drawers yielded anything of interest. I looked on top of the wardrobe, then through every drawer, crevice or crack inside the wardrobe. Tabitha searched the trunk that stood at the foot of the bed.

Nothing.

'I can't think where else to search,' I said in despair, my hands on hips in the middle of the room.

'I remember what I used to do when I was a little girl and I wanted to keep something hidden,' said Tabitha dropping to her knees, and slipping her hand underneath the mattress.

'Eureka!' she cried a moment later.

'You speak Greek?' I asked.

'Here it is,' she said, pulling out a small, black

leather-covered book and handing it over to me. I flipped though the pages.

'Is it what you were hoping to find?' she asked.

'It is exactly what I was hoping to find,' I replied. 'A little book full of names, addresses and phone numbers.'

'But what does it mean? What is the significance?'

'You'll see that the day after tomorrow—at Tullus's committal hearing. Make sure that you bring Quaresimus with you when you come to the court-room. If all goes well, I just might be able to get Tullus released and the charge dropped at the com-mittal stage.'

Tabitha threw her arms around me, 'Oh, Ben,' she said, 'you're great.'

I walked back to the Gideons' house feeling elated, but also very homesick. The thought of all that love—the bond that existed between Tabitha and Tullus—made me miss Rachel very much.

As soon as I got back to the house I dialled our number in Caesarea, speaking to Rachel for ages. I told her everything that had happened so far in Damascus, then whispered a lot of the foolish things that young married couples so often do. Then, finally, remembering how much money the phone call would be costing I reluctantly brought our conversation to an end.

'You be very careful,' were Rachel's last words to me, 'it's the presence of Paul Benson in Damascus that worries me. I love you Ben, look after yourself—for my sake.'

That night there was a group of us at the dinner table: David, Miriam and Phoebe Gideon, Joe Barnabas, myself, Nicolaus, and Ananias. George, the Abyssinian, was on guard duty on the city wall.

Over the meal there was much discussion of the murder case, and much speculation about Paul Benson and his plans in Damascus. Burger had said that he was not well. What would he be doing once he was recovered?

After dinner I sought out Barnabas, because I had a question to ask him.

'About what you were saying this morning,' I said, as we settled down on a sofa at the quiet end of the room, 'it still doesn't make sense to me.'

'What, exactly, doesn't make sense?'

'The connection.'

'What connection?'

'The connection between human beings ignoring God and all the suffering and evil in the world. What you said about the human race is true, I have no doubt about that. It is true that we, all of us, rebel against God, or ignore God, or shunt God off to some insignificant corner of our lives. Some of us invent our own religions as a way of ignoring God. Some of us pretend that we are self-created, self-dependent, self-sustained. Some of us just never give God a thought. And some of us think that by being a bit religious we can control God when, in fact, God should control us. We have all found ways of ignoring God, of shutting him out of controlling our lives, of cutting ourselves off from him.'

'Yes, quite true. So what's the problem?'

'How can that absolutely typical human behaviour actually *cause* suffering and evil, let alone *all* the suffering and evil in the world?'

'Have you got a minute to listen to a story?'

'Sure.'

'It's a sort of fable called "The Kingdom of Kings". A long time ago,' continued Barnabas, 'a delegation of citizens went to see their king, complaining that it was unfair that there should only be *one* king in the whole kingdom. "We should *all* be kings!" they insisted. Reluctantly the king agreed to their request, and issued a decree proclaiming every citizen in his kingdom to be a king.

'The king's proclamation was warmly welcomed. Everyone was delighted to be a monarch in his or her own right. But almost at once, problems began to arise.

'In every home in the land children suddenly became uncontrollable. Whenever they were told to go to bed, every child would simply issue a royal decree postponing bedtime by an hour.

'Husbands and wives issued opposing royal decrees about who had to do the washing up, and the result was often an ugly argument.

'Neighbours issued opposing royal decrees about fixing their dividing fence, and the disputes would sometimes come to blows.

'The notion of everyone being their own king ended in tears, hurt, anger, and frustration.

'In fact, just like the real world we live in today,' concluded Barnabas.

'A good yarn,' I responded, 'but explain the point to me.'

'The point is,' said Joe Barnabas, 'that there are only two kingdoms that you and I can live in: the kingdom of God or the kingdom of Me. Human relationships so often end up collapsing in a heap because they are so much like diplomats from two self-governing nations arguing over a piece of disputed territory.'

'And our ignoring God, rebelling against God, means that we all live in the kingdom of Me rather than the kingdom of God. So . . . we are . . . all of us . . . I think I see.'

'If we reject the right of the maker and ruler of the universe to rule our lives,' added Barnabas, 'self creeps in and quietly steals the throne: that's the kingdom of Me. And that is what the Bible calls sin!'

'And it's the rule of self that causes human beings to inflict suffering on each other?'

'Correct.'

'And to behave in ways that are unkind, or even cruel and evil?'

'Precisely.'

'Let me think about it.'

I went off to bed with my head buzzing.

CHAPTER 17

The next morning after breakfast I sat down at the telephone with Quaresimus's book beside me, and began dialling.

Half an hour and seven phone calls later, I had the evidence I needed for the committal hearing! I made the arrangements I needed to make, and hung up the phone.

I was still sitting there, beside the phone, writing up my notes, when Ananias came into the room, looking as if he had seen a ghost. Or perhaps a very large number of heavily armed ghosts.

'What's wrong?' I asked.

'God has just spoken to me in a vision,' he stammered, trembling, his face pale. He looked, I now decided, not so much like a man who had seen ghosts but a man who has just read his own name in the obituary column!

'Are you sure?' I asked, thinking he more likely needed sympathy, and possibly therapy.

'The Lord spoke to me in a vision, calling out "Ananias"!'

'Really! And what did you reply?'

'Yes, Lord!'

'I see,' I murmured sympathetically, 'and was that the whole conversation, or was there more?'

Ananias stumbled on breathlessly, 'The Lord said to me, "Go over to Straight Street and find the house of a man named Judas and ask there for Paul Benson. He is praying to me right now, for I have shown him a vision of a man named Ananias coming in and laying his hands on him so that he can see again!"

' "But Lord," I exclaimed,' continued Ananias, ' "I have heard about the terrible things this man has done to the believers in Jerusalem! And we hear that he has arrest warrants with him from the chief priests, authorising him to arrest every believer in Damascus!"

'But the Lord said, "Go and do what I say. For Paul Benson is my chosen instrument to take my message to the nations and before kings, as well as to the people of Israel. And I will show him how much he must suffer for me." That's what God said to me and that's what happened!'

'Very interesting' I responded, in a soothing voice, 'I suggest you have a nice, quiet lie down and think about what all this really means.'

'I'm not lying down,' said Ananias, still pale and trembling. 'I am going to do what I was told. I am on my way to the house of Judas in Straight Street to find Paul.'

'Come now, Ananias,' I said firmly, 'get a grip on yourself. You musn't go and visit Paul, you know that. He would just arrest you. Perhaps torture you. Possibly even have you killed. This vision you've had can't be from God. Maybe it's just last night's dinner playing up with your digestion?'

'It was a clear instruction from God,' insisted Ananias.

'Your imagination is probably playing tricks on you,' I said, still trying to be calm. 'Wait until all the others come back, and discuss your vision with them.'

'It was a clear instruction from God!' he said, his mouth set in a grim line of determination.

'Then it must have been a parable. You know, symbolic. Yes, that's it—a parable. I wonder what 'Paul Benson' stands for in the parable?'

'I don't think it's a parable.'

'God can't possibly mean for you to go and speak to our worst enemy!' I exclaimed. 'It can't be meant literally!'

'You'd be surprised how often God means things literally,' replied Ananias quietly, 'and I'm off right now. When God speaks, it is stupid to do anything but obey. All the objections you've raised I've already thought of myself—'

'Why not fax him,' I interrupted, 'Benson can't torture a fax!'

'No,' replied Ananias, 'God said, "go", so I am going.'

'In that case, I'm coming with you,' I said, giving up the argument and grabbing my cloak.

We walked side by side in a kind of solemn silence, down the alleyway and out into Straight Street. Ananias did not have to ask anyone for directions, he seemed to know exactly where he was going. Perhaps the address had been part of the vision.

'This is the place,' he said, stopping in front of an old terrace block at the northern end of Straight Street.

On the front door was a brass plate that read 'Burger and Justus, Counsellors at Law'!

'Now, listen—' I began, when I saw that sign.

'Just wait here,' interrupted Ananias, 'I'm going in alone.'

There was no stopping him, so I had no alternative but to let him go.

The minutes ticked by, and I paced up and down the kerb waiting for him.

At one stage a curtain was lifted at one of the upstairs windows and a face appeared. It was Weasel Face himself! He stared down into the street and our eyes met, then he let the curtain fall back into place and disappeared from my view.

Still I waited, more and more anxious as the minutes ticked by.

At last the front door opened and Ananias re-emerged. And leaning on his arm was Paul Benson!

I could see at a glance this was a very changed Paul Benson. He was blinking in the sunlight, as if he found it hard to adjust to the bright morning light. His skin was pale, and he looked thinner than when I had last seen him.

He had the same strong features—prominent hooked nose, dark, brooding eyes, thick, black beard, and thinning hair above his high forehead—but there was something different about him, something indefinably, indescribably different.

I opened my mouth to speak but Ananias interrupted me.

'Don't say anything, Ben. Just give me a hand with Paul. We are taking him back to the Gideons' house.' There were such urgency and command in his voice that I didn't question him.

Back at the house Paul lay down on a sofa in the front room, and Ananias told the servants to prepare some food for him. Then we left him resting, and went back to the sitting room to talk.

I was bursting with questions: 'What happened at

Judas's house? What is Paul Benson doing here of all places? What is going on? What does it all . . .'

'Hold on, Ben,' said Ananias, holding up a hand, 'let me explain.'

'Please do.'

'What happened is that I went into the house and said that I had come for Paul Benson. The servant who let me in at the front door took me to two men who, I was told, had travelled from Jerusalem with Paul. I asked these men to take me to Paul, and one of them said, "Are you a doctor?". The other one asked, "Do you know what his problem is?"

'So I asked them to tell me, and the first one said that as they had neared Damascus, three days before, Paul suddenly stared at the sky, as if he could see something, and then fell to the ground. The men could see nothing but they heard a voice sort of coming out of mid-air. It shook them up, I can tell you.'

Ananias stopped to catch his breath, and then continued.

'The voice said: "Paul! Paul! Why are you persecuting me?"

'Paul asked, "Who is speaking?"

'And the voice replied, "I am Jesus, the one you are persecuting! Now, get up and go into the city and await my further instructions."

'And when Paul picked himself up off the ground he discovered that he was blind. So the two men I was talking to—both Temple Guards—led him into Damascus, to the house where he was due to lodge, and they have waited with him for three days, while Paul has refused to eat or drink anything.'

'Amazing!' I said, running my fingers through my hair, and trying to take this in.

'How were these Temple Guards coping with all of this?' I asked.

'I have never seen two such tough bullies look so weak and confused,' replied Ananias, with a cheeky grin.

'Go on then,' I said. 'Tell me what happened next.'

'I went upstairs,' continued Ananias, 'and found Paul, and laid my hands on him, and said, "Brother Paul, the Lord Jesus, who appeared to you on the road, has sent me so that you may be filled with the Holy Spirit and get your sight back." Instantly, as though scales fell from his eyes, Paul said he could see. He asked to be baptised, so I brought him here.'

That was it. It was stunning. It was breathtaking. But it had happened! The chief persecutor of the believers was lying down recovering on a couch in the front room, and asking to be baptised!

The house was in uproar for the rest of the day. When David and Miriam returned home from a visit to Miriam's mother, they were confronted with Ananias's amazing story. At first they couldn't believe it. They kept muttering, 'It's a trick of some sort.'

'He's deceiving us,' said Miriam, 'trying to trap us.'

They went and talked to Paul where he was still resting in the front room and came back with stunned expressions on their faces, saying, 'It's all true!'

Later when Joe Barnabas arrived and was told the story he almost jumped out of his skin with excitement.

'Isn't it just like God,' he exclaimed, 'to catch us by surprise like this and turn our worst enemy into a brother!'

Then there was the matter of Paul's baptism. I

suggested that he be baptised in Damascus's Barada River, but everyone howled that down saying the Barada was so polluted that plunging into it could be fatal. Then someone thought of using the pool around the fountain in the courtyard. In the end that's what was done: the fountain was turned off, and Paul was baptised in the decorative pool at about midday.

Then, exhausted by three days of lack of food, drink and sleep, and by everything that had happened, Paul fell into a deep sleep soon after he was shown into his new room.

No-one else felt like sleeping—they all wanted to sit around and talk endlessly about what had happened, even in the steamy heat of the middle of the day!

Paul woke up and ate again, then fell asleep again after asking Joe to obtain a copy of the Scriptures for him, saying he had a lot of serious studying and thinking to do.

Meanwhile, I had a committal hearing to prepare for, and I spent much of the afternoon hunched over a borrowed desk, preparing the documents I needed.

Late in the afternoon I caught a cab to the District Court to lodge the necessary documents with the court before the hearing.

The registrar's office was, as usual, a hive of inactivity. Once again, there was a queue, and I had to take a number and wait. At last the clerk called my number and I approached the counter.

'Good afternoon,' I said with a big smile, doing my best to break through the civil service sourness on the face of the clerk.

'If you say so,' he replied. 'What have you got there?'

I handed over my documents.

'These will take a moment. Wait here please.'

I know what a 'moment' means to these civil servants, so I leaned against the counter, and settled in for a longish wait. Bored, I began reading the documents spread out on the bench behind the counter.

My eye was running in a casual way over a range of legal documents—bail applications, settlements that needed to be registered, and so on—when suddenly I felt as though a thousand volts had shot through my system.

There on the bench was a charge sheet—and under the heading 'conspiracy to murder' was the name of the person being charged: Tabitha Mason! And the charge was signed by Aaron Burger!

CHAPTER 18

As soon as my own documents were returned—duly
stamped and signed—I stuffed them into my pocket,
ran out into the street, and hailed a passing taxi.

When he dropped me at the front door of the
Mason villa, I told the driver to wait, leaped out and
pounded urgently on the door.

Septimus opened the door, an alarmed look on his
face.

'Oh, it's you, Mr Bartholomew. What's the prob—'
he started to wheeze.

'Is Miss Mason home?' I asked, pushing past him.

'She's still in the dining room, sir, if you . . .'

His voice faded behind me as I ran through the
courtyard into the dining room.

Tabitha was sitting alone, the remnants of a meal
still on the table before her—she hadn't eaten very
much. The Gideons had tried to persuade her to come
and stay with them until the murder trial was over,
but she'd insisted she would rather be alone. In her
hand was a letter.

'Tabitha!' I said, striding through the doorway, and
noticing tears glistening in her eyes.

'Ben! I didn't expect you tonight! A letter has
arrived from Tullus in prison. The poor dear . . .'

'I want you out of here. Tonight!' I interrupted.

'I don't understand.'

'Pack a suitcase, just one, just the basics. And take

one of your maids along to keep you company and look after you.'

'But Ben, what's wrong?'

'Come on,' I urged, 'start packing. I have a taxi waiting at the front gate.'

'But . . . but . . .'

'I'll explain while you're packing.'

Moved by my sense of urgency Tabitha hurried to the door, called one of her maids and issued instructions.

'Now that's under way,' she said, 'perhaps you'll explain what this is all about. Why the big drama?'

'You're about to be arrested, Tabitha. And I'm trying to prevent that, or at least postpone it.'

'Arrested? Whatever for?'

'Conspiracy to murder is what it says on the charge sheet.'

'Murder? Ben this is ridiculous! And who would want to charge me with murder, anyway?'

'Aaron Burger, that's who.'

'Oh,' her face suddenly solemn.

'Burger has sworn out a warrant for your arrest on a charge of conspiracy to murder.'

'Why would he do that?'

'There is none so vicious as a District Attorney spurned in love. Burger is going to try and make your life even more miserable than it is now.'

'It would be in character. But which murder am I charged with?'

'I couldn't read that on the charge sheet, but a good guess would be the murder of your own father.'

'My father! But how could anyone think—'

'I don't believe Burger does think—he's just taking revenge. He has persuaded a judge that you might have conspired with Tullus in the murder of your father—that's what I'm guessing.'

'All for revenge?'

'Not entirely. This charge knocks over two birds with one stone. The first is his desire for revenge because you rejected him. The second is his need to weaken your evidence in support of Tullus, which was so powerful at the bail application hearing.'

'How does he do that?'

'If you're under arrest, charged with the same murder, your testimony in support of Tullus becomes, in effect, null and void.'

'But what can we do about it?'

'To arrest you, they have to find you. And we are going to make that as difficult as possible.'

'You want me to go into hiding?'

'Exactly!'

'No, I won't do it! If Tullus can face this sort of persecution, so can I!'

'That's very brave of you, Tabitha, but also very foolish. You are of more use to Tullus if you are free, right?'

'I suppose so.'

'Then do what I tell you.'

The maid returned, struggling with two large suitcases.

'All right then, what do I do now?' asked Tabitha.

'Do you have your own car?'

'Yes.'

'Good, then send the taxi away, and you can drive yourself to a place of safety.'

Tabitha rang for Septimus, gave him some money, and told him to pay off the taxi.

'Now,' I said, when Septimus left, 'take your car, and your maid and these two suitcases, and drive to a motel well outside of Damascus—something out in the desert would be ideal. Register under your own name—so you can't be accused of flight. Don't tell me, or anyone else, exactly where you are going. That way if I am asked where you are, I can truthfully reply that I don't know.'

'But how will you get in touch with me?'

'I won't. You'll get in touch with me. Call me tomorrow afternoon at the Gideons' house. Now, clear off.'

'Goodbye, Ben,' Tabitha said, pecking me on the cheek, 'I'm sure you know what's best.'

A few minutes later her car drove away from the front of the house. I rang for Septimus, ordered coffee, and settled down to wait.

Within half an hour a police car, siren screaming, came to a screeching halt in front of the house. Out tumbled Captain Tragg of the City Watch Crime Squad, accompanied by four uniformed officers. They pounded on the front door until Septimus admitted them.

I was waiting in the courtyard as Tragg came striding in, waving a piece of paper.

'You! I should have expected to find you here, Bartholomew. I have an arrest warrant for Miss Tabitha Mason, so I suggest you produce her at once—unless you want to be arrested for concealing evidence, and obstructing the police.'

'I'm not obstructing you, Tragg,' I said. 'Search wherever you like. She's not here.'

'Where is she then?'

'She drove off in her car earlier this afternoon.'

'Was she alone?'

'I believe she was accompanied by her personal maid.'

'Where did they go to?'

'Miss Mason neglected to tell me.'

'And I suppose you neglected to ask?'

'I'm afraid I did, Captain.'

'As a lawyer, Bartholomew, you are an officer of the court, and you are bound to reveal the whereabouts of a suspect wanted by the law.'

'If I knew I would tell, Tragg. But I honestly don't know. Even torture would be a waste of time, I can't tell you what I don't know.'

Tragg looked at me thoughtfully for a moment, then said, 'You'd be smart enough to ask her not to tell you. That's what you've done, isn't it?'

'All that you need to know, Captain, is that I don't know where Tabitha Mason is, or where she has gone.'

Tragg's men returned from their search of the villa, reporting that they had found no trace of Tabitha. Tragg ordered them to put out an all-points bulletin.

'One of the patrols will find her, never you fear,' he snarled at me.

'Oh, I have no fears for Miss Mason's safety at all,' I replied, with a smile.

'We're going now, Bartholomew,' snapped Tragg, 'but one of these days you'll pull a trick that's just a bit too smart, and end up in prison yourself. So watch your step.'

'Thanks for the advice, Captain,' I said, cheerfully.

Tragg turned on his heel and stormed out, still muttering under his breath.

When I got back to the Gideons', it was late, and I was tired.

Most of the household had gone to bed, but Joe Barnabas was still awake, and still excited. I found him at the big kitchen table, drinking coffee, staring into the distance, his eyes sparkling with life.

'What a great day, Ben!' he enthused.

'In lots of ways, yes,' I said.

'And it demonstrates what we were talking about the other day.'

'What's that?'

'The relationship between suffering and human rebellion against God.'

In all that had happened since I had almost forgotten our conversation.

'Paul's persecution of believers, and the terrible suffering he has inflicted on them and their families, was directly related to his rebellion against the real purposes of God in this world.'

I was tired, and simply nodded in agreement.

'But Paul is only an obvious example of what is, in reality, universal to humankind.'

'I guess so,' I said. 'In fact, I've often been asked why God allows so much suffering in this world.'

'Next time someone asks you that, tell them that suffering in this world is like measles.'

'Measles?'

'Measles,' repeated Joe. 'When you get measles you get spots on the skin. But the spots are not the disease, they are just the symptoms of the disease. The real disease of measles is an infection in the bloodstream. In the same way, suffering and evil are just the symptoms; the real disease, the infection in the bloodstream of every human being, is rebellion against God—usually by ignoring him, and running our lives without him. That's the disease of living in the kingdom of Me—the disease of self, of sin, of rebellion.'

'That's interesting, but I still have a problem,' I

said. 'What you have just told me explains half of the suffering in the world—the half caused by the bad things that people do to other people. But it does not explain the other half.'

'What other half?'

'The suffering caused by accidents floods and droughts and disease. Like that dreadful accident we saw in Straight Street the other day, when the horse bolted and several people were killed. There was no human evil involved there. It was just an accident. Why does that kind of suffering happen?'

'The answer to your question is difficult for human minds to understand, perhaps in the end only God can understand it. But according to the Scriptures, God's message to the human race is that even that suffering is basically caused by human rebellion against God's rule.'

'How can that be?'

'It is very difficult to see how that can be at all, isn't it? But the Scriptures say that it is so. It's not just this generation of humans that has rebelled, it is every generation—right back to the very first. And when that first generation rebelled against God's rule, in some way their rebellion infected the world in which they live—in which we now live.'

'Infected?'

'Somehow our rebellion has corrupted the physical world around us. It is, as I said, beyond human comprehension, but when human beings cut themselves off from God, it is as though the molecular structure, the very nature, of the planet was affected. Ever since then the world has been the way it is—a world of floods, drought and disease. A world in which a bolting horse can take human lives. The physical world around us is dysfunctional because of us.'

'That's a very hard notion to get my head around.'

'I know. But if you look at the very beginning of the Scriptures, in the book called Genesis, there you will find the story of the rebellion of our primaeval parents. And in their action you find the true reason why the world is the way it is.'

'Hhmm. I must give some thought to this.'

'Do that, Ben,' Barnabas urged. 'It is a difficult but important matter. And remember, the world not only had a beginning, it will have an end. And when that end comes, when God finally rolls up the scroll of human history and all things are judged, then the creation around us will be liberated from the effects of the great fall of the human race. All creation is waiting patiently and hopefully, for on that day thorns and thistles, sin, death and decay will all disappear, and the world around us will share in the glorious liberty of God's kingdom.'

'I'll do some reading and thinking about it,' I promised with a yawn, finding it all a bit heavy at the end of a long, dramatic, day. 'I'll see you in the morning,' I said, stumbling off to bed.

CHAPTER 19

The morning brought the first day of Dr Tullus Matthias's committal hearing.

Over breakfast I had a request for George, 'Could you do me a favour this morning?' I asked.

A huge smile creased his face, 'Sure thing, Ben, what is it?'

'I want you to go over to the Mason villa and ask for a servant named Quaresimus. It's important that he is in court for the hearing this morning. Can you make sure that he's there?'

'He won't argue with me, Ben,' said George, the huge grin still on his face. He was roughly the size of a rhinoceros—I was sure that he would meet little opposition from Quaresimus.

'Be gentle with him, though, George. Tell him that his mistress wants him to appear in court.'

'Will do, Ben,' said the big Abyssinian, making a mock salute as he departed.

It was right on the dot of ten o'clock when Judge Hezion entered the courtroom. We all rose.

'Committal hearing into a charge of murder—The *Empire versus Dr Tullus Matthias*,' chanted the clerk of the court.

I glanced over towards Aaron Burger who scowled at me, a bitter expression on his face. My rescue of Tabitha from his grasp had obviously displeased him.

But she couldn't avoid detection long, both of us knew that.

'Mr District Attorney,' said the judge, 'do you have an opening address before you call your first witness?'

'I will spare the court a lengthy opening address,' said Burger, rising to his feet. 'The only preliminary comment I need to make is this: in all murder cases it is necessary to show motive, means and opportunity. In this case the motive is obvious, is easily established, and is not denied by the accused. As for the means—the murder was committed with the accused's own antique dagger, a fact which, again, the accused does not deny. As for opportunity, the prosecution will show that the accused, and only the accused, had the opportunity to commit the murder.'

As Burger spoke I glanced over to where Tullus stood in the dock. Paying no attention to the proceedings, his eyes were raking the public gallery. Clearly, he couldn't understand why Tabitha wasn't there.

'Very well, Mr Burger,' said the judge. 'Call your first witness.'

'The prosecution calls Captain Tragg of the City Watch Crime Squad.'

Tragg took the stand and was sworn in.

'Captain Tragg, please describe to the court the room in which you found the victim's body on the day of the murder.'

Tragg ostentatiously opened up his notebook. 'The victim was found in his own bedroom. It is a square, sparsely furnished room with solid, white-washed walls. There is only one door in the room and two windows. Both windows, I should add, are heavily barred against intruders.'

'Are those bars secure? Did you check them?'

'I examined them personally, and I had a scene-of-crime officer examine them scientifically.'

'With what results?'

'The bars are solid and had not been tampered with,' Tragg replied smugly.

'So, how then could the murderer have got to his victim?' asked Burger, a self-confident smile on his face.

'Only through the door,' said Tragg.

'There was no other way in or out?'

'That is correct.'

Burger turned to the judge: 'A little later, your honour, the prosecution will be presenting medical evidence establishing the time of death as between 10.00 a.m. and 2.00 p.m. Now, Captain Tragg,' he said, turning back to his witness, 'during that critical period, was the door under observation at all times?'

'Yes, it was.'

'And who entered the murder room during that time?'

'Only the defendant—Dr Tullus Matthias.'

'Objection, your honour!' I said, leaping to my feet.

'On what grounds, Mr Bartholomew?' asked the judge.

'This is not best evidence, your honour. All that Captain Tragg can offer is hearsay. It should be stricken from the record.'

'Objection sustained. That last answer will be stricken. Do you have any further questions, Mr Burger?'

'I most certainly have, your honour. Captain Tragg, during your interviews with the defendant, did he at any time deny having entered the room in question and having seen the victim on the day of the murder?'

'No, he did not!'

'So his presence at the scene of the crime has been established out of his own mouth?'

'It has!'

'If the court pleases,' I interrupted, 'the defence is perfectly happy to concede the presence of my client in the victim's room on the morning concerned, but only as a physician.'

'The reason for the visit doesn't matter,' Burger interjected quickly, 'as long as the defence is prepared to concede that Dr Matthias was in the murder room on the morning of the crime, the prosecution is satisfied. Now, Captain Tragg, let's turn our attention to the murder weapon. Have you succeeded in identifying it?'

'Yes, we have. The murder weapon is a distinctive antique dagger—the property of the accused.'

'Once again, your honour,' I said, rising to my feet, 'The defence is prepared to concede that the knife in question was indeed once the property of my client.'

'You are being so helpful,' said Burger, making a mock bow. 'The prosecution thanks you for your co-operation.'

'Anything to help the court,' I replied with a smile and a nod in the direction of the judge.

'Now, Captain Tragg,' continued Burger, 'what have you discovered about the relationship between the defendant and the victim's daughter.'

'Malachi Mason has—or, rather, had—a daughter named Tabitha. My investigations indicate that an attachment had formed between her and Dr Matthias—an attachment that the murdered man took strong exception to.'

'Objection, your honour,' I said, 'Once again, this is not best evidence. Captain Tragg has no personal knowledge of the relationship he is reporting to the court. This account is inadmissible hearsay. If the prosecution thinks this is relevant let him put the principals on the stand.'

'Now, your honour! That's outrageous!' snorted Burger. 'Mr Bartholomew knows full well that Miss Tabitha Mason has disappeared, quite possibly at his connivance.'

'That's a serious accusation, Mr Burger,' murmured Judge Hezion. 'Are you making an official complaint? Do you have any evidence of misconduct?'

'Not at the present time, your honour,' replied the District Attorney, 'but when this case is over my office will be investigating most urgently.'

'In that case, if you have no formal complaint to make against Mr Bartholomew, and no evidence against him, I will rule on his objection.'

'As your honour pleases,' muttered Burger, a sour look on his face.

'The objection is sustained. You'll have to produce some more direct evidence to establish a relationship between the defendant and the daughter of the deceased.'

'Very well, your honour. In that case, I have no further questions of Captain Tragg.'

'Mr Bartholomew,' said Judge Hezion, 'do you have any questions of this witness?'

'Just a few, your honour,' I said, rising to my feet and approaching the witness stand. 'Captain Tragg, tell me some more about the murder weapon.'

'What would you like to know, counsellor?'

'How did you first come to identify it as the property of my client?'

'Well . . . because . . . well, actually, he told us.'

'When did he tell you?'

'On the day of the murder. He told one of my officers that he recognised the dagger.'

'One of your officers? Which officer?'

'Well, the first officer on the scene.'

'So Dr Matthias made no attempt whatsoever to conceal his ownership of the dagger?'

'I guess not.'

'In fact, he revealed it to the very first officer of the City Watch Crime Squad to arrive on the scene. Is that correct?'

'Yes.'

'And is that the action of a guilty man?'

'Guilty men behave in many different ways!' snapped Tragg.

'Objection!' shouted Burger, leaping to his feet, 'The question calls for a conclusion on the part of the witness.'

'Do you have anything to say to that, Mr Bartholomew?' asked the judge.

'Indeed I have, your honour. Captain Tragg has been presented to this court as an expert witness. As the head of the Crime Squad one area of expertise that he must have—that neither he nor the District Attorney can deny—is knowledge of criminal behaviour.'

'That seems fair enough to me. Objection denied,' said with a sharp rap of the gavel.

'Now, Captain Tragg, let's get back to that question. Is it likely that a guilty man will identify a murder weapon as his property?'

'As I said earlier, guilty men behave in many different ways!' snarled Tragg.

'Let's see if we can get at this a different way,

then,' I said thoughtfully. 'How long have you been in the Crime Squad?'

'Over thirty years.'

'How many criminals have you arrested over those years?'

'I have no idea! Thousands!'

'And how many of those thousands turned to you at the scene of the crime and said: "By the way—the murder weapon belongs to me"?'

'Well . . .'

'How many, Captain Tragg?'

'Actually . . . none.'

'No. Not none. One. Dr Matthias. Is that true?'

'Yes.'

'His behaviour clearly indicating his innocence, right?'

'I don't know that I would—'

'No further questions,' I snapped, before Tragg could say any more.

'The witness may stand down,' said Judge Hezion. 'Mr Burger, you may call your next witness.'

'Call Dr Achilles Galen.'

CHAPTER 20

In response to the call a tall, thin, almost completely bald man entered the courtroom wearing the robes of a Greek-trained physician—and a haughty, arrogant expression.

He stated his full name and profession, then turned his attention to the District Attorney.

'Dr Galen, you examined the body of Malachi Mason?'

'I did.'

'When and where did you make your first examination?'

'On the day the body was discovered, and in the room where the body was found.'

'And you later conducted a more thorough investigation?'

'I did. I conducted a complete autopsy at the City Morgue.'

'As a result of those two examinations, did you come to a conclusion as to the cause of death?'

'I did.'

'Will you please tell the court about your conclusion.'

'I concluded that the apparent cause of death was indeed the actual cause of death—the stab wound to the chest.'

'There were no complicating factors?'

'None. The dagger entered the chest cavity

between the seventh and eighth ribs and penetrated the heart to a depth of one inch.'

'Would death have been instantaneous?'

'Not quite. But it would have been very quick.'

'Could the victim have moved, or cried out in some way?'

'Most people would, if stabbed in that fashion.'

'Most people,' persisted Burger, 'but what about Malachi Mason?'

'I have been given to understand that the victim was suffering from an illness—a severe virus—and was deeply asleep. It is quite possible that in such a case he could have died before he was awake enough to stir or cry out.'

'Finally, doctor, can you tell us the time of death?'

'Based on body temperature, rigor, lividity, and stomach contents, I would say somewhere between 10.00 a.m. and 2.00 p.m.'

'Thank you very much, doctor.' Turning to me, Burger added with a sneer, 'Your witness, counsellor.'

'About the stab wound, doctor,' I said, slowly rising to my feet, 'was it the only wound?'

'Yes, it was.'

'Were there no other wounds or suspicious marks on the body at all?' I asked. I was on a fishing expedition, but the doctor was not to know that.

'As a matter of fact . . .' he paused.

'Yes, doctor? Please continue.'

'Well, they are so insignificant, really . . .'

'Let the court be the judge of what is significant and what is not. What did you find, doctor?'

'I found a cluster of tiny scratches around the point of entry.'

'A cluster? How many is a cluster?'

'Oh, perhaps half a dozen,' murmured the doctor, looking down his nose at me and the rest of the court.

'And just how tiny were these tiny scratches?'

'No more than half an inch in length.'

'And how did they come to be there?' I persisted.

'I haven't the faintest idea.'

'Come now, doctor! You are here as an expert witness. What is your "expert" opinion?'

'The best I can offer is a guess.'

'Then guess for us.'

'Perhaps the murderer was looking for the best place to insert the blade.'

'In other words, these scratches were most likely made with the point of the dagger—the murder weapon?'

'It seems the most likely possibility.'

'Let me see if I can picture this. Before inserting the blade, the murderer scratched around finding the best entry point?'

'Something like that.'

'So the murderer was not only homicidal, but clumsy?'

'I cannot explain my observations, merely report them.'

'You've taken this line of inquiry as far as it will go, Mr Bartholomew,' said the judge. 'Move on.'

'Very well, your honour. The time of death, doctor, you set at somewhere between 10.00 a.m. and 2.00 p.m.?'

'That is correct.'

'That's a rather broad range, isn't it?'

'It is an accurate range.'

'I'm sure it is. But can't you narrow it down a little?'

'It can be scientifically unwise to be too precise as to time of death.'

'I assure you, doctor, that I don't want to push you to conclusions that are not scientifically justified. However, considering all the factors you took into account—body temperature, rigor, lividity and stomach contents—surely you can be a little more precise than a four-hour range? Or is that the best your scientific ability can manage?'

'There is nothing wrong with my scientific ability!' snapped Dr Galen, drawing himself up to full height.

'Show me!' I challenged, 'Tell the court when Malachi Mason died. Was it ten o'clock? Eleven? Noon? One o'clock? Two o'clock?'

'Midday,' blurted the doctor, and out of the corner of my eye, I could see Burger squirming in his seat.

'Twelve noon?' I persisted.

'That is the most likely time.'

'Two hours *after* my client saw the deceased!' I commented. 'I'm finished, your honour.'

'Re-direct,' yelped Burger, leaping to his feet.

'Go ahead, Mr Burger,' said the judge, with a weary sigh.

'Doctor,' said the District Attorney, approaching the witness stand, 'you said the most likely time of death was twelve noon?'

'I did. Based on the scientific data. That's the most likely'

'Likely, but not certain?' insisted Burger

'There is always a margin of uncertainty in forensic science,' replied Dr Galen, with a solemn nod of his head.

'We know from other evidence that the victim was alone in his room, with the door constantly watched at twelve noon—so that proves that noon was *not* the time of death, doesn't it?'

'Objection,' I said, jumping up.

'On what grounds, Mr Bartholomew?' said the judge, looking at me over the top of his glasses.

'The question calls for a conclusion on the part of the witness.'

'But this is an expert witness, your honour,' protested Burger, 'and recognised as such by the court. Under the rules of evidence, expert witnesses are allowed to draw conclusions.'

'The question is outside of the witness's area of expertise,' I persisted. 'It asks him to draw a conclusion based not on his own forensic examination but on the reports of other witnesses.'

Judge Hezion, rubbed his chin thoughtfully, 'Unless you have further arguments to offer, Mr Burger, I intend to sustain the objection.'

'In that case I have no further questions, your honour,' Burger grumpily resumed his seat.

'Thank you, Dr Galen,' said the judge. 'You may leave the stand.'

'One moment please, your honour,' I interrupted, 'I have one or two more questions on re-cross.'

'Very well. Remain on the stand doctor, and remember you are still under oath. Mr Bartholomew?'

'Dr Galen,' I said, walking towards the stand, 'Mr Burger's misguided question has drawn our attention to an apparent clash in the evidence. On the one hand the forensic evidence you have brought us indicates midday as the most likely time of death. Other evidence suggests this is impossible. How strong is your opinion on the time of death?'

'Forensic medicine is an inexact science, your

147

honour,' replied Galen, ignoring me and turning towards the judge, 'However, there are good reasons . . .'

'Body temperature, rigor, lividity, and stomach contents?' I interrupted.

'Precisely those things,' replied Galen, sneering in my direction, 'that suggest to me—all other things being equal—that the time of death was most likely around twelve midday. However, all other things are *not* equal. When Captain Tragg pointed out to me the evidence of the guard on the door of the victim's room, I came to the conclusion that I was being too precise.'

'So you rewrote your evidence to suit the police, is that what you are telling the court?' I challenged.

'Most certainly not!' Galen snorted indignantly.

'But you *are* telling the court,' I continued, 'that you dismissed midday as the possible time of death not because of forensic factors, but because of other factors?'

'Yes, as I explained . . .'

'That's all, Dr Galen. I have no further questions of this witness your honour.'

'In that case, this strikes me as an opportune moment for the court to rise for lunch. Court will resume at two o'clock.'

During the recess I hurried back to the Gideons', where Miriam served a chicken salad to whoever happened to be in the house at the time. David and Miriam practised an 'open house' policy, and people were coming and going all the time.

'How's Paul now?' I asked through a mouthful of lettuce and tomato.

'Much better,' said Miriam with a warm smile.

'Physically much better,' corrected David, 'but emotionally he's very depressed.'

'How come?'

'Guilt,' chipped in Ananias. 'He is prostrate with guilt over persecuting the followers of Jesus. That's why he's not eating lunch with us. He's finding it hard to face us all.'

'To be honest, I'll find it hard to face him,' I admitted. 'Back in Jerusalem we were all terrified of him. I'll find it very hard to look on him as a friend and brother.'

'You must try, Ben,' said Joe Barnabas earnestly. 'You must try. Paul has been accepted and forgiven by God. We can do no less. We must accept, forgive, and love him.'

I was still thinking about the difficulty of doing this as I bustled back to court for the afternoon sitting.

Once the judge was seated and the court in session, Burger rose to call his next witness.

'Call Didimus Quaresimus.'

So, I thought, I needn't have worried about asking George to get Quaresimus to court after all—he was a prosecution witness all along.

CHAPTER 21

Quaresimus took the oath, and took his place on the witness stand.

'Will you please tell the court your full name and occupation,' said Burger, not bothering to look up from the pages of notes he held.

'Didimus Marcus Quaresimus. I am a steward and senior servant of the household at the Mason villa.'

'By the Mason villa you mean the home of the late Malachi Mason, the victim of the murder currently before the court?'

'Yes, sir, that is correct.'

'How long have you been employed at the Mason establishment?'

'I have been there for eight years now, sir.'

'Are you happy there?'

'Oh, yes. Mr Mason was a very reasonable employer.'

'And Miss Tabitha Mason, do you get on well with her?'

'Yes, sir. As the mistress of the house she is very efficient, and a very fair employer as well, sir.'

'You hold no feelings of dislike, or spite towards any members of the Mason household?'

'That's quite correct, sir,' said Quaresimus, sticking his chest out with self-importance.

'No grudges of any sort?'

'I had no reason for any, sir.'

'And you got on quite well with the other members of the household staff?'

'It is only a very small staff, sir. Some of the young women are rather empty-headed, and old Septimus is a bit vague at times, but I got on well with all of them.'

'Is this getting us anywhere, Mr Burger?' snapped Judge Hezion querulously.

'I'm seeking to establish the reliability of the witness, your honour,' simpered Burger. 'He is a key witness for the prosecution, and his credibility is all-important.'

'Well, you've done that. Now move on,' growled the judge.

The judge's attitude I took to be a good sign for the defence. Perhaps, I speculated, Judge Hezion resented being overruled at the bail hearing. In which case he would, psychologically at least, be leaning towards us.

'Mr Quaresimus,' resumed Burger, 'cast your mind back to the day of the murder. Do you remember that day clearly?'

'I'll never forget it, sir.'

'Your master was sick that morning, wasn't he?'

'Very sick, sir. Worse than he'd been since the illness started.'

'And when was that?'

'About three days earlier, sir.'

'But no doctor had called to see him?'

'I was in the room, sir, when he told Miss Tabitha that he would see no-one but his own doctor.'

'Who was unavailable?'

'Yes, sir.'

'Did this concern Miss Tabitha?'

'She looked very worried, sir. We all talked about

it in the servants' hall. About how worried she looked, I mean. She was very anxious about her father's health, sir.'

'We don't want you to draw any conclusions, Mr Quaresimus. Just tell the court the facts as you know them from your own personal experience!'

'I'm sorry, sir,' stuttered Quaresimus, 'very good, sir.'

'Your honour,' added Burger, turning towards the bench, 'it is appropriate for this court to know that a warrant has been issued for the arrest of Tabitha Mason on the charge of conspiracy to murder—'

'No!'

Everyone in the court turned around at this wounded roar from Tullus Matthias, bellowing his protest at the news.

Judge Hezion banged his gavel several times, 'The accused will remain silent, or he will be removed from the court. Do you understand that?'

'Ah . . . yes . . . your honour . . . I understand,' Tullus muttered quietly. 'I apologise for my outburst.'

'Very well then. Continue Mr Burger.'

As Burger rose to his feet, I looked towards Tullus. He looked back with a frightened and worried expression on his face. I mouthed the words, 'I'll see you later', then turned my attention back to what Burger was saying.

'That being the case, your honour, you will understand that the real attitude and intention of Miss Tabitha Mason is a matter over which the prosecution will be offering evidence in the course of this trial.'

'I take your point, Mr Burger,' nodded the judge, sagely. Then he turned to Quaresimus, still waiting patiently in the witness stand, and said, 'It is most important that you do not draw any conclusions about the attitudes of others, simply report your observations.'

'Yes, your honour. Certainly, your honour,' stumbled Quaresimus anxiously.

'Please resume, Mr Burger,' muttered the judge.

'Mr Quaresimus, we were focusing on the day of the murder.'

'Yes, sir.'

'And we had reached the point where you had reported your observations of the illness of Malachi Mason.'

'Yes, sir. He was very sick, sir. Sicker that day than before, sir.'

'Very well. Let's move on. How long did you spend in the courtyard of the Mason villa that day?'

'I was there for most of the day, sir.'

'How did that come about?'

'My first job on most days is to draw the household water supply for the day from the well in the courtyard.'

'And you did that?'

'I did, sir.'

'When?'

'It took me until around the middle of the morning, sir.'

'And then what happened?'

'Then Dr Matthias arrived, sir,'

'You were there at the time and saw him arrive?'

'I did, sir.'

'What did you see him do?'

'He spoke to Miss Tabitha, and then he went into Mr Mason's room, sir.'

'Now—and this is very important, Mr Quaresimus—who else had seen Malachi Mason that morning?'

'Miss Tabitha had, sir. And her personal maidservant.'

'Tell the court about that, please Mr Quaresimus,' said Burger with a confident sneer, as he strolled slowly from the bar table to the witness stand.

'Well, they were looking after him, sir. Caring for him.'

'By "they" you mean Tabitha Mason and her personal maidservant?'

'Yes, sir.'

'For the information of court,' said Burger, turning towards the judge, 'Tabitha Mason has fled to avoid arrest under the warrant I referred to earlier. And, perhaps significantly, this same personal maidservant appears to have fled with her.'

'Objection, your honour,' I said. 'The fact that Tabitha Mason cannot be found by the City Watch is not, of itself, evidence of flight. It may only be evidence of the incompetence of the City Watch Crime Squad,' at this I glanced at Captain Tragg, who glared daggers at me. I continued, 'Furthermore, the charge against Tabitha Mason is not currently before this court. The only matter on trial here today is the guilt or innocence of my client, Dr Tullus Matthias, and I would ask the court to direct the District Attorney to refrain from raising irrelevant matters in this hearing.'

'Mr Bartholomew has a good point, Mr Burger,' said the judge, 'What do you have to say?'

'Miss Tabitha Mason *is* relevant, your honour! Highly relevant! She couldn't possibly be more relevant! She is the motive, the reason why the accused committed this murder, your honour. Furthermore, if the charge of conspiracy is proved against her she will be implicated in this very murder.'

'Mr Bartholomew?'

'Your honour, with all due respect to my learned colleague, the District Attorney of Damascus, it is not the murder of Malachi Mason that is before this court, but only the charge against my client. Any other charges to do with the same crime will be heard in another court, at another time. If, indeed, they are ever heard at all.'

'But, your honour . . .' moaned Burger.

'That's enough, gentlemen,' said the judge firmly, 'I have heard your arguments. Mr Burger you must confine yourself to the matter in hand—namely the charge against Dr Matthias. I am prepared to give you latitude when it comes to establishing the motive of the accused. But that latitude does not extend to arguing for guilt or innocence in the matter of other accused persons or other charges. Is that clear?'

'Very clear, your honour,' Burger said in a subdued voice.

'Very well. Continue with your examination of the witness.'

Burger shuffled his papers, drew a deep breath, then turned his attention back to Quaresimus.

'You told us,' he said, 'that you saw Tabitha Mason and her personal maidservant visit the room of Malachi Mason on the morning of his death.'

'That is correct, sir, they did. A number of times.'

'How many times?'

'I couldn't say for sure, sir, but maybe seven or eight.'

'Seven or eight times?'

'Yes, sir.'

'What were they doing?'

'Nursing him, sir—to the best of my knowledge.'

'And who else saw Malachi Mason that morning?'

'Only me, sir.'

'You?'

'Yes, sir. I was the only other person who saw Mr Mason. Before the doctor, that is.'

'Exactly when did you see Mr Mason?'

'A few minutes before Dr Matthias.'

'A few? How many is "a few"?'

'Perhaps three minutes, no more.'

'And why did you go into see him?'

'I took a fresh jug of water into his room.'

'I see. And was Malachi Mason alive when you saw him?'

'Yes, sir.'

'How do you know?'

'He tried to talk to me, sir.'

'What did he say?'

'I couldn't make out any words, sir. It was a mumble. Like he was delirious.'

'But he definitely spoke?'

'Yes, sir.'

'So you can tell us, definitely, from your own knowledge, that Malachi Mason was alive some three minutes before the accused saw him?'

'That is correct, sir.'

'Who went into Mr Mason's room with the doctor?'

'No-one, sir. He went in alone.'

'Not even Miss Tabitha Mason?'

'Only the doctor, sir. Alone.'

'How long was he in there?'

'About ten minutes.'

'And where were you during this time?'

'Still in the courtyard, sir.'

'When the doctor came out, what happened?'

'He talked to Miss Tabitha, sir. Then Miss Tabitha

told me to take a seat at the door to Mr Mason's room and stop anyone from going in or out, so that Mr Mason could sleep, sir.'

'And did anyone go in or out?'

'No sir, no-one.'

'When did you next see Mr Mason?'

'Late that same afternoon, sir. The doctor summonsed me, just after he and Miss Tabitha had walked into the room.'

'And in what condition was Malachi Mason when you saw him for the second time that day?'

'He was dead, sir.'

'So, let's be quite clear about this. You saw Malachi Mason twice that day—the first time he was definitely alive and the second time he was dead?'

'That is correct, sir.'

'And the only person who entered the victim's room between your two visits—the *only* person—was the accused, Dr Tullus Matthias?'

'Yes, sir.'

Burger turned towards me with an evil grin on his face, and said, 'Your witness, counsellor.'

CHAPTER 22

I rose slowly to my feet and walked across the courtroom floor to the witness stand. For a moment I stood in front of Quaresimus and stared him in the eye. He looked uncomfortable and licked his lips.

'Get on with it, Mr Bartholomew,' snapped the judge, 'the court doesn't have all day!'

'Certainly, your honour. Mr Quaresimus, Miss Tabitha Mason placed you on "guard duty"—if I can call it that—outside Malachi Mason's room at what time?'

'I don't know exactly.'

'Approximately then.'

'Late in the morning.'

'So, that means about what time?'

'Maybe ten-thirty to eleven o'clock.'

'And that's when you took a seat, in the shade of the lemon tree, in front of Malachi Mason's door.'

'That's correct.'

'When were you relieved from that duty?'

'I beg your pardon? I don't understand.'

'When were you told,' I said, speaking slowly and deliberately, 'that you no longer needed to remain on guard at Malachi Mason's door?'

'I was never told.'

'So when did you stop being on duty at the door?'

'When the corpse was found, I guess. Didn't need

anyone on duty after that. As soon as the body was found I was given errands to run.'

'And when was that?'

'Late afternoon.'

'Can you give us a time?'

'I couldn't see a clock.'

'Guess. Give us an approximate time.'

'Maybe four, or four-thirty,' replied Quaresimus with a shrug of his narrow shoulders.

'So you were posted on door duty at, say, eleven in the morning, and that duty ended between four and four-thirty in the afternoon. Is that correct?'

'Yes, sir. That's about right.'

'Who did you see during that time?'

'No-one went in or out of Mr Mason's room, I've already said that.'

'I didn't ask you that. I'm not asking who you saw enter or leave the room, I'm just asking you who you saw at all during that time.'

'Well . . . just the household staff . . . I mean . . . just the people who happened to walk across the courtyard.'

'And who were they—precisely?'

'But, your honour,' complained Quaresimus, turning to the judge, 'I can't remember that sort of detail.'

'Just do your best,' Judge Hezion offered no sympathy. 'Answer the question as best you can.'

'Well, all I can say,' muttered Quaresimus sullenly, 'is that I probably saw all the members of the household at one time or another, and that's all. Apart from the doctor, there were no visitors until the City Watch officers arrived late in the day. Is that what you want?'

'That will do,' I said. 'Now, if that's who *you* saw—who saw you?'

'Objection, your honour!' said Burger, leaping to his feet. 'This is pointless harassment of the witness, it is revealing no information not already before the court, it's taking us around in circles, and is wasting the court's time.'

'I'm inclined to agree with the District Attorney,' said the judge, looking at me sternly. 'What do you have to say for yourself, Mr Bartholomew? Is this line of questioning taking us anywhere?'

'If the court will just grant me a little more latitude, I will show its relevance to my case.'

'I expect you to show relevance very soon, otherwise I will ask you to move on. Objection dismissed, Mr Burger.'

'Briefly,' I said, turning back to Quaresimus on the witness stand, 'tell the court who saw you during your time in the courtyard, at the door of Malachi Mason's room.'

'Well . . . everyone, I guess. I mean everyone who walked across the courtyard. At least, until siesta started, then everyone had a rest—except me.'

'So, during siesta time you were alone, and were seen by no-one?'

'Of course!'

'Do you have a girlfriend?'

'You know I have. Dinah told me you went to see her.'

'Just answer the question, Mr Quaresimus,' the judge said wearily.

Quaresimus, shrugged his shoulders, 'Yes, I have a girlfriend called Dinah.'

'And do you sometimes sneak out and visit her when you are supposed to be on siesta duty?'

'Yes, sometimes I do.'

'Did you visit her on the day of the murder?'

'No! I didn't! She wasn't even in town. She and her mistress were in Jericho for the whole week.'

'This line of questioning seems to have come to a dead end, Mr Bartholomew,' muttered the judge, darkly.

'Not quite, your honour,' I replied, 'There's one more step to go.'

'Then be quick about it!' he snapped.

'Mr Quaresimus, is Dinah your only girlfriend?'

'Eh? I don't understand.'

'Come now, Quaresimus. The question is straightforward enough. Do you have any other girlfriends?'

'Well . . . I'm still a young man . . . I mean to say, I'm not engaged to Dinah or anything.'

'In fact, you're quite a ladies' man, aren't you?'

'I'm popular with the girls, you could say that.'

'Is one of your many girlfriends Leah Levinson?' Quaresimus looked uncomfortable, and pulled his tunic a bit looser around his throat.

Burger realised that his key witness was about to get into trouble and leapt to his feet again.

'Objection, your honour. The court has extended great leniency to Mr Bartholomew and all he has done in return is to take us on a wild-goose chase and waste the court's time. I respectfully ask your honour to direct my learned colleague to move on to another line of questioning.'

'I disagree, Mr Burger,' said Judge Hezion. 'Objection overruled. Answer the question Mr Quaresimus.'

'Well . . .'

As Quaresimus lapsed into silence I turned towards the public gallery and said, 'Would Leah Levinson please stand up?'

An attractive, dark-haired woman in her early twenties stood up in the middle of the public gallery.

'As you can see, Mr Quaresimus, Leah Levinson is present in the courtroom today. If you will not co-operate I can call her as a witness. So now, bearing in mind the penalty for perjury, please tell the court—is she a girlfriend of yours?'

'Yes,' admitted Quaresimus, very quietly.

'Louder please,' I said.

'Yes!'

'And did you visit her during the siesta hour on the day of the murder?'

There was a long silence.

'Well, did you?' I persisted.

'Yes.'

'Louder please.'

'Yes!'

'During what times?'

'About twelve till two,' he almost whispered.

'Louder.'

'About twelve till two!'

'So, from twelve till two you were not on duty in front of Malachi Mason's door?'

'That's right,' Quaresimus admitted reluctantly.

'At the same time as the rest of the Mason household were resting during siesta?'

'Yeah.'

'So during those hours the murdered man's room was unwatched and anyone could have entered, killed Malachi Mason, and left again, unseen?'

'I guess so.'

'You know so, don't you Quaresimus?'

'Yeah, I know so.'

'I have no further questions for this witness, your honour,' I said, resuming my seat.

'Do you have any questions on re-direct, Mr Burger?' asked the judge.

Burger was engaged in a whispered consultation with Captain Tragg and his junior counsel.

'Ah, no, your honour. Not at this time,' muttered Burger, 'although, with your honour's indulgence, I may recall this witness for further questioning later.'

'Very well. In that case I will adjourn the court for today. This hearing will resume tomorrow morning at ten o'clock.'

I scooped my papers into my briefcase and stood up. Turning around to leave the courtroom I found myself face to face with Aaron Burger. There was a long, heavy silence between us.

'Don't think you've won. That's all, just don't think you've won!' he said finally, then stalked off.

I made my way to the holding cells in the basement of the court building, and asked to see my client.

Tullus looked grey and pallid when he was brought into the interview room, but in his eyes burnt a bright fire.

'What's happened to Tabitha?' he asked, the moment the door closed behind him.

'Calm down. She's all right,' I said, motioning him to take a seat.

'But this charge of conspiracy to murder. What does it mean?'

'It means that Aaron Burger is a dangerous enemy,' I said, seating myself opposite him.

'Not only dangerous, powerful,' said Tullus, glumly. 'If he's after Tabitha then . . .'

'Then there is some risk. But he hasn't got her yet, so don't lose hope.'

'Why has he turned on her?' asked Tullus, a puzzled note in his voice. 'I always imagined that he wanted me out of the way so he could have her for himself.'

'That was his original plan,' I agreed, 'but I overheard him pushing himself on Tabitha and being firmly refused. He's now turning on her to exact vengeance.'

'I see.'

'I have arranged for Tabitha to be "out of the way"—let me put it like that. With the result that she may not even be found before we have this matter settled and the whole charge against you cleared up.'

'Is she safe?'

'Yes.'

'And well?'

'Completely. Except for her worry about you.'

'Poor kid.'

'Tullus, we have to talk about your dagger.'

'My what?' His mind was still on Tabitha.

'Your dagger—the murder weapon.'

'Yes, of course.'

'When was the last time you saw it?'

'I've been wracking my brains trying to remember. The trouble is, it's like a lot of bits and pieces that you inherit—you never give it any thought from one year's end to the next. The last time I can really remember seeing it was months ago—so that doesn't help, does it?'

'I'm afraid not. Who knew you had it?'

'Everyone who ever visited my house. It was on display. Or, sort of on display. On a mantelpiece, in fact, with a lot of other things.'

'Before the murder, had you noticed it was missing?'

'I'm afraid not. It was just a piece of the scenery on a rather crowded mantel.'

'So it could have been missing for weeks, or even months?'

'As far as I can tell, yes.'

'And lots of people knew it was there?'

'Yes, heaps of people.'

'So anyone could have taken it in the past few weeks or months?'

'I suppose so.'

'Were you burgled at any time in the last few months?'

'No. Mind you, I'm not very security-conscious.'

'Time's up,' a guard said, opening the door.

Tullus stood up and walked over to the guard. At the door he turned and said, 'By the way. Thanks for what you did in court today—you were brilliant.'

'We try, Tullus old son, we try.'

'What you achieved today has given me enormous confidence in you. I'm certain you can get me off.'

As he left, and the steel door clanged closed behind him I thought to myself, 'Well, at least that means one of us is confident.'

CHAPTER 23

At the Gideons' that night, Paul Benson joined us at the table for the evening meal. Before we sat down he took my elbow, led me to a quiet corner and, with tears in his eyes, asked my forgiveness for any suffering he had caused me. Later I discovered that he had done the same with everyone else.

I couldn't take my eyes off him throughout the meal. This was the man I had thought of as a monster. Yet here he was eating with us. He gradually became more relaxed and joined in the conversation. I don't think I could have been more dumbfounded if David Gideon had brought a tame rat to share our meal and give a speech afterwards!

'Do you have any plans for tonight?' Joe Barnabas asked me later, as we cleared plates from the table.

'Why do you ask?'

'We were planning to sit around and study the Scriptures together. Paul has asked us to, and I'll lead the study. Can you stay with us?'

'I'm afraid I've got a job to do, and I have to keep working,' I replied, pleased to have a genuine excuse. Being in the same room as Benson still made me nervous.

'I understand,' said Joe. 'What are your plans for tonight?'

'I'm starting to look for Malachi Mason's *real*

murderer. I still think that's the surest way to get Tullus off the hook.'

'I wish you well then,' said Barnabas. 'We'll pray for you when the group meets.'

After I'd done my share of washing and wiping up, I pulled an extra cloak over my shoulders and stepped out into the cool night air.

From the Gideons' I walked to Straight Street. The busy thoroughfare was filled with lights, the cafes packed with people, and many of the shops were still open for business, emitting a noisy barrage of conversation as shoppers bargained with shopkeepers.

I stopped for a cup of strong, sweet coffee at one of the sidewalk cafes—I was starting to get addicted to the stuff—and then continued on my way. In the evening the buskers came out onto Straight Street— playing their flutes, singing, dancing, and begging the passing parade for 'any small coin, any small coin will be most welcome'. Straight Street seemed less of a bazaar at night, and more of a circus.

As I walked, the humidity in the air warmed me up, and I had to stop and take off my extra cloak. As I did so I caught a fleeting glimpse of a dark cloaked figure hovering nearby. I soon became aware that if I stopped the figure seemed to stop too. If I turned to look, it darted away or melted into the crowd. Could this be Otto Strong, I asked myself, planning another attempt to 'persuade' me to leave town?

About halfway down Straight Street I turned left and headed towards the river front. I was looking for a seedy bar and grill called The Bilge Pump, where, according to Paul Mallard's notes, I would find the old sea captain Ahab Ishmael.

The narrow alleyway was poorly lit, and my footsteps echoed like the footsteps of a phantom follower. Several times I stopped suddenly and looked around, but there was no-one there. No-one I could see, anyway.

At the end of the alley I turned into Barge Pole Lane. This turned out to be a long line of cheap bars and gambling joints interspersed with the backs of warehouses. There were drunks staggering down the street, drunks lying on the footpath, and drunks vomiting in the gutter. But at least there were a lot of people around.

I found The Bilge Pump under a flickering neon sign with several of the letters broken, giving the impression that the place was called 'The Big Pup'. Bilge pump? Big pup? I couldn't care less, as long as Captain Ishmael was inside.

The place was crowded, the ceiling was low, and the air was filled with smoke and murmured conversation. I walked up to the bar.

'What'll it be?' growled a barkeeper with more scars than teeth to decorate his face.

I looked up at the bottles on the shelves behind him, and saw that my choice was restricted to rum or else rum. I ordered a small one and, when it arrived, leant my back against the bar, surveyed the room, and took a sip. I had heard of 'rot gut' rum before, but this stuff started rotting at the back of the throat and continued all the way down.

I took a suspicious look at the liquid in my glass. This stuff would be more useful, as a spray to kill termites than a drink. I wouldn't risk another swallow.

At a number of the tables, small groups of men were gambling with greasy decks of cards. Several of the customers were slumped in their chairs, having drunk themselves into oblivion.

Finally, in a far corner, I spotted my man, Captain Ahab Ishmael: black eye patch, greasy tangled beard, and wooden stump replacing his left leg below the knee.

'Can I buy you a drink?' I asked, approaching the table where he was sitting alone.

'Now why would ya want to do a damn fool thing like that for?' he growled, his voice slurred after permanent pickling in cheap rum.

'In return for a little conversation,' I replied.

'I can tell ya some tales of the sea that will curl the hairs on ya chest. Assuming, that is, that you've got any hairs on ya chest!' he said with a gap-toothed grin.

'Not tales of the sea,' I explained, pulling out a chair and sitting down, 'tales of merchants and ship owners.'

'Them lot!' he growled, spitting in disgust on the floor. 'Your average ship's rat has got more moral fibre than them!'

'So I'm told, so I'm told,' I hastily agreed, 'and that's exactly what I want to talk to you about.'

'Ya did say somethin' about a drink didn't ya? Or have me ears gone as dry as me throat?'

'Name your poison,' I replied.

'Ah, poison is all they serve in this fish barrel of a place. But the more I drink, the better I forget,' he said, and waved to the only waiter then ordered a double rum.

'Forgetting is not what I want you to do,' I explained. 'It's remembering I'm interested in.'

'Rememberin' what?'

'Not what—who. Malachi Mason.'

'Him!' yelped Captain Ishmael, then burst into an amazing array of profanities that included bits of Egyptian, Phoenician, Aramaic, Latin and Greek.

'Don't like him then?'

'Hate 'im. Hate 'im with every drop of acid in me twisted guts.'

'Why.'

'See this!' growled the captain, slapping his wooden leg. 'A gift from Malachi Mason this is. But I had to pay for it. The same day he gave me this he took away me ship, me life savings and me lovely wife and daughters.'

His eyes filled with tears.

'Tell me about that day,' I said, wanting to avoid dealing with a maudlin, weeping drunk.

'The ship was called *The Jonah*,' he sniffed, wiping his nose with the back of his hand. 'A bad name for a ship. Should never have been called that. And badly designed. Too broad across the beam and inclined to wallow whenever the seas came up. But still and all, a safe enough ship when it was properly looked after.'

He stopped talking, and seemed to be looking a long way into the distance.

'Yes, captain?' I prompted. 'You were saying?'

'Where was I? Oh, yes. That last voyage of *The Jonah*. We was takin' a mixed load of cargo from the port of Tyre across to Crete. Should 'ave been a milk run.'

'You were captain of *The Jonah* on that voyage?'

'More than that! Much more. I was thinkin' of retirement see. So I had me wife an' daughters with me. We was goin' to settle on Crete, where I was born. And 'alf the cargo consisted of dressed timber—cedars from Lebanon—that I'd bought with me life savings. I knew I could sell that timber for a fair profit on Crete. Maybe buy a little inn with the profits. Settle down. Spend more time with me family,' he took another deep swig of his rum. 'More fool me. Mason had other plans.'

'What other plans?'

'Quick profits. Them was the plans. Never mind anyone else, just quick profits, and let others pay the price.'

'And how did Mason plan to make these quick profits?'

'By sinking 'is own ship, that's 'ow! *The Jonah* 'ad been into dry dock for repairs the summer before. And 'e 'ated to spend any brass did old Mason. So 'e told the shipyard just to give 'er a coat of paint, and not to bother with caulking the boards, or doin' anythin' proper like.'

'So the ship was unsafe?'

'Aye, lad, that's what it was.'

'And Mason knew it was unsafe?'

'He knew all right. He knew the first good storm would sink 'er. That's why 'e overinsured 'er. And every cargo 'e put in 'er after that, as well. All overinsured. He knew she'd go down to Davy Jones's locker sooner or later. An' she did. An' 'e collected on 'is insurance. An' I collected this,' Captain Ishmael slapped his wooden leg again, and took another slug of rum.

'It was a storm that did it?' I asked.

'Aye, lad. A bad 'un. Waves higher than the top mast. Mind you, we would have survived if *The Jonah* hadn't started takin' water. Which she did. An' if the timbers hadn't started to break up. Which they did. The mizzen mast fell across the deck and I got this leg, and I was helpless—just helpless—as me lovely wife and daughters drowned.'

He paused to wipe the moisture out of his eyes with his gnarled fingers. I waited until he'd recovered.

'You know that Malachi Mason's dead now, don't you?' I asked.

'Aye, so I 'eard. An' good luck to whoever killed 'im, I say.'

'Was it you who did it?'

'Me who what? Killed 'im! Is that what this is all about? Not satisfied with takin' me ship, me family, me life savings, and most of me left leg, the ghost of Malachi Mason 'as come back from the grave to take me life for murder, 'as 'e?'

'That's no answer,' I said, leaning forward across the table, and staring directly into the old sea captain's eyes. 'Did you kill him?'

There was a long silence before he answered. His watery blue eyes drifted down to the table where he saw the remains of my tot of rum. He picked it up and drank it down in one gulp.

'Ah, that's better lad,' he said, licking his lips, then he put down the glass and returned my stare. 'I wish I could say I did it, lad. Aye, I truly wish I could.'

For a while he sat and stared at the tabletop, shaking his head as though lost in some sad, private thought.

'But I didn't,' he continued at last, 'I didn't. I was a bonny fighter when I was younger. But all the losses just took all the fight outta me. Once I was back on me feet again I should 'ave come straight 'ere to Damascus, and found that swine Mason's office, and rammed a harpoon straight through 'is gullet. I should 'ave—but I didn't.'

'Why not?'

'I didn't care any more. Without me wife and daughters. Without any future. I just didn't care.'

'So what did you do?'

'I drifted and drank, lad. Aye, that's what I did. I drifted and drank. I ended up 'ere, doin' casual work as a deck 'and on them river barges. An' gettin' drunk every night. That's all that's left for me, lad. I'm glad the worms are eatin' Malachi Mason's carcass. But I didn't do it, lad. There's no fire in me belly any more. And the sad truth is, I just don't care enough about anything.'

CHAPTER 24

'Anything I can do for you?' I asked, wanting to do something—anything—to help this wreck of a man.

Captain Ishmael looked at me for a moment, as if he hadn't heard me right.

'Anything I can do for you?' I repeated.

'Aye, lad, there is,' he said at last. 'There's just one thing ya can do for me. One thing.'

'And what's that?' I asked earnestly.

'Just this, lad, just this—buy me another double rum!' growled the captain, and then threw back his head and laughed raucously. The laugh subsided into a hacking cough. I threw a few sheckles onto the table. How he spent the money was up to him.

Ishmael had persuaded me he was not the murderer—I was one hundred per cent certain of that. He lived at the bottom of a rum bottle, hurting no-one but himself.

I waded back through the The Bilge Pump's thick atmosphere—composed of equal parts smoke, sweat, garlic, and stale rum—pushed open the bar-room door, and stepped out into the cool, night air. For a minute I just stood there inhaling deeply. Then I pulled on my heavy cloak, and turned to walk up the narrow street.

As I walked I glimpsed a movement—a definite movement this time—on the opposite side of the street. Every nerve in my body tingled with danger.

I relaxed my muscles, trying to give no sign by my body language that I was aware of the lurking threat. At the same time my mind became more alert, my senses more acute than ever.

I caught a faint scrape of sandals on cobblestones that told me my pursuer was moving behind me.

The lane's lighting consisted of a few single-bulb lampposts at long intervals. In between were deep wells of darkness. I walked in a slow, unconcerned fashion, then, as soon as I was totally invisible in the middle of a pool of inky blackness I stopped, pressed myself against a brick wall and looked for a place to hide.

I found the corner of a warehouse, and squeezed myself into the narrow gap between two high brick walls of neighbouring buildings.

Silently, almost not breathing, I waited. My phantom follower was moving closer, creeping noiselessly on the balls of his feet. For a moment the silence was absolute, then I heard a breath exhaled and realised my follower was standing still, directly opposite my hiding place, less than two yards away.

How long the two of us were frozen in that position I don't know. It felt like an eternity. My pursuer started to move forward, thought better of it, and stood still again.

Perhaps I made some small noise. Perhaps he could smell me—the odours of *The Bilge Pump* tended to linger. Perhaps he just guessed. In a sudden movement he swung towards me, pulled a flashlight out from under his black cloak, and shone it full on my face.

I lashed out with my foot and kicked the flashlight out of his hand, sending it spinning through the air for several yards. It crashed onto the cobblestones and went out. As the light spun out of my pursuer's hand the hood on his cloak fell back, and I briefly saw the distinctive bullet-shaped head of Otto Strong.

Having no desire for a return bout with him, I turned and ran. As I pelted down the narrow gap between the two buildings my right hand trailed along the brick wall beside me. As soon as it located a doorway, I stopped and tried the wooden door. It was unlocked. I pushed it open and stepped inside.

More darkness. I had stepped from a pitch black night, into a pitch black building. I stumbled forward, bumped my knee on a large, heavy barrel, then proceeded more cautiously. I had got only a few yards from the door when it opened again—Otto Strong had come into the warehouse after me.

My searching hands told me that the whole building was stacked high with barrels—one on top of another, far beyond my reach. Between the rows of barrels were narrow walkways. Strong began to stalk me.

Small sounds were amplified in that vast, echoing building. We could see nothing—not even a hand held an inch in front of the eyes—but every sound echoed, and travelled.

Safety, I thought, might lie in keeping very still. So I tried this. But with every second I could hear Strong getting closer. When he was within a few yards of me, I broke into a run.

After running headlong into the pitch blackness for ten yards my nerve failed, and I skidded to a stop. I was breathing heavily, my breath whistling and hissing in and out of my lungs like an old steam locomotive. There was no way Otto Strong could fail to find me now.

I turned and waited for him, hearing the soft

approach of his leather sandals on the stone floor. The sound stopped. Then there was a crackle, and suddenly I saw Strong holding a flickering match in his hand.

'You wouldn't listen to my first message, Mr Bartholomew,' he whispered, 'so I'm afraid this time I shall have to deliver a more permanent one.'

He transferred the trembling match to his left hand, reached towards his belt, and pulled out a gleaming steel blade.

'A completely permanent message, Mr Bartholomew,' he whispered. 'One final demand notice, you might say.'

The match burned down to his fingers. He flicked it out and the darkness returned. Otto had been closer to the bright little flame than I had, and would, therefore, find the darkness more abruptly blinding than me. To take advantage of this, I dropped down onto my haunches. If he came at me with his knife, I figured, he would come in too high, and hit the air over my head.

But he didn't attack.

Instead he lit another match.

'Good move, Mr Bartholomew,' whispered Strong, 'but it won't do you any good.'

He dropped the still burning match onto the floor, and came at me with the knife. He came low and hard, like a charging charioteer. I waited until the last moment, then rolled to one side.

Strong slid past me, his knife slicing my ear he was so close. He couldn't stop, and crashed—hard— into a stack of barrels behind me.

I staggered to my feet and turned to face him. He had already caught his breath and recovered his balance. He turned to face me, the gleaming steel blade still held firmly in his right hand.

There was a creaking noise and I glanced up and saw the stack of barrels he had collided into swaying precariously over Strong's head.

'Look out!' I yelled.

'No! You look out!' shouted Strong stepping forward, his knife hand swinging savagely. And as he started towards me, he stepped straight into the path of the falling barrel. It crashed onto his head, knocking him down, and shattering itself. The sound of the crash, and of Otto's last scream, echoed around the warehouse like an explosion.

I stood frozen in my tracks. Then I glanced up at the stack of barrels—the rest of them looked secure enough. I hurried forward, knelt down beside Strong, and felt for his pulse. But there was really no need to—I knew that he was dead.

I turned around and discovered a warm, yellow glow trickling across the warehouse floor. Strong's match had fallen into a pile of dry straw which was now burning.

I looked around for something to put it out.

An empty barrel, or a bucket, and a water supply— that's what I needed.

I hurried up and down the walkways of the warehouse searching, without success, for something to fight the fire. Then I was knocked off my feet by an invisible hand, and deafened by the roar that raged around me.

I staggered back to my feet. A wall of flames now engulfed half the building. It was barrels of brandy that had exploded and were now feeding the fire.

There was nothing I could do. By the brilliant light of the burning warehouse, I found my way to the side door, let myself out, and hurried between the two buildings. When I got back to the lane I collapsed from smoke inhalation and exhaustion.

By the time I had recovered, the street was full of people. The patrons of the bars and inns that filled the street were organising themselves into a bucket brigade and, as I watched, the City Watch arrived to take charge. Realising there was nothing I could contribute in my exhausted state, I left them to it, and turned my feet towards home.

I had another reason for not staying at the scene of the fire. I didn't want to give Captain Tragg an excuse—even a feeble one—for arresting me. Nothing would please Tragg and Burger more than having Tullus's lawyer under lock and key!

I limped back towards the Gideons', feeling a warm trickle down the side of my face. I touched it, then looked at my hand—blood!

CHAPTER 25

My ear was bleeding from where it had been sliced by Otto Strong's knife. I pressed my scarf against the cut and hurried on.

I arrived to find most of the house in darkness, the occupants retired for the night. Joe Barnabas was the only one still awake. He was in the kitchen making a cup of coffee when I walked in.

'Ben! What's happened to you! You're a mess!'

'It's nothing,' I murmured. 'You should see the other guy.'

Then I realised that my joke was in bad taste, because the other guy was dead.

'What happened?' asked Barnabas again, as I wet a cloth and cleaned the cut on my ear.

'Well,' I replied, 'I interviewed one possible suspect in the Mason murder case. And then I ran into a cheap hood with a sharp knife.'

'It looks more like he ran into you,' said Barnabas, cutting off a piece of plaster to stick over the cut on my ear.

'Ran into me? Yeah, I guess that's what happened all right,' I agreed, remembering Otto Strong's savage attack in the warehouse. 'And what about you? Did you have a good night?' I continued, dabbing the ear dry and applying the plaster.

'Us? Yes, we did as it happens. A terrific night, in fact.'

'Oh, yes? In what way?'

'Well, as we had planned, we sat around to study the Scriptures. I was going to lead the discussion, but as the evening went on Paul contributed more and more. Ben, that man knows so much about the Scriptures! He was able to point out prophecy after prophecy that was fulfilled in Jesus. His knowledge is just breathtaking!'

'Hhmm. I'm still finding it hard to come to terms with Paul being such a completely changed person.'

'You will, Ben, you will,' said Barnabas confidently, 'but tell me more about your night.'

I told him everything that had happened, omitting no details.

'Well, considering what could have happened,' he said when I had completed my narrative, 'I'm pleased that you survived. In fact, I'd say that your survival is an answer to prayer. We did pray for you here this evening, as we promised to.'

'Thank you for that. And tonight's events seem to confirm what you were saying.'

'About what?'

'About the source of suffering and evil in the world being the evil in human hearts.'

'Yes,' said Barnabas, 'And that corruption of the human heart is caused by rejecting God and God's rule over human lives.'

'Knowing that doesn't actually stop it hurting,' I commented, touching my ear and wincing at the sharp pain. 'That's how most people are going to react to what you've been telling me.'

'In fact, I've noticed that most people have one of two reactions to suffering and evil—one of them right, the other wrong.'

'Explain.'

'Well, the first common reaction is for people who are going through great trials to say "Why me? Why is this happening to me?" '

'Yes, that's right,' I agreed. 'I've heard that often.'

'And that's the wrong reaction. The answer to the question "Why me?" is "Well, why not?". In other words, anyone who lives in a world of suffering—a world in rebellion against God—must expect to suffer. To live in this world and say "Why am I suffering?" is like someone who lives in the tropics saying "Why am I hot?". That's just the way the world is.'

'And what's the other common reaction?'

'The other one is to say, "It shouldn't be like this!" '

'Yeah, I guess I've heard that said too. Although, perhaps not quite as often.'

'True. Anyway, that response—"It shouldn't be like this"—is the correct one. That's how God reacts to suffering. God did not create a world in which there was suffering. He created a perfect world into which suffering and evil were introduced by human beings declaring their independence from Him and His rule. God looks at the suffering caused by our rebellion and says "It shouldn't be like this!" '

'If that's what God says, then why doesn't He do something about it?'

'What would you like Him to do?'

'Well, for starters, whenever anyone behaves cruelly to someone else, snuff them out!' 'That'd stop them doing it again!' After my encounter with Otto I wasn't feeling very patient or compassionate.

'If God snuffed out a person's life whenever that person hurt someone else, you and I would both be dead. And so would everyone else. None of us would survive!'

'Speak for yourself!' I protested.

'I am,' said Barnabas, 'and for you and for the entire human race. Are you going to tell me that you have never hurt another human being? Because if you are, you are not being honest with yourself. You can think of times when other people have hurt you? Of course you can. Well, the bad news is, other people can clearly remember times when you have hurt them! None of us is innocent. None of us can escape condemnation. The very fact that we are *not* snuffed out instantly, the very fact that the human race goes on surviving, is a tribute to God's great patience, and love, and mercy, and compassion.'

'But surely God could do *something* about suffering?'

'God has done something. He has done the most important "something" that could ever be done.'

'Which is?'

'He has suffered for us. He has entered this world of suffering. He has become the "Suffering God". And it is because of his suffering that we can be healed, and forgiven, and restored.'

I had opened my mouth to ask another question when I heard the Damascus City Hall clock strike midnight, and I remembered that I had to appear in court tomorrow.

'Unless I get some sleep,' I protested, 'I will be no use to Tullus in court tomorrow.'

'In that case,' said Barnabas, 'I mustn't keep you up a minute longer!'

Exhausted by the events of the day, I slept very deeply. Ananias woke me finally at nine o'clock to tell me that the court was sitting in one hour.

I leapt out of bed, had a short cold shower, and hurried downstairs for a quick breakfast of coffee and bagels.

When I walked into the kitchen Paul Benson was there. I halted in my tracks, feeling uncomfortable in his presence. If he noticed my discomfort he ignored it, said good morning, poured me a coffee, and passed the bagels.

As we sat talking briefly over breakfast, I discovered just how changed this man was. 'The monster of Jerusalem' was, well, the only word is—gentle! More than that, he was . . . humble. I was flabbergasted.

I left half an hour later, with a briefcase stuffed full of legal documents under my arm.

Despite my late start I was in the courtroom in time to spread out the documents I needed on the bar table, and engage in some friendly chat with the clerk of the court.

At a half a minute to ten, Aaron Burger walked in accompanied by several flunkies from his office, and by Captain Tragg.

While I was staring at them, Tragg looked up, caught my eye, and smiled at me in a sly and sinister way. Then he turned his back on me. He seemed to be taking a special interest in this case.

'Good morning,' I said to Burger, with forced cheerfulness.

He grunted in reply, not even looking at me.

'How's your cousin?' I asked. That made him look up.

'My cousin?'

'Yes. Paul Benson. How is he?' I asked, mischievously.

'He's sick!' snapped Burger. 'He should be in

hospital. In fact, he should be committed to an asylum for his own good!'

That sounded like a threat, and gave me something to think about briefly. Then Judge Hezion entered, we all rose, and the court was in session for the morning.

'Has the prosecution finished its case?' asked the judge.

'Not yet, your honour,' replied Burger. 'We still have one or two witnesses to call.'

'Proceed, Mr Burger.'

'Call Shem Danielson.'

The call was repeated by the clerk of the court, then out in the corridor. An elderly man tottered into the courtroom, took the witness stand, and took the oath.

'Tell the court your full name and occupation,' said the clerk, after administering the oath.

'Shem Korah Danielson. I am the senior steward in the household of Dr Tullus Matthias.'

Tullus's servant! What did Burger have up his sleeve?

The District Attorney walked over to the exhibits table, picked up the silver dagger and handed it to the witness.

'Mr Danielson, do you recognise this weapon?'

'I most certainly do,' answered the old man.

'Please tell the court where you have seen this dagger before.'

'In Dr Matthias's house.'

'It was the property of Dr Matthias?'

'Yes, sir, it was. And of his father before him, and of his father before that.'

'It's an old family heirloom then?'

'Yes, sir, that is correct. Although why the family

wanted to keep it I could never understand. It's an ugly thing.'

'I'm not interested in its aesthetic value, Mr Danielson, merely its identification and its ownership.'

'Oh, it's Dr Matthias' dagger, sir, there's no doubt about that,' he said then turned towards Tullus. 'I hope I haven't got you into trouble by saying that, sir.'

'Don't worry, Shem,' said Tullus, 'I was in trouble already.'

'Thank you, sir. I'm glad you understand, sir. But they gave me this legal piece of paper, sir, and said I had to come to court.'

The judge banged his gavel angrily.

'The witness and the accused will cease from engaging in private conversation across this courtroom!'

'I'm sorry, sir,' Shem Danielson, quavered.

'Mr Burger,' continued the judge, ignoring this last remark, 'have you any further questions of this witness?'

'I've finished your honour,' said Burger, then, turning to me, 'Your witness, counsellor.'

CHAPTER 26

I left the bar table and walked across to the witness stand. When I held out my hand, the witness passed the dagger to me.

'Definitely from the Matthias household?' I asked.

'Definitely, I'm afraid,' said Shem Danielson.

I looked at the intricately carved handle on the silver dagger. Then curled my fingers around it, as if to use it as a weapon.

'Ouch!' I exclaimed, startled to feel a sharp pain in my hand.

'What is the problem, Mr Bartholomew?' asked the judge.

'Some sharp edge on the handle just caught my hand, your honour,' I explained.

'Impossible,' interrupted Danielson, 'there are no sharp edges on that handle. It was worn smooth generations ago.'

I looked at the dagger. He was right. Elaborately carved though the handle was, it was quite smooth to the touch. I looked at my hand, and buried in the point of my thumb, was a sharp splinter of wood. How had I picked up a splinter of wood from a solid, silver-plated steel dagger?

'When was the last time you saw this weapon?' I asked the witness.

'Saw it?' he replied. 'I'm not really sure.'

'Was it last week?'

'Objection your honour. This witness couldn't have seen this dagger last week since it has been in police custody for more than a week. The defence should stick to the facts and not indulge in foolish fantasies.'

'Objection sustained. You only waste the court's time, Mr Bartholomew, when you speculate on the impossible.'

'I apologise, your honour,' I said, then turned back to the witness, 'Well, when *was* the last time you saw it? Was it two weeks ago?'

'I'm not sure?'

'Three weeks?'

'I don't know.'

'Possibly four weeks ago?'

'I really don't know.'

'Is this getting us anywhere, Mr Bartholomew?' interrupted Judge Hezion.

'I believe so, your honour.' I pushed on, 'Mr Danielson, from your own certain knowledge, when *was* the last time this dagger was in the Matthias villa?'

'From my own certain knowledge? Well, about six months ago.'

'You're certain of that?'

'Quite certain. That was the time of the annual spring-clean. It's the one time of the year when I personally clean the dagger.'

'Who cleans it in between?'

'No-one. I'm the only person in the household who cleans silver. Once a year I clean the silver ornaments and decorations around the place—the pieces that are never handled, in other words.'

'So, we can definitely locate this dagger in the Matthias villa six months ago?' I repeated.

'Objection your honour,' said Burger. 'We can

definitely locate the murder weapon in Dr Matthias's house *and nowhere else* at any time prior to the murder. This line of inquiry by the defence is irrelevant, incompetent and immaterial.'

'Can you show relevance, Mr Bartholomew?' asked the judge.

'It is the contention of the defence, your honour, that this dagger was stolen from the home of the accused by the real murderer some time prior to the killing of Malachi Mason.'

'And you think this witness can establish that?'

'Up to a point, your honour,' I replied.

'Objection overruled. You may continue, Mr Bartholomew.'

'So, Mr Danielson. We have established that the last time you were aware of the presence of this dagger in your master's house—aware, that is, from your own personal and certain knowledge—was some six months ago?'

'Yes, sir, that is correct.'

'If the dagger was missing from the villa after that time, why would you not have noticed?'

'Because of where it was located, sir. On a mantelpiece along with a lot of other ju . . . items.'

'Items? Or junk—as you were about to say?'

'Indeed, sir.'

'So the dagger may have been missing for weeks, or even months, and its absence have gone quite unnoticed and unremarked?'

'That is correct, sir.'

'No further questions.'

'Do you have anything on re-direct, Mr Burger,' asked the judge.

'I certainly do, your honour,' Burger said, leaping to his feet.

'Mr Danielson, you tell us that you were not in the habit of noticing the dagger in between its annual cleanings, is that correct?'

'Yes, sir.'

'So, not only would you not notice if it was missing, you wouldn't even notice if it was *there*, would you?'

'I suppose not, sir.'

'Consequently, you cannot tell the court, of your own personal and certain knowledge, that the dagger was missing, can you?'

'Ah, I suppose not, sir.'

'No further questions.'

'The witness may stand down. Call your next witness, Mr Burger.'

While old Shem Danielson hobbled off the witness stand and out of the court, Burger played with the papers in front of him. Then he glanced sideways at me, giving me a peculiar look.

'If it please your honour,' he said, 'the prosecution calls . . . Tabitha Mason to the stand!'

Tabitha! They had located her after all. All eyes—including mine—shot to the back of the courtroom. The large double doors opened slowly, and in walked Tabitha, handcuffed to two large officers of the City Watch.

She looked pale and terrified. I glanced at Tullus. He was on his feet in the dock leaning forward. As Tabitha passed the bar table I touched her sleeve.

'Are you all right?' I asked.

She nodded her head as she gave me a faint trembling smile, then she mouthed the words, 'I'm sorry.'

Once she had been led to the witness stand and sworn in, Burger stood up and said, 'If your honour pleases, this witness is now under arrest on a charge of conspiracy to murder Malachi Mason. Hence, she is implicated in the case currently before the court. Nevertheless, I have brought her before the court today—in response to the earlier challenge by the defence,' he said this with a sneer in my direction, 'in order to establish the relationship between this witness and the accused. This relationship goes to the question of motive in the case before the court. She is, however, a hostile witness, and I would ask the court to designate her as such.'

'Do you raise any objections to this, Mr Bartholomew?' asked the judge.

'No, your honour, no objection.'

'In that case, Mr Burger, you may treat Miss Mason as a hostile witness, with the extra latitude in questioning which that implies. Carry on, Mr Burger.'

'Thank you, your honour. And I thank my learned colleague, the counsel for the defence, for his co-operation in this matter.'

'Just get on with it, Mr Burger,' snapped the judge.

That's what I liked to see—Burger irritating the judge!

As Burger rose to his feet I noticed an officer of the City Watch hurry into the court and whisper in Captain Tragg's ear. Tragg stood up, bowed to the judge, and left the courtroom in a hurry. Burger looked as puzzled as I was by this behaviour, but he went on with his planned interrogation.

'Miss Mason, please tell the court about your relationship with the accused,' he said.

'No!'

'What?' bellowed Burger, round-eyed and disbelieving.

'You heard me, Mr Burger,' said Tabitha, quietly but firmly. 'I refuse to answer your questions.'

'Your honour, please instruct this witness that she is required to answer my questions.'

'Miss Mason,' said Judge Hezion, in a quiet and father-like manner, 'I'm afraid the law requires that you answer his questions, or else I must hold you in contempt.'

'And I'm afraid I must continue to refuse to answer,' said Tabitha.

'Do you have any grounds for your refusal, Miss Mason?' asked the judge.

'Yes, your honour,' she replied, 'on the grounds that a wife cannot be compelled to give evidence against her husband.'

'What?' yelled Burger, leaping out of his seat as if hit by an electric shock.

'Settle down, Mr Burger,' said the judge sternly. 'I will handle this. Miss Mason, are you telling the court that you are married to the accused?'

'That is so, your honour.'

'Do you have any proof to support your claim?'

'I have brought my marriage certificate with me, suspecting I might need to produce it.'

Tabitha dug into the folds of her tunic, and produced an official-looking parchment which she handed over to the judge.

'This looks to be in order,' he murmured, looking up at the bar table. 'Would either of you gentlemen care to examine this document?'

'No,' growled Burger, slumped in his chair, his head in his hands, 'what's the point!'

'I beg your pardon, Mr Burger?'

'I'm sorry, your honour. I meant, no thank you, your honour.'

'Mr Bartholomew? What about you?'

'Yes please, your honour,' I replied, approaching the judge's bench, and accepted the parchment he held out.

'Now, Mr Burger, I think we may conclude that your attempt to question this witness is over, and she may leave the stand.'

'Just a moment, your honour,' I said quickly. 'I wonder if Miss Mason would agree to answer some questions from the defence?'

'Miss Mason?' said the judge, raising his eyebrows quizzically.

'I have no objection to that, your honour.'

'Then you may carry on, Mr Bartholomew.'

'Miss Mason,' I said, approaching the witness stand, 'I have just been examining this certificate of your marriage to Dr Tullus Matthias, and it strikes me that the date of the marriage is significant. Would you please tell the court just *when* you were married.'

'Five days before my father was murdered.'

'Did your father know of the marriage?'

'No. No-one knew. We married in secret.'

'Why did you do that?'

'We couldn't wait any longer. My father was becoming more and more difficult. And I thought that once we were actually married, he might come to accept it. Tullus was dubious, but I talked him into it.'

'So it was a strategy to win over your father?'

'More or less.'

'What were your plans?'

'That I would tell him that we were married, and that we both regarded marriage as being for life. Let him fume and foam at the mouth. Then I thought he would accept the reality, and welcome Tullus into the family. When that happened Tullus and I planned to have a second celebration of our marriage—in front of all our Christian friends.'

'I see. And how did it work out?'

'I never told my father at all.'

'Why not?'

'Because he became ill. I decided—we decided—that it was impossible to tell him about the secret marriage until he had fully recovered. But . . . of course . . . he never did.'

'So on the day when your father died, Dr Tullus Matthias was already your legal husband?'

'Yes,' she replied, her face shining, a true smile lighting up her face for the first time.

'The prosecution has been arguing to this court that Dr Matthias's motive for murdering your father was his refusal to let you marry. But if you were already married—as this certificate proves—then there was no such motive?'

'That's right. No motive at all.'

'One final question: Why did you tell no-one about the marriage until now?'

'We were . . . well, we were a little ashamed of having done something as important as this in secret.'

'I have no further questions of this witness, your honour.'

CHAPTER 27

As Tabitha left the stand, the handcuffs were refastened and she was led away in custody.

'Your honour,' I said, 'I move at this time that the prosecution has failed to establish a *prima facie* case against my client, and I ask that all charges be dropped and my client released.'

'Your response, Mr Burger?' said the judge gravely, 'I will hear arguments on this motion.'

'Your honour,' spluttered the District Attorney, 'we have more evidence still to present, and witnesses still to call, and I would ask that you hold over your judgment on the motion until at least the end of the prosecution's case.'

'Very well, Mr Burger, I am prepared to do that much. If you have further evidence to present I will listen to that before I make a ruling. Call your next witness.'

Tragg had hurried back into the courtroom and begun to whisper in Burger's ear.

'With the court's indulgence,' said Burger to the judge, 'may I have a brief consultation with the arresting officer in this case?'

'As long as it's brief,' snapped the judge impatiently.

The whispered conversation continued for more than a minute, and when Burger rose to his feet to face the judge, he was smiling broadly.

'The prosecution calls Decimus Septimus.'

Septimus? The old servant employed by Tabitha? What possible help could he be to the prosecution's case?

Tragg must have had Septimus standing by, because he was led into the court almost at once. He took the oath.

'Please tell the court your full name and occupation.'

'I am Decimus Titus Septimus, and I am a steward at the Mason villa.'

'How long have you been employed at the Mason villa, Mr Septimus?' asked Burger.

'Oh, since I was a boy, sir. It's more than fifty years now,' replied the old man.

'What are your duties?'

'Nowadays, just light kitchen work. When I was younger and fitter I used to do the heavy work—the lifting and carrying. Like Quaresimus does now.'

'You work in the kitchen, you say. Do you have a view from the kitchen into the courtyard?'

'Oh, yes, sir. From my kitchen window I can see almost the whole of the courtyard.'

'Do you remember the day that Malachi Mason died?'

'Yes, indeed I do, sir. A dreadful day, a dreadful day it was.'

'I'm sure it was. Now, do you remember seeing Dr Tullus Matthias enter Mr Mason's room around the middle of the morning?'

'Yes, sir, I do remember. I was at the kitchen window peeling potatoes. There's a bench just inside the window, and that's where I usually work, sir.'

'Thank you, Mr Septimus, that's very clear. Did you also see Dr Matthias leave Mr Mason's room?'

'Yes, sir. Only about ten minutes later it would have been.'

'Shortly after that Quaresimus was put on duty outside Mr Mason's door. Guard duty I suppose we should call it, since his orders were to stop people from going into Mr Mason's room. Did you see him there?'

'Quite clearly. There's nothing wrong with my eyesight. I saw Quaresimus sitting on a wooden stool, in the shade of the lemon tree, just outside Mr Mason's door.'

'Very good. Now—Quaresimus had been ordered to remain on duty, in that position, for the whole of the day . . .'

'I wouldn't know about that, sir. I didn't hear the orders that Miss Tabitha gave to him.'

'No, of course not. However, would you have been able to see whether or not he carried out any such orders?'

'I don't understand what you mean, sir?'

'I am asking you how long you kept the courtyard under observation from your kitchen window!'

'Oh, I see, sir. All afternoon, sir.'

'All afternoon? Isn't that a little unusual? Did you take an afternoon siesta like everyone else?'

'No, indeed I didn't, sir.'

'Why not?'

'I'm a twitcher, sir.'

'A what?'

'A birdwatcher, sir.'

'So I take it that you sat up through the siesta hour birdwatching! Is that correct?'

'Quite correct, sir. There was a pair of yellow-throated tree sparrows, sir. I had been watching them for several days. They were building a nest in the lemon tree in our courtyard.'

'And you were watching these birds . . .'

'Yellow-throated tree sparrows, sir.'

'Yellow-throated whatevers, on the day that Malachi Mason died?'

'I was, sir. It was a rare opportunity to observe their nest building habits up close, so to speak. The yellow-throated tree sparrow is smaller than your . . .'

'Very interesting, I'm sure. And you were watching this pair of sparrows throughout the siesta hour?'

'I was, sir. I have found siesta to be an excellent birdwatching time. There is no work to do, the place is quiet, and I can concentrate in peace.'

'Are you certain that you were watching for the *whole afternoon* on that particular day?'

'Absolutely certain, sir. I'll never forget the day my old master, Mr Malachi, died. It was a dreadful day. It's etched on my memory. It was also, as it happens, the day the sparrows finished their nest. And I saw them do it. I watched all afternoon, sir.'

'Let's come back now to Quaresimus, and his orders to stand watch outside Mason's door all afternoon. Did he follow those orders?'

'Well, sir, that's a little awkward. I don't want to get one of my fellow servants into trouble.'

'You have sworn an oath to tell the truth, Mr Septimus. So tell the court the answer to my question: was Quaresimus on duty all afternoon?'

'No, sir. I'm afraid not, sir.'

'When was he absent?'

'He slipped away when everyone else had retired for their afternoon siesta, sir.'

'And how long was he gone for?'

'I didn't time him, sir. But I would guess an hour and a half. Perhaps a little less.'

'I see. Now during the absence of Quaresimus did you have the courtyard under observation at all time?'

'I never took my eyes off those delightful little birds nest building in our lemon tree, sir. I watched them the whole time.'

'And that means you could see the whole courtyard at the same time?'

'Well . . . yes, sir, I could.'

'Would you have seen anyone who entered or left Malachi Mason's room?'

'I most certainly would, sir.'

'And who did you see? Who entered or left Malachi Mason's room during that time?'

'No-one, sir. Not a blessed soul.'

'You're certain of that?'

'I couldn't be more certain, sir.'

'Thank you, Mr Septimus,' said Burger, then turned to me and sneered, 'Your witness, counsellor.'

'Septimus,' I said, rising to my feet, 'would you mind telling the court how old you are?'

'I wouldn't mind at all. I'm sixty-two years of age.'

'Your eyesight, you tell us, is excellent?'

'Yes, sir.'

'What about your bladder?'

'I beg your pardon, sir?'

'Quite often, Septimus,' I said, 'gentlemen of your age need to go to the bathroom rather more often than they did when they were younger. Is that true in your case?'

'Ah . . . well . . . yes, I suppose it is, sir.'

'And did you leave your birdwatching during the afternoon to go to the bathroom?'

'I suppose I must have done, sir.'

'So the courtyard was *not* under observation at all times!' I prompted.

'Oh no, the courtyard was still under observation, sir,' insisted Septimus.

'How could that be?' I asked.

'I went to the bathroom just before Quaresimus left, and I didn't go again until after he came back.'

'You're sure of that?' I challenged.

'Yes, sir.'

'Absolutely sure?'

'I'm afraid I am, sir.'

'At the age of sixty-two, is your memory as strong as your eyesight, or as weak as your bladder?'

'There's nothing wrong with my memory, sir,' blurted Septimus. 'I remember that afternoon very well.'

'And you want this court to believe that there was no time—not even a few seconds when your attention was elsewhere—when someone might have slipped, unseen, into Malachi Mason's room?'

'That's right, sir,' said Septimus, puffing out his chest, 'I'm a very sharp old man.'

Tragg had coached this witness very well. He had appealed to his pride, and persuaded him that nothing could have slipped past his 'keen eyes'.

'In that case, I have no further questions of this witness, your honour.'

'The witness may stand down.'

'That completes the prosecution's case, your honour,' said Burger.

'In that case,' said the judge, 'I will hear arguments

on the defence's dismissal motion. Mr Bartholomew I will hear you first.'

I got up and walked over to the judge. 'In a murder case the three key elements are motive, means and opportunity. The prosecution has failed to establish any motive whatsoever in this case. First they offered us speculation that Malachi Mason's opposition to his daughter's marriage was the motive. Then it was revealed that the marriage has already taken place, and that motive no longer existed. In its place, the prosecution has offered us nothing—nothing at all. Motive is non-existent in this case.'

I glanced down at my notes, and continued.

'Secondly, there is the question of means. This revolves entirely around access to the murder weapon. The defence readily agrees that the dagger in question was originally the property of the accused. However, there is no evidence before this court to show that only the accused had access to that weapon or, indeed, that someone else did not remove the weapon for the purpose of committing the murder and framing my client. At best, the evidence as to means proves nothing.'

I noticed, with pleasure, that the judge was nodding slightly as I made my remarks.

'Finally,' I continued, 'there is the question of opportunity. And here I would simply remind the court that the prosecution's case—namely that the accused, and only the accused, had opportunity—now rests entirely upon the testimony of one man. An elderly man at that. To commit for trial on such evidence would be unsafe, your honour, and unlikely to lead to a conviction. And hence, I would ask you to rule that the prosecution has failed to establish a *prima facie* case, and to release my client without a stain on his character.'

'Mr Burger?' murmured the judge.

'Your honour, everything my learned colleague has said about motive and means I am prepared to grant. But I would point out to the court that there are other elements to consider in both these areas. If the investigating officers have failed, thus far, to uncover the motive for this horrible crime, that does not weaken our case. Motive is the least important of the three key elements needed to make out a strong *prima facie* case against the accused.'

Burger wiped the sweat from his brow with a large, white handkerchief. I wasn't sure whether this was meant to be a theatrical gesture, or whether he was really feeling the pressure of this case.

'As to means. The dagger was and is the property of the accused. The defence has failed to connect the dagger to anyone else. In the absence of such a connection there must be a very strong presumption that the dagger points to the guilt of the accused.'

Again Burger mopped his brow. He really *was* very tense, I realised.

'But in the end, your honour, the case against the accused rests upon the unanswerable question of opportunity. There is one person, and only one person, who *could* have committed this appalling crime. One, and only one, person who had access to the victim. And that is the accused—Dr Tullus Matthias.' Burger turned and pointed dramatically at Tullus in the dock.

'If only that man *could* have committed the murder, then that man *did* commit the murder! As for depending upon only one "elderly" witness. Well, really your honour! I have just been looking into the pages of *Who's Who in Damascus* and have discovered that your honour is exactly the same age as the witness Septimus. I leave it to your honour to judge the reliability of sixty-two-year-old men! The witness in question was very clear and very definite. I put it to you, your honour, that his testimony cannot be dismissed, that a *prima facie* case has been well and truly established, and that the accused should be bound over for trial.'

For a few moments the judge shuffled the papers on his bench, then he made a note, and raised his head to address the court.

'Mr Bartholomew put his argument very well. And if this was a full trial I would be inclined to agree that conviction on the testimony of one witness is unsafe. However, this is *not* the full trial, it is only the committal hearing, and all that I need to decide is if the accused should face a jury of his peers or not. Given the weight of the evidence on opportunity I am persuaded that the charge cannot be dismissed at this time. Hence, I hereby find that the prisoner is to be remanded in custody, to appear in court on the charge of having murdered Malachi Mason on a date to be fixed.'

The judge banged his gavel, and I leapt to my feet.

'Your honour, the matter of bail . . .' I began.

'My hands are tied,' said the judge quickly, 'The Ethnarch has opposed bail, and hence I cannot grant it. The court is adjourned.'

CHAPTER 28

With a heavy heart I made my way out through the imposing stone portals of the Damascus Central Criminal Court, and down the sweeping stone staircase.

Joe Barnabas hurried up the stairs towards me.

'I couldn't get here any earlier, Ben,' he said, breathing heavily. 'What happened?'

I told him.

'Hhmm. Bad news. And Tabitha under arrest now too?'

'That's right.'

'Still, you'll get them both off when the trial proper comes on. I'm sure of that.'

'Thanks for the vote of confidence, but, truth to tell, I don't feel very confident just at the moment.'

'Let me buy you some lunch, and we'll talk about it,' said Barnabas.

He took me to a little Greek restaurant that was built on a pier over the Barada River. We ate salads piled high with fetta cheese, black olives and anchovies, and I told Barnabas about the things that were weighing heavily upon me.

'Tabitha should not be under arrest!' I complained. 'She has done nothing except refuse the advances of the odious Aaron Burger. And for that she's arrested for conspiracy to murder? It is so horribly, wickedly, unfair!'

'Yes, it is unfair,' agreed Barnabas, 'but then, this is an unfair world. That unfairness is part of the suffering and evil that characterise this world.'

'Knowing that doesn't stop it hurting,' I moaned.

'True. If we live in the tropics we will be hot—if we live in this world we will hurt. That's unavoidable.'

'But it shouldn't be like this!'

'No, it shouldn't,' agreed Barnabas, 'that's God's attitude exactly—it shouldn't be like this.'

'Well, why doesn't He *do* something about it!' I complained.

'He *has* done something about it!'

'Not that I've noticed,' I muttered.

'Well, what would you like God to do?'

'Strike down Burger when he behaves in this vile and evil way—strike him dead!'

'If God struck everyone dead who hurt someone else, both you and I wouldn't be here, Ben. God hasn't done what you or I would do—He has done something more important than that.'

'What, exactly?'

'Instead of dealing with the symptoms, God has struck at the infection in the bloodstream. Instead of dealing with the manifestations, God has dealt with the heart of the matter.'

'How?'

'He has suffered for us, and it is through his suffering that our suffering comes to an end.'

'You're talking about the suffering of Jesus on the Cross?'

'That's right.'

'How does that work to end our suffering?'

'Let me explain by telling you a story.'

Barnabas was silent for a moment, then he cleared his throat and continued.

'Some years ago I lived in a small village high in a valley, in the foothills of a great mountain range. There was a river flowing through the village, and one year it flooded. The floodwaters ripped through, tearing down houses, carrying off sheep, cattle, and goats, and threatening human lives.

'A young man named Dardanus got into a small wooden boat and paddled to the edge of the village, where the slope fell away, and the waters should have been draining away.

'There he found the water blocked and backed up in a narrow valley. The floodwaters had carried so much rubbish and debris along with them that they had blocked the narrow way between the rocks. The rubbish and debris had formed a natural dam, and were holding the waters back.

'Dardanus stripped off his cloak and tunic and dived into the water to try to drag some of the branches and rocks and debris out of the natural dam, so the water would break through and drain away.

'Again and again he dived.

'Eventually he succeeded in loosening some rocks and branches. When he did that, the pressure of the floodwaters did the rest. It swept away the rest of the rubbish and the water thundered through.

'But it carried Dardanus with it. He had saved hundreds of lives in the village by his action—but it had cost his own life.

'That is what Jesus has done. He has plunged into the suffering and evil in this world, just as Dardanus plunged into those floodwaters.

'Jesus has given his life to clear away the rubbish and debris that we—by our rebellion against God—

have created. All the rubbish in our lives has blocked the road back to God. In his death Jesus clears the road, he clears away all the debris and rubbish that our rebellion has piled up there, and opened up the way back to God. Jesus suffered to clear the road, so that we can travel God's Way.'

When Barnabas stopped speaking I just nodded. His story had given me much to think about. We ordered two cups of Damascan coffee—and drank it in silence.

'What are you going to do next?' Barnabas finally asked.

'I'm going after the real murderer,' I said grimly. 'And I'm determined not to stop until I have nailed the person who *really* killed Malachi Mason! That's the only way I can make Tullus and Tabitha safe.'

'Where will you start?'

'I think with Mason's old partner—Seth Yentob. Listen, will you do me a favour?'

'Sure. What is it?'

'Take my briefcase—it has all the legal papers in it—back to my room, and I'll go straight from here to Yentob's office.'

'Consider it done. On top of which, I'll pay for lunch,' said Barnabas, with a smile.

I found the offices of Mason and Yentob in an old sandstone building, not far from the riverside docks and warehouses. There was no elevator, and I had to climb an ancient dark timber staircase to the seventh floor.

There I found a frosted glass door with chipped gold lettering that read:

MASON AND YENTOB INCORPORATED
IMPORTERS AND EXPORTERS
MERCANTILE AGENTS
COMMERCIAL CONSULTANTS
Inquire Within

Within I found a young secretary with a mass of blonde hair, bright red fingernails, and a slow typing speed, labouring over a letter.

'Good afternoon,' I said, interrupting her slow tap, tap, tap.

'Oh, hello,' she said brightly, welcoming an excuse to stop typing. 'Can I help you?'

'You sure can. Is Mr Yentob in right now?'

'Yes, he is. Do you have an appointment?'

'I have now, sweetheart,' I replied, striding past her, and pushing open the door that had 'Seth Yentob' lettered on its frosted glass panel.

The office was large and dark, with account books, files and documents piled precariously around the floor.

Dwarfed by an enormous desk was a small man, pencil thin, with a bald head and a Roman nose. He was making some calculations with an abacus when I entered, and scribbling occasional numbers on a scrap of paper.

He looked up and saw me, and at the same moment one of the many phones on his desk rang.

'Yentob,' he snapped into the receiver as he picked it up.

'Yeah . . . Yeah . . . Okay . . . I see . . .' he muttered into the phone. 'Sell when they go up another half point, and move the profit into pork belly futures.'

He put the phone down and looked at me.

'I'm sorry, Mr Yentob,' squeaked the blonde secretary, who had come into the office behind me, 'but he just walked in. I couldn't stop him.'

'That's all right, Doris,' said Yentob, 'I'll take care of it.'

'You're in here now—you might as well take a seat,' he said waving me to a chair. Doris clicked her way out of the office on her high-heeled shoes.

I opened my mouth to speak but another of the phones rang.

'Yentob,' he said, grabbing it. 'No . . . No . . . Definitely not . . . Salt is a drug on the market . . . I'm not making a bid . . . Yeah . . . Call me back.'

He hung up the phone and looked back in my direction.

'A denarius for your thoughts,' he said, 'Mr . . . whoever you are.'

'Bartholomew is the name. Ben Bartholomew.'

'Ah, you're the guy who's defending Malachi's murderer? I wish you well. Whoever slipped a blade into my old partner deserves a medal not a noose!'

Two phones rang at once.

'Yentob—hold the line,' he said into one, then turned to the other and snapped, 'Yentob . . . Is that so? . . . It's a possibility . . . What say I trade you the granite for the timber . . . Best Lebanese . . . Whadda ya say? . . . Straight trade . . . Okay it's a deal . . . Send over the paperwork.'

Then Yentob grabbed the other phone, 'Hello? . . . How many? . . . I never buy slaves without a medical report . . . No, not *your* man, *my* man . . . Give me the details . . . Uh, huh . . . I'll send someone over tomorrow.'

Yentob hung up the phone, scribbled a note, and then looked up at me.

'Now, where was I?' he asked. 'Ah yes. You're trying to defend that young doctor who slipped a scalpel into Malachi.'

'Not a scalpel, a dagger,' I said, 'and it wasn't the doctor who did it.'

'Then who did?'

'That's what I'm trying to find out. You mind answering a few questions?'

'Not a problem—fire away.'

CHAPTER 29

'You make no effort to disguise your dislike of Malachi Mason?' I said.

'I didn't dislike him,' said Seth Yentob in mock protest. Then he leaned forward across the desk and snarled, 'I despised him!'

'Mind telling me why?'

'No, I don't mind. He was a crook, that's why.'

'Not like you?'

'Not like me at all!' snapped Yentob. 'I'm a merchant. A businessman. An entrepreneur. He was just a crook!'

'What sort of crook? What did he do?'

'What didn't he do? That's a better question! If he wanted to get a government contract he would bribe an official—'

'Not like you?' I interrupted, gently raising one eyebrow.

'Not like me! Bribes are bad economics! It's like being blackmailed—the price goes up with every payment. Besides which, it leaves you open to actually *being* blackmailed. Messy business. Bad business. I never bribe.'

'But Mason did?'

'All the time!'

One of the phones rang again.

'Yentob . . . Sure I've got money in road building futures . . . This is the Roman Empire, road building futures are a sure bet . . . No, not often traded . . . They're blue chip . . . Turn over is very low . . . Yeah . . . I'll take whatever you can get under the one thousand shekel mark . . . Yeah . . . Talk to you later.'

'The deals never stop,' I remarked.

'If the deals stopped, the Empire would stop,' replied Seth Yentob. 'Now—where were we?'

'Malachi Mason was a crook—you were just explaining that to me.'

'Well, he was. Every deal he did, he skimmed out a secret commission for himself.'

'What did that do to the profitability of this firm?'

'It cheated me out of my fair share of the trading profits! That's what it did!'

'So, you're better off with Mason dead?'

'I certainly am!'

'Did you kill him?'

'Me? That's ridiculous. I almost never leave this office. I have a little apartment next door. I only sleep four hours a night. The rest of my time is spent at this desk, trying to turn an honest denarius or two.'

'So you claim you couldn't have killed him?'

'That's right! Because I never leave this building! Ask anyone! I challenge you, ask anyone!'

'But, of course you could have paid someone to kill him, couldn't you?'

'Get out!' screamed Yentob, rising to his feet, his voice rising to the pitch of a boy soprano on a bad day, 'Get out! Get out! Get out!'

The abacus off his desk came whistling through the air, aimed directly at my head. I ducked, and decided to leave.

'I'm going, Mr Yentob,' I said, 'but don't think

you've convinced me of your innocence—because you haven't.'

I ducked again as an account book whizzed through the air on the same flight path as the abacus, then stepped quickly out of the office and closed the door behind me.

'That's what happens to people who walk into offices unannounced,' said the blonde bimbo smugly, then went back to polishing her fingernails, her nose stuck in the air.

I left the offices of Mason and Yentob with a lot of ideas rushing through my mind. What did Yentob's behaviour mean? Had I seen aggrieved innocence? Or irritated guilt?

When I arrived back at the Gideon household there was a message for me: Aaron Burger had phoned, and would I call back as soon as I came in? I called back.

'Bartholomew, how nice to hear the sound of your voice again,' said Burger, his greasy tones oozing down the phone line at me.

'Yes, I just love socialising with you too!' I said sarcastically, 'But there must be some point to this. Why did you leave the message?'

'Just keep calm, Bartholomew, and you will learn all. I wanted to talk to you about the full trial for Dr Tullus Matthias on the charge of murder.'

'What about it?'

'Would you be ready to go to trial on Monday?'

'Two days away?'

'You can read a calendar? Good. Now, let me ask you again. Would you be ready to go to trial on Monday?'

'How come a date is available so soon?'

'One of the defendants in another matter has fallen ill, so a five-day hearing period, starting Monday, has become vacant. Judge Hezion phoned me in my office to offer us the five days. Well, I want it, Bartholomew, I certainly want it. The sooner I have Matthias convicted and hung the happier I'll be. Unfortunately, the judge won't give us these days unless you agree. So, what do you say?'

I thought furiously. Which was better? An early trial, or a later one? How close was I to having my case together? Could I have my investigations completed in two days? What was in the best interests of my client?

'I'm waiting,' Burger's nasal voice came sniffling down the line.

'Yes, and I'm thinking,' I snapped.

What to do? What to do? If I said 'no', then almost certainly it would be months before we could get another date in the criminal list. That would give me a lot of time to investigate and prepare the case. On the other hand, my client had been denied bail, and was rotting in a filthy, damp, dark prison. The more I thought about Tullus in his prison cell, the more certain I became that the right move was to get it over with.

'All right,' I said. 'We'll be ready to proceed on Monday. I'll call the judge.'

'Wonderful!' crowed Burger. 'And Bartholomew, let me tell you—I intend to have you on toast on Monday!'

'I'll see you in court,' I said coldly.

'See you in court, Bartholomew,' replied Burger with an evil, wheezing laugh.

I quickly rang Judge Hezion and confirmed my

approval. Then I put the phone down and stood for a moment, just staring into space.

'What's on your mind, Ben?' asked David Gideon, walking into the hallway at that moment.

'Tullus's trial,' I explained, 'the full trial before a jury, starts on Monday.'

'That's a bit soon, isn't it?'

'A hearing date became available and I thought it best to take it.'

'Will you be ready by Monday?'

'I'll have to be, David. I'll just have to be.'

'All the best then, and we'll be praying for you.' David slapped me on the shoulder, and sailed out through the front door.

Right, I thought, I've got to get straight back to work. Where to next? It was getting near closing time for most office workers, so I thought it might be a good time to catch Silas Levi. I checked his work address on the note Paul Mallard had given me, and set off.

At the northern end of Straight Street, in the outlying suburbs of Damascus, lay the warehouses of the great trading companies. It was from here that the camel trains set out on the Great North Road bearing boxes of dates, copper pots and bronze swords. They returned with silks, spices and exotic perfumes.

Not far out of the city the road split in two: one arm heading north-east towards Alleppo and then Turkey, and the other turning westward towards Baghdad, Isfahan, and the riches of India.

I found the address I had been given. The sign across the front of the giant warehouse said 'Arabian Express—Trading and Credit Company'. It was a famous firm. I carried one of their gold Abex cards in my wallet. Just about everyone did.

I entered the building through vast sliding doors large enough to admit Hannibal and all his elephants side by side. Ahead of me the warehouse disappeared in an unimaginable echoing, twilight vastness. To my right, a dim yellow glow showed where a bunch of offices huddled against the front wall of the complex. I entered the offices, and found myself at a small reception desk.

Behind the desk was a blousy brunette filing her fingernails. Before I could speak a voice like a gravel pit shouted from an inner office: 'You busy, Rosie?'

'Yes I am, Mr Jacobs,' screamed back the brunette. 'I'm doing the filing.'

The response was a grunt from the inner office, and then silence. Rose kept working on her fingernails. I was about to speak to her, when she spoke first.

'Yeah? Whadda ya want?' she whined in a nasal voice, without looking in my direction.

'I'm looking for Mr Levi?'

'Oh yeah?' she said, looking up at me, and chewing gum as she spoke. 'Which one? About half our clerks are called Levi.'

'Mr Silas Levi,' I explained.

'Oh, Silas? Why didn't you say so. He's the long streak of misery at the corner desk.'

She nodded towards the far corner. I started walking in the direction she had indicated, then I turned back and said, 'I'm impressed by your concentration.'

'Whadda ya mean, my concentration?' she whined.

'Your ability to do two things at once—chew gum and file your nails!'

I turned on my heel and marched off towards Silas Levi before she could respond.

CHAPTER 30

Silas Levi wore cuff-protectors over the sleeves of
his tunic, and an old tennis shade over his eyes.

'Mr Levi?' I asked, approaching his desk.

He looked up from the ledger he was scratching
in, and blinked at me blindly. His face was as boney
as a skeleton's, with only a thin covering of pale skin,
and large, bloodshot eyes.

'Huh?' he said, in response to my inquiry.

'You're Silas Levi?' I asked.

'Who wants to know?'

'Ben Bartholomew's the name. May I have a few
words?'

'I'm working,' he said, in a gloomy voice.

'And in a few minutes you won't be,' I persisted.
'Can I buy you a drink, and ask you a few questions?'

He thought about this for a moment.

'I can't see why not,' he said eventually.

With that he went back to scratching with a quill
pen on the parchment pages of the ledger. I sat down
on a wooden clerk's stool, and waited for him to
finish.

I didn't have to wait long. After a few minutes a
steam whistle blew, and the office shut down. Levi
took off his sleeve protectors and tennis shade, and
pulled an old grey cloak over his tunic.

'Where can we get a drink around here?' I asked,

walking beside him out of the office, and out of the vast warehouse.

'Just down the road is my usual watering hole,' he said. He made it sound as if going for a drink after work was the worst punishment in the world.

A block and a half down the street, we came to The Thirsty Camel. Inside it was dark and cool—a welcome relief from the hot, humid evening.

'What'll you have?' I asked.

'Well, if you're paying?'

'I am.'

'Then I'll have a brandy—the genuine Egyptian stuff.'

I ordered two, and we took them to a quiet table in the corner.

'What do you want?' grumbled Levi, after he'd taken a sip of the brandy.

'It's about Malachi Mason . . .'

'Forget it!' he growled, showing a flash of life for the first time since we'd met. 'Wrong topic. Thanks for the drink. Conversation's over.'

'No it's not.' I leaned across the table and grabbed his lapels. 'You wanted the drink, you'll answer the questions! Unless you do, I'll drag you out into the road and knock you around until you're eating camel dung!'

I didn't mean it, of course, but it was an impressive sounding threat. His bloodshot eyes, dull and vacant, stared at me for a moment, then he shrugged his shoulders.

'Okay?' he said, then finished his brandy in one, large swallow.

'How did you know Mason?' I began.

There was a longish pause. Then Levi began to talk, not looking at me, but at his empty glass.

'I wasn't always like this, you know,' he said in a voice so low it was almost a whisper. 'I owned my own business. Wine merchant. None of that Galilean rubbish! Only the best Judean vintages. And I used to import a very nice Roman red.'

'You did business with Mason?'

'We traded. He would buy from me in bulk. For export. He bargained very hard. Drove me down to the thinnest of profit margins. But I reasoned that it was discount for bulk. And anyway, he wouldn't sell in my market and undercut my regular profit.'

He stopped for a long time, staring at the stains on the tabletop.

'And . . .?' I prompted.

'And he did,' moaned Levi.

'Did what?'

'Sold into my market. Here in Damascus.'

'Let me get this clear. He bought wine from you in bulk?'

'Yes.'

'At bulk discount rates?'

'Yes. Up to sixty per cent off recommended retail price. That's a big discount. It cut my profit margin to shreds. Normally I would only give retailers thirty per cent.'

'But you gave him sixty?'

'He insisted. He drove a hard bargain. But it was always for a big order.'

'This was a problem for you?'

'Instead of exporting, as he had promised, he resold the wine here in Damascus—into my home market. I was selling my product at thirty per cent discount, and he was selling it at forty, or forty-five. I lost all my regular customers to him.'

'What did it do to your business?'

'Closed it. I had high overheads. I couldn't keep operating without decent margins. The bills mounted up. I fell behind with the rent. I couldn't pay wages. I couldn't service my debt at the Damascus Savings and Loan. They had my company declared bankrupt. Put in a receiver. Sold the stock cheaply. Mason bought it. Then they sold the whole business—trading name, goodwill, premises, staff. Sold it cheap. Mason bought it.'

'Did he keep you on to manage the business?'

'Are you joking? He thought that if he could cheat me out of my own business I wasn't worth employing!'

'And then?'

'Then I was destitute. My wife left me. She hadn't bargained on poverty when we married. And she took the children with her. And I had to take any job I could scrounge. For lousy pay. And in the meantime Mason put the wine prices back up, and saw the company turn in a handsome profit under his new manager. That . . . that . . . stinking, rotten, carcass of a camel rat's flea!'

There was real energy in Levi's voice as he said these last words, and a flash of genuine hatred in his eyes.

'If he walked in here right now,' he continued, 'I would wrap my fingers around his throat and strangle the life out of him. And never give a thought to the consequences.'

'Interesting thought. But impossible, of course.'

'Why impossible?' Levi looked puzzled.

'Because someone's already done it,' I replied.

'Done what?'

'Killed Mason.'

'What . . .? You mean . . . murdered him?'

'That's right.'

The stick figure of gloom opposite me suddenly began to tremble and shake, and utter strangely strangled sounds. At first I thought he was sick. Then I realised that he was laughing.

'How? Tell me how?' he said when the laughter subsided.

'Stabbed. Through the heart,' I explained.

'Too quick,' said Levi, 'too painless. He should have died slowly. And painfully.'

'You really didn't know?'

'Know what?'

'That Mason was dead.'

'No, I really didn't know.'

'But it's been in the daily paper—the *Acta Diurna*.'

'I never see the paper. Why should I? What is there in it for me? What is there left in life for me?'

'So Mason's death is news to you?'

'It's wonderful news to me! The best news I've had since . . . since . . . since it all happened.'

'Did you kill Malachi Mason?' I snapped.

'Now, wait a minute. I didn't even know that he was dead until you told me,' he muttered his bushy eyebrows crawling up his forehead like a couple of surprised spiders.

'So you say.'

'I really didn't know,' pouted Levi.

'All right—where were you then on the day Mason died?'

'I was at work.'

'All day?'

'All day. You can ask anyone in the office.'

'That's interesting—because I haven't told you yet what day it was that Mason was murdered!'

'Well . . . but . . . I just assumed it was a weekday. A working day, that is. I just assumed.'

'Sure you did. And you were working at the time. And you didn't even know he was dead. And you want me to believe that,' I snarled.

'Now, look here Mr . . .'

'Bartholomew.'

'Mr Bartholomew—don't you go trying to get me into trouble. I don't know what it's got to do with you anyway.'

'I'm a lawyer,' I explained. 'I'm representing the man charged with the murder.'

'So that's it! So that's it!' squeaked Levi, his voice rising in panic. 'You're trying to get your client off by pinning the murder on me!'

'All I want is the truth, Levi. Believe it or not, that's all I want.'

'I don't believe it. You're trying to get me into trouble. I don't want to talk to you any longer,' he said, staggering awkwardly to his feet. Without taking his eyes off me, he backed away towards the bar, then turned around and fled, in panic.

I was still wondering about his puzzling behaviour as I reached the Gideons' house, arriving just as the others were finishing their evening meal.

'I've kept yours hot for you in the oven,' said Miriam.

She returned from the kitchen a moment later, and set my meal on the table. Although the others had finished eating, Joe Barnabas and Paul remained at the table to keep me company while I ate.

'I mentioned your name to your cousin in court this morning,' I told Paul.

With a smile he asked me how Burger had responded.

'He said that you were sick,' I replied, chewing my food. At that both Paul and Barnabas laughed heartily.

'That clinches it!' said Barnabas with determination, 'I think you should do it.'

Paul agreed.

'Do what?' I asked.

'Well, tomorrow is the Sabbath, so Paul is going to preach in the synagogue tomorrow morning!'

'About what?' I inquired, innocently.

'The truth about Jesus, of course!' laughed Joe, 'that'll pin a few ears back, I can promise you that!'

It certainly would! It seemed to me they were just asking for trouble.

CHAPTER 31

Later that night I sat down with all the papers for the court case spread out around me, doing the hard grind that needed to be done to be ready for Monday morning's hearing.

Some time later I leaned back in my chair yawning, and heard a clock somewhere strike midnight. The time had flown away while I was working. A minute or so later, I heard the sound of fire engine sirens screaming to the other side of town.

Needing a break from my work, and feeling curious, I climbed the stairs to the Gideons' flat roof to see if I could spot the fire from there. I scanned the horizon, and there it was, over to the north-west—a flickering, ruddy glow.

For several minutes I stood watching. Just where was the fire burning? From the distance involved it was clearly on the other side of Straight Street. And up towards the high-rent end of town, by the look of it. In fact, very close to the apartment building where Aaron Burger lived!

For a moment I considered this possibility, then finding it too intriguing to leave alone, I hurried downstairs, pulled on a heavy cloak, and walked briskly across town.

The closer I got, the more certain I was that my guess was correct. The glow of red and yellow flames was growing stronger, and the sounds of fire-fighting louder.

As I rounded the last corner I saw that it was Burger's building burning. I pushed my way past the crowd of disaster sightseers, until I reached the front line and could see the fire-fighters pumping water. Through the billowing smoke I saw that it was not the whole building that was burning, just the top floor—Burger's penthouse apartment!

After watching the fire-fighters at work for some time, I began to make my way back through the crowd, scanning faces as I went. There was something smelly about this, and it wasn't just the smoke.

The crowd was a sea of faces, all craning upwards, all lit by the hellish glow of red and yellow flames. Then, I saw Burger himself.

He was dressed in a formal tunic and robe. So, he hadn't been undressed for bed when the fire broke out. I pushed my way through the crowd towards him.

'Please accept my sympathies,' I said.

At the sound of my voice Burger turned, looking startled, and a little guilty (or was that just my imagination?)

'Thank you,' he managed to croak, after a moment's delay.

'Are you all right?' I asked. 'Not injured in any way?'

'No. No, I'm fine thank you,' he said formally.

'It must be heartbreaking to see your valuables go up in smoke,' I said, mustering as much sympathy as I could.

'Oh, it's all insured,' replied Burger, casually, 'Well insured, in fact.'

'Still, there must be some things that can't be replaced,' I remarked.

'I keep my few personal treasures down at the office,' snapped Burger.

'Well, that's good then,' I muttered.

We were silent for a few minutes as we watched another hose being unrolled and attached to a high-pressure pump.

'Look, if you're hoping,' said Burger, breaking the awkward silence between us, 'that any of my legal work has gone up in flames, forget about it!'

'I beg your pardon?'

'You're hoping that my brief in the Mason murder case is burning in those flames, aren't you?' growled Burger.

'No! Honestly, I hadn't given it a thought!' I protested.

'I'll bet you hadn't!' came the sarcastic reply. 'Well, you can just forget about that possibility, Bartholomew. All the paperwork is at my office, and the trial will commence Monday as scheduled!'

'I had never imagined otherwise.'

'Good!' he snapped.

I was about to leave when a thought struck me. 'Do you have somewhere to sleep tonight?'

'Thank you for your concern,' said Burger, with exaggerated politeness, 'but my friends will take care of me.'

'Good. Well, I'll see you on Monday then.'

With that I turned my back on the flames, and walked back to the Gideons'.

That night my sleep was disturbed by nightmares of fires, and I awoke late to the sound of members of the household bustling to get ready to leave for the synagogue. I showered and dressed quickly so that I would be in time to join them.

The main synagogue in Damascus was an imposing building: huge bronze double doors and marble columns on the outside, polished Lebanese cedar panelling on the inside. The women from our group went upstairs to the women's area on the gallery level. We men took our seats at the back of the main hall.

I noticed Barnabas slip over to where the Chief Rabbi stood and whisper in his ear. Barnabas pointed over to where our group sat. The rabbi looked around with surprise, then nodded in agreement.

The synagogue was constructed so that all the seats were facing Jerusalem. On the platform at the front was an intricately carved wooden chest. This was the 'ark' that held the scrolls of the Law—that is to say, of God's Great Book. In front of this hung an oil lamp called the 'eternal light' because its constant flame symbolised God's eternal presence in His world.

The service began with prayers led by the cantor. Then several men from the congregation read from the 'Books of Moses' and from the Psalms. The last reading was from 'Psalm 23', which seemed to speak directly to my concerns about the suffering in the world.

'Because the Lord is my shepherd, I have everything I need!

'He lets me rest in the meadow grass and leads me beside the quiet streams. He restores my failing health. He helps me do what honours him the most.

'Even when walking through the dark valley of death I will not be afraid, for you are close beside me, guarding, guiding all the way.

'You provide delicious food for me in the presence of my enemies. You have welcomed me as your guest; blessings overflow!

'Your goodness and unfailing kindness shall be with me all my life, and afterwards I will live with you forever in your home.'

When this scroll was carefully packed away, and the reader had sat down, the Chief Rabbi rose and said: 'We have a distinguished visitor in our congregation this morning. None other than Paul Benson, who has come all the way from Jerusalem. It's my pleasure to ask him to come up now and say a few words to us.'

At this Paul rose from his seat and made his way to the front. There was an air of expectation as he surveyed the seated crowd. Then he began.

'Fellow Jews,' he said, 'and all others here who reverence God, let me begin my remarks with a bit of history.

'The God of our nation Israel chose our ancestors and honoured them in Egypt by gloriously leading them out of their slavery. And he nursed them through forty years of wandering in the wilderness. Then he destroyed seven nations in Canaan, and gave Israel their land as an inheritance. Judges ruled for about 450 years, and were followed by Samuel the prophet.

'Then the people begged for a king, and God gave them Saul, son of Kish, a man of the tribe of Benjamin, who reigned for forty years. But God removed him and replaced him with David as king, a man about whom God said, "David, son of Jesse, is a man after my own heart, for he will obey me." And it is one of King David's descendants, Jesus, who is God's promised Saviour!

'But before he came, John the Baptist preached the need for everyone to turn from sin to God. As John was finishing his work he said, "Who do you think I am? I am *not* the one you are waiting for. But listen! He is coming after me, and I am not good enough to take the sandals off his feet."

'Brothers—sons of Abraham, and also all of you Gentiles here who reverence God—this salvation is for all of us! The Jews in Jerusalem and their leaders fulfilled prophecy by killing Jesus; for they didn't recognise him, or realise that he is the one the prophets had written about, though they heard the prophets' words read every Sabbath. They found no just cause to execute him, but asked Pilate to have him killed anyway. When they had fulfilled all the prophecies concerning his death, he was taken from the cross and placed in a tomb.

'But God brought him back to life again! And he was seen many times during the next few days by the men who had accompanied him to Jerusalem from Galilee. These men have constantly testified to this in public witness.

'And now Barnabas and I, and these others, are here to bring you the Good News that God's promise to our ancestors has come true in our own time, in that God brought Jesus back to life again. This is what the second Psalm is talking about when it says concerning Jesus, "Today I have honoured you as my son."

'For God had promised to bring him back to life again, no more to die. This is stated in the Scripture that says, "I will do for you the wonderful thing I promised David." In another Psalm he explained more fully, saying, "God will not let his Holy One decay." This was *not* a reference to David, for after

David had served his generation according to the will of God, he died and was buried, and his body decayed. No, it was a reference to another—someone God brought back to life, whose body was not touched by all the ravages of death.

'Brothers! Listen! In this man Jesus, there is forgiveness for your sins! Everyone who trusts in him is freed from all guilt and declared righteous, something the Jewish law could never do. Oh, be careful! Don't let the prophets' words apply to you. For they said, "Look and perish, you despisers of the truth, for I am doing something in your day—something that you won't believe when you hear it announced." '

CHAPTER 32

As people filed out of the synagogue I heard several ask Paul to return and speak to them again next week.

Then I saw Aaron Burger, his face purple with fury, in an angry huddle with the Chief Rabbi and a number of other leaders of the community. This could only spell trouble for Paul. For the time being I had enough trouble of my own to worry about, and a mountain of work to do.

'Joe, old friend,' I said to Barnabas, as we were walking home, 'could you arrange for me to visit both Tullus and Tabitha in prison later today?'

'Sure,' he replied, 'any preferred time?'

'I have a job to do straight after siesta, but any time after that would be fine.'

'I'll see to it,' he promised.

After my siesta, I set out to visit Della Rhodes, Malachi Mason's former secretary. Her address looked like simplicity itself to find: Apartment 3, 1127a Straight Street. In reality, it was a nightmare.

1127 Straight Street was a rug seller's shop. But there appeared to be no 1127a. To the right was 1125, to the left 1129. Between each shop was a narrow alley, stacked high with garbage bins awaiting collection. At the end of the alley between 1125 and 1127 was a small courtyard with a clothesline filled with washing. At the end of the alley between 1127 and 1129 was a brick wall.

I made inquiries. None of the passers-by could help. The rug seller at 1127 was constantly busy with customers and waved away my attempts at asking questions as if I was a fly at a family picnic.

Finally, I made my way back to the tiny courtyard at the end of the narrow alley between 1125 and 1127. Wading through damp washing I looked for a door. To my delight, there it was! A green-painted door, with small brass numbers screwed to its upper panel spelling out 1127a.

I tried the door handle, which turned. Inside I found myself in a small, dimly-lit hallway, with a narrow staircase rising in front of me. To my left and right were numbered doors—one and two respectively. I walked up a flight of stairs to the next landing, and knocked on number three.

It was opened a minute later by a dark-haired, attractive young woman. Her face was round and friendly, and she smiled with her eyes as well as her mouth when she said, 'Hello. Can I help you?'

'Yes, you can,' I replied. 'Or, at least, I hope you can. I'm investigating the murder of Malachi Mason, and I'd like to talk to you about him.'

The smile disappeared from her face, and she hesitated for a full minute. Finally she said, 'No. think I'd rather not,' and began to close the door.

I put my hand on the door to prevent it closing in my face, and made a split-second decision that it would be more effective to appeal to her better nature than to try threats.

'Please,' I said, 'an innocent man has been charged with Mason's murder. I'm conducting his defence. Anything you can tell me will help.'

There was another pause, and then she said, 'Very well. You'd better come in.'

I stepped inside and she closed the door behind me. The apartment was very feminine: all chintz fabrics, and pink lampshades, with lace cafe curtains on the window and little pots of African violets lining the windowsill.

She waved me to a seat, then went into the tiny kitchenette to make a pot of coffee. I sank into an overstuffed armchair with creaking springs, and a minute or two later she returned carrying a tray laden with coffee pot, cups, sugar and cream. While she cleared away a pile of magazines and found a place on the small coffee table to rest the tray, I introduced myself and briefly explained the plight of Tullus Matthias.

'I didn't work for him for long, and I never knew him very well,' she said as she poured, 'so I don't know that I'll be able to help you very much.'

'How did you come to get a job with him in the first place?'

'An ad in the paper—as simple as that. I'd just arrived back in Damascus after graduating from the Cairo Secretarial College and I was looking for work. His was one of a number of jobs I applied for.'

'What was the job exactly?'

'Secretary–receptionist. And the odd thing was that I was offered the job almost as soon as I arrived for the interview.'

'How do you mean?'

'Well, I walked into his office, Mr Mason looked me up and down, asked my name and my age, told me how much the job paid, and asked me when I could start.'

'As quickly as that?'

'As quickly as that. He never even asked me for my typing or shorthand speeds. I soon found out why. In the first place, the job was very simple. Both Mr Mason and Mr Yentob did a lot of their deals verbally with handshakes. They seemed to regard committing things to paper as to be avoided if at all possible. So I answered the phones, and typed the occasional letter. There were only a few people who ever called in person. So it was a very easy job.'

'I see.'

'But the main reason,' she went on, 'was that Mr Mason wanted his secretary–receptionist to be decorative, so he employed entirely on the basis of appearance. And not decorative only, but friendly too. Very friendly.'

'Meaning . . .?'

'Meaning that Mr Mason was a widower—had been for many years. He seemed to think that he had a right to expect his secretary to comfort and entertain him.'

'How did you respond to that notion?'

'With considerable anger, Mr Bartholomew, considerable anger. I hadn't spent two years at the Cairo Secretarial College to become the plaything of an employer!'

'How did you show your anger?'

'I slapped his face, more than once, when he became improper. The third time I slapped him, he fired me. On the spot. With no severance pay, and still owing me a week's wages.'

'What did you do?'

'I sued him for wrongful dismissal.'

'Successfully?'

'No! And that's what rankles. The hearing was a farce. Mason produced witnesses I'd never seen before, people who had never been to the offices of Mason and Yentob, who all swore that I typed badly and lost files. They were the most offensive lies! I'm really a most efficient secretary, Mr Bartholomew.'

'I'm sure you are,' I said soothingly. 'Where are you working now?'

'In the office of "Arabian Express—Trading and Credit Company". You must have seen their big warehouse on the edge of town?'

'Not only have I seen them, I was out there yesterday. I can't recall seeing you there.'

'You were probably only in the general office,' she explained. 'I work in the executive area as a specialist stenographer.'

'I see. And how do you feel about Malachi Mason now?' I asked.

There was a long pause before she replied, 'I've forgotten about him. I've put all that behind me.'

'I suppose it's easy to do that, now that he's dead?'

'I dealt with my anger, and left that all behind long before Mr Mason was murdered!' snapped Miss Rhodes.

'So you admit to feeling anger then?'

'Of course! Who wouldn't, given what that . . . that . . . snake put me through.'

'Yes, of course. Perfectly understandable. You must have been boiling like Vesuvius on a bad day when it happened.'

'You bet I was,' she said with vigour.

'So how did you deal with that?'

'I . . . I . . . I just forgot about it. That's all.'

'No, I don't think that is all,' I said slowly. 'There's a feeling coming through your words. You did more than just forget—didn't you?'

She turned her head away, and for a moment gazed

out at the brick wall that was the only view she had through her tiny window. I waited as the silence became oppressive.

'All right,' she sighed, 'I'll tell you—in strictest confidence! This must never be passed on to anyone else. And if you do tell anyone, I'll deny it.'

'Strict confidence,' I promised.

'I've never told anyone this before, but time has passed now. I felt guilty about it after I'd done it, and I still feel that guilt even now, so long afterwards. Perhaps if I tell someone, the guilt will go away.'

'Guilt? Guilt over what?' I prompted.

'Immediately after the court case, when Mr Mason had paid all those witnesses to tell all those awful lies about me, I couldn't think about anything but revenge.'

'Did you just think? Or did you act?'

'Oh, I acted all right. I knew that everyday for lunch Mr Mason ate two egg sandwiches on rye bread. He ordered them from a little deli not far from his office. I got a job at the deli making sandwiches, and bought myself a powerful emetic. After a few days, when the bimbo who had replaced me came in to order Mr Mason's egg sandwiches I made them up.'

'Mixing in a large dose of the drug?'

'Correct. About an hour later I saw an ambulance pull up in front of the offices of Mason and Yentob. A little while later Mr Mason was brought down on a stretcher, and carried off in the ambulance. At the time I worried that I had put too much of the drug in his sandwiches. I only wanted to make him feel ill and uncomfortable, I didn't want to kill him. Two days later he was back at work, and I was satisfied then that I'd had my revenge, so I quit my job at the deli and found a new secretarial job.'

'That was enough to satisfy your desire for revenge?' I asked.

'Absolutely,' replied Miss Rhodes firmly.

Shortly afterwards I took my leave of her, and walked back to the Gideons'.

Was one vomiting attack sufficient revenge for that very capable young woman? Perhaps it was. On the other hand, if she was capable of poisoning Mason enough to make him ill, did that show that she was also capable of killing him? Did her anger ever come boiling back again? And was that enough for her to take a second revenge—a fatal one?

CHAPTER 33

'I've got them, Ben,' said Barnabas, as I walked in the front door of the Gideons' house.

'Got what?'

'The prison passes you asked for,' he explained. 'So that we can visit both Tullus and Tabitha today.'

I glanced at the time.

'It's getting late,' I said. 'We should get going now, if we want to be at the jail before visiting hours end.'

'Let's make tracks then,' said Barnabas, grabbing a cloak and heading for the door.

Half an hour later we found ourselves approaching the grim, fort-like prison again.

We were admitted by the same surly prison officer as on our first visit. We asked to be taken to the women's wing of the jail, to see Tabitha.

As her cell door swung open, we saw her, huddled in one corner like a frightened kitten that has been accidentally locked in a cupboard. She looked pitiful. The rough, grey prison smock she wore could not detract from her striking beauty. But her face was pale and frightened, and her bottom lip trembled.

She rushed over to us and hugged Barnabas.

'Oh, Uncle Joe,' she whimpered. 'Why has this happened? Why is the world such a horrible place?'

Barnabas didn't try to answer, he just patted her shoulder and murmured a gentle, 'There, there.' He realised she just wanted comfort, and a guarantee of her friends' support.

But over her shoulder he deliberately caught my eye. Tabitha's question was exactly the question that I had been wrestling with. I think he wanted me to recognise that the problem of suffering is universal. Anyone who is not suffering at this moment, either has, or else will.

I pushed this cheerful little thought to the back of my mind and said, 'Sit down for a moment, Tabitha. There are some questions I have to ask you.'

'Yes, of course,' she said, dabbing her eyes and nose with a damp handkerchief, and perching herself on the edge of the one bunk in the tiny, dark cell.

'Firstly,' I said, 'how did Tragg and his men catch you?'

'I don't really know. But I guess they were looking very hard.'

'Where were you?'

'My maid and I booked into a motel called the Desert Inn on the northern road, well out of town. I did what you told me to do and booked in under my own name. 'Anyway, a few days later officers of the City Watch Crime Squad came to the front desk and demanded to see the register. Of course, they found my name and arrested me.'

'It didn't seem to take them long,' I remarked.

'Well, there were a lot of them looking,' said Tabitha. 'On the way back into town I saw official City Watch chariots on every road, and road blocks at every intersection. And there were officers on foot just about everywhere.'

'They must have thrown almost all their resources into hunting for you.'

'I guess so.'

'But why?' I asked. 'Why are they treating this one case as being so important? Why is so much official muscle being thrown into it?'

Tabitha just looked at me and shrugged her slim shoulders. Then, as she wiped away a tear with the back of her hand, she asked, 'When can you get me out of here?'

'I've thought about that,' I replied, 'and I think the best approach is to concentrate on the main murder charge against Tullus, and to try and find the real murderer. After all, you are charged with conspiring with him. If the charge against him is dismissed, the charge against you automatically fails.'

'How is Tullus?' asked Tabitha.

'We're going to see him as soon as we leave you,' said Joe Barnabas, patting her hand comfortingly.

Tabitha's eyes were as large as saucers, her face open and trusting.

'I keep hitting brick walls,' I said. 'Can you think of anyone who wanted your father dead? Can you think of anything suspicious, or strange, or out of the way that happened in the days before your father died?'

'No, nothing,' she replied slowly, thinking as she spoke, 'there was nothing like that. If there was I would have told you.'

'Yes, I know. But think. Cast your mind back. Concentrate!'

Tabitha closed her eyes and concentrated.

'No, still nothing,' she said with a sigh when she reopened her eyes. 'There's nothing that has any connection with father's death. The only thing . . .'

'Yes?'

'But it happened weeks before father died. So I don't think there can be a connection. You see, at

least two weeks before the murder there was a suggestion that someone was watching the house.'

'Who made this suggestion?'

'One of the servants.

'Which one?'

'Old Septimus.'

'He thought your villa was being *watched*?' I
persisted.

'That's right.'

'Did he tell you why he thought that?'

'He had been birdwatching and he was observing
some bird in a tree across the street from our villa.
Anyway, he said that he kept seeing the same person,
standing in the shadows, watching our villa.'

'What did this person look like, did he tell you?'

'Heavily cloaked, I think he said. It couldn't have
been anyone he recognised, or he would have told
me.'

'Was this followed up at all?'

'My father was angry about it,' said Tabitha, 'but
after Septimus's report the watcher seemed to go
away, and we all forgot about it. Until now. Is it
important?'

'Possibly not. But I'll check it out,' I promised.

We took our leave of Tabitha, Barnabas giving her
a farewell hug and assuring her that all the Christians
in Damascus were praying for her. She retreated to
the corner of her cell, when the turnkey came to let
us out.

We were then taken to the much larger men's wing,
where we found Tullus pacing up and down in his
small cell like a caged tiger.

'How is Tabitha? Have you seen her? Can you get
her released? Is she all right?'

'Tabitha is no happier about being locked up than

you are,' said Barnabas soothingly, 'but she is as well as can be expected. We've just come from her and she is not being treated any worse than any other prisoner.'

Tullus punched his right fist into the open palm of his left hand. 'She shouldn't be here! She *mustn't* be here! You must get her released!'

'Any suggestions as to how?' I asked. 'We're up against powerful forces in this case.'

'But surely you can do something?' said Tullus, despair overtaking his anger.

'The best we can do is to defeat the charge against you,' I explained for the second time that afternoon, 'then the charge against Tabitha will collapse.'

'I see. And when do we tackle that?'

'Almost at once. That's what I've come to tell you,' I explained. 'Your case will be heard before a jury, beginning on Monday.'

'That's quicker than I expected,' commented Tullus.

'It is unusually quick,' I agreed, 'but I thought it best to accept an early date.'

'How will it go?' he asked, a tremble of real uncertainty in his voice.

'I never promise clients outcomes,' I replied, 'just my best efforts.'

'Yes,' he said, sinking down onto the bunk, and lowering his head into his hands, 'I guess that's all you can do.'

'Joe will be here,' I continued, nodding in his direction, 'bright and early Monday morning to ensure that you are shaved and showered and smartly dressed. Appearance has a powerful effect on juries. And that means that you must look confident, relaxed, open-faced, and innocent.'

'I'll try to look all of those things. But I don't know if I can manage it.'

'Now I have a question for you.'

'Yes?'

'Why on earth didn't you tell me that you and Tabitha were married?'

'Well . . . I guess because . . . we had agreed . . . before the murder that is . . . I didn't think I could break the agreement without talking to Tabitha first . . . and I just never had the chance to . . . to talk to her about that,' said Tullus, shrugging his shoulders.

'It would have helped if I had known,' I said. 'That sort of thing can have an impact on tactics, on strategy.'

'Yes. I understand. I am sorry.'

It was almost sunset before Barnabas and I left the prison. We made it back to the city walls just as the gates were being shut for the night.

'So much suffering, Barnabas,' I said as we walked, 'all around us.'

'Sadly true, Ben,' he replied, 'And you know why.'

'Yes, because people live in the kingdom of Me, instead of in the kingdom of God?'

'That's exactly right. That's the disease that's causing all this pain.'

CHAPTER 34

My first priority the next morning was to check out Tabitha's suggestion that the Mason villa was being watched in the weeks prior to her father's murder.

I found old Septimus in the kitchen of the Mason villa, peeling an apple for his breakfast. He looked up, startled, when I entered.

'Oh, it's you, Mr Bartholomew,' he looked a little guilty as he spoke, 'I'm sorry about the evidence I gave in court the other day. But I had to tell the truth, didn't I?'

'Yes, you did. Don't worry about that now, it's something else I want to talk to you about.'

'Yes?'

'Two weeks before Mr Mason died—or thereabouts—you told your employer that someone was watching this house.'

'Did I? Oh, yes, so I did. I'd forgotten about it in all that has happened since.'

'Tell me what you told Mr Mason.'

'Well, let me see now. I had been birdwatching and I was watching a pair of doves nesting in the sycamore tree on the opposite side of the street.'

'And what made you suspect that someone was watching this house while you were watching the birds?'

'I saw someone, sir. Not very clearly, to be sure. But I definitely saw someone.'

'Who? Where?'

'Well, opposite this villa is, as you know, an apartment block, and the front door of that building is right next to the sycamore tree. So I couldn't help noticing him lurking about there.'

'Him? Who?' I interrupted, frustrated by the drips and dribbles in which the information was trickling out.

'The watcher, sir. The man in the dark-blue cloak. The first time I saw him lounging in the doorway I paid no attention. And then I saw him again. And again.'

'Always in the same place?'

'Yes, sir.'

'And where was that place?'

'Like I said, in the front door of the apartment building opposite. In the shadows made by the awning over the doorway. Always hanging back in the shadows, he was, and wearing that dark-blue cloak. Anyone who just glanced in his direction wouldn't have noticed him at all. Perhaps that was his intention. At any rate, I wasn't glancing, I was observing the nesting doves, and so I couldn't help but observe him as well.'

'And this was two weeks before Mr Mason died?'

'That was when I told him. But I first saw the man a week before that. Perhaps a week and a half.'

'So, after watching this man lurking opposite for a week—or possibly a week and half—you finally told Mr Mason.'

'You make it sound as though I was lax in my duties, Mr Bartholomew. I can assure you that I was not. The first few times I saw the watcher I thought nothing of it. But when he was there again and again,

I became suspicious, and that's when I told Mr Mason.'

'Was the "watcher", as you call him, definitely looking at this house? Was he keeping the villa under observation?'

'That I couldn't say for sure, sir,' replied Septimus, 'but I think he was. And that's what I told Mr Mason.'

'And how did he react when you told him?'

'He was angry, sir.'

'Did he make any suggestions as to who it might be?'

'From what he said, I got the impression that he thought it might have been one of his business competitors, sir.'

'And it was definitely a man doing the watching? Could it have been a woman?'

'Ah, that I couldn't say for sure, sir. It was a large, dark-blue cloak and it completely covered this person.'

'What did Malachi Mason do, when you told him and he became angry?'

'He stormed out of the house to confront the person, sir. But the person was gone. And never came back again. At least, I never saw him again, sir. I think Mr Mason decided that I had imagined it. But I didn't imagine it, sir. I really saw the watcher, I swear I did.'

'Show me where,' I said, and led the old man out to the front steps of the Mason villa.

'Over there, sir,' he said, pointing to the opposite side of the road.

Sure enough there was an apartment building there—a narrow, four-storey, whitewashed affair. And in the front, covered by a canvas awning, and right beside a flourishing sycamore tree, was the front entrance.

'That's where he stood, is it?' I asked, pointing to the entrance porch.

'That's the place, sir,' said old Septimus, 'back from the street in the shadow of the porch.'

'Thanks, Septimus, you've been a great help,' I said, slapping him on the shoulder in a friendly way before briskly crossing the street.

I stood for a moment where the watcher had stood—in the shadows of the porch, facing the Mason villa. If the intention was to keep the Masons under observation, the place was well chosen. There was a clear view of the front and one side of the villa, and a view of whoever entered or left by the main front steps.

I turned around and entered the cool, dark lobby of the apartment building, and rang the bell for the concierge.

At first I thought my ringing had been ignored, but when I rang again a voice called from inside 'I'm coming! I'm coming!'

At last the door to the concierge's flat opened, and a slovenly middle-aged woman appeared in a grubby house dress.

'Yeah? Whadda ya want?'

'Any empty apartments?' I asked.

'Only on the top floor,' she replied, and began closing her apartment door.

'Hang on, sweetheart!' I protested. 'What makes you think I'm not interested in the top floor?'

'We haven't got a lift, only stairs. It's a long way up. Only poor students take the top floor apartments.'

'Well, I'm interested—show me!' I insisted.

She looked at me dubiously, then, perhaps thinking

of the consequences if the building's owner learned she had refused to show a flat to a potential tenant, shrugged her shoulders.

She disappeared inside her flat for a moment, and returned holding a large bunch of brass keys.

'After you,' she said, waving me towards the stairs.

It was a long climb, up four steep flights, and by the time I reached the top I realised that I wasn't quite as fit as I'd imagined.

If I was unfit, it was worse for the concierge. She waved her hand to indicate that she couldn't speak for the moment, and sat down on the top step to recover her breath.

'Which ones are vacant?' I asked, after waiting for a couple of minutes.

'The back . . .' she started to say, but the sentence died in a fit of smoker's cough, that, once it had begun, hacked on for a full minute.

When she had recovered she took a deep breath and tried again, 'The back two.'

'The front two are occupied then?' I asked.

'The front right is occupied by students. The front left is paid for, but no-one is living there.'

'That's a bit strange, isn't it?'

By way of reply she just shrugged her shoulders as if to say: the whole world is strange, but as long as they pay their rent it's none of my business.

'I'd like to see it.'

'See what?' her eyes narrowed in suspicion.

'The front left apartment. The one that's paid for but unoccupied.'

'I can't do that,' she protested. But her protests died away when I pulled a purse of coins out of the pocket of my tunic and started counting out one denarius after another. When I got to five I stopped.

'Another five after I've seen inside the apartment.'

'Very well. But I'm coming in with you. I can't leave you alone in an apartment someone else is paying for.'

'Suit yourself.'

She unlocked the apartment door with one of the brass keys on the large keyring. I stepped in and walked over to the front window. As I suspected, it had an even better view of the Mason villa than the porch below.

'Who's renting this place?' I asked.

'Didn't give a name.'

'Man or woman?'

'Man.'

'Young? Old? What did he look like?'

'I never saw his face. He always kept the hood on his cloak pulled up, even indoors.'

'What colour was the cloak?'

'A dark colour. Dark-blue I think. What's this all about?'

'It's about your earning a few more coins,' I said, going back to the window. Yes, the view was excellent. Because of the height it was possible to see the whole of the house, part of the courtyard, as well as the street in the front of the Mason villa, and the laneway that ran down one side.

I began searching the room.

'You leave everything the way you found it!' growled the concierge, lighting up a cigarette.

The tiny room was sparsely furnished, and there wasn't much to search. But under the single bed I found a long, thin, wooden box, and when I slid it out and opened it up, I found that it contained a telescope!

That settled it. Septimus wasn't mistaken. The

Mason villa really had been spied on. And when the spy became concerned that Septimus might have spotted him—or, perhaps, just because he wanted a better view—he moved from the porch up to this room and continued his spying from here.

What had he seen? Had he been watching on the day of the murder? Had he seen the murderer? Or was he himself the murderer or someone employed by the murderer to report on the Masons?

'The man who rented this room—does he spend much time here?' I asked.

'An hour or two each day. Never any more than that.'

'Has he always come here alone?'

'Always.'

'And when was the last time you saw him?'

'About two weeks ago, I guess.'

In other words, at about the time of Malachi Mason's murder!

CHAPTER 35

I let a further five coins dribble into the hungry palm of the concierge, then departed.

Instead of heading straight back to the Gideons' for lunch, I decided to stop off at the courthouse, and check which court, and which judge, had been allocated to the murder trial for the following day.

The public area in the clerk of the court's office was as crowded as always. On one wall was a long noticeboard containing all the listings. Under the criminal list I found *The Empire v Matthias*—listed for court number one. We had drawn the same judge as last time—Judge Hezion—which I was happy about.

As I was about to turn and leave I heard a familiar voice. It was Aaron Burger—his back towards me—growling at some poor junior clerk of the court.

'You will let the media know when the prisoner is arriving, and at which entrance. Do you understand?'

'Yes, but I'm not supposed to . . .' the poor clerk was blustering.

'You're supposed to do what I tell you to do,' said Burger.

'But what if someone finds out?'

'Then you make sure that they don't find out!'

'But . . .'

'Just do it!' snapped Burger, then strode off.

I shrank back into the crowd so that he wouldn't

see me. So, I thought, he was planning to subject poor Tullus to 'trial by media'. Well, there wasn't much I could do about that—except humiliate Burger by proving Tullus innocent in court.

What else was Burger planning, I wondered? What other nasty surprises did he have up his sleeve? Perhaps if I followed him, I could find out.

I hurried out of the courthouse in time to see Burger's distinctive figure disappearing down the broad, stone steps at the front of the building. Keeping at a discreet distance, I shadowed him.

He walked quickly, never looking behind him. He entered Straight Street and pushed his way through crowds of shoppers and merchants. He thrust aside a startled rug seller loaded down with his wares, who cried, 'Hey! Who do you think you are!'

Once he reached the centre of Straight Street—the part reserved for horse-drawn vehicles—he was more cautious. But his pace hardly slowed as he ducked his way around chariots, farm carts, and mounted riders, his cloak flapping behind him.

I let some distance develop between us, to avoid being spotted, and almost lost him when he suddenly turned and ducked into a side alley. I ran to make up lost ground, and entered the alley as he emerged at the far end, and turned right. I sprinted to the end of the alley, and looked cautiously out into the narrow street into which it emptied.

The footpath was deserted! Burger had vanished. Where could he have got to? The street was lined with small coffee shops, so I began to check these out.

Halfway down the street I spotted Burger sitting in a huddle with a group of men at a back table in a coffee bar, called The Manna House. Pulling the hood of my cloak up to cover my face I stepped inside and took a side table as close as I dared to Burger and his group.

When the waiter came I ordered coffee and a bagel with cream cheese. Then I tried to turn my ears into radars and pick up at least some of what the Burger group was saying.

Burger was leaning forward across the table, his back to me, talking rapidly in an earnest whisper to a group of young ruffians with three-day stubble and sour expressions.

After he'd been talking for a few minutes, one of the others said in a loud voice: 'But isn't this the same man who persecuted Jesus's followers in Jerusalem?'

'Keep your voice down!' snapped Burger angrily, as he waved his hands to hush the young man.

So, it was Paul they were talking about.

Another of the young men facing Burger started to speak and although he tried to keep his voice low, I could still pick up some of the words.

'. . . understand,' he hissed, '. . . came here . . . arrest . . . in chains . . . chief priests.'

'He did,' I heard Burger say, then his voice dropped to a quiet murmur and I couldn't hear the rest.

My coffee and bagel arrived, and I began eating while still straining both ears to pick up the odd word.

'. . . drastic action . . .'

'. . . only one way . . .'

'. . . what if . . . escape . . .'

At this Burger raised his voice enough for me to pick up a complete sentence.

'All the gates in the city wall are being watched,'

he said, 'both day and night. There's no way he can escape.'

Escape? Why should Paul want to escape from Damascus?

As the conference reached its climax, the voices dropped even further, and I could no longer pick up even the odd word. But one of the young thugs had pulled a wicked-looking knife out of his tunic, and was fingering the blade in a loving and sinister fashion.

Finally some sort of agreement seemed to be reached. There were handshakes all around, then Burger dug into his belt and pulled out a money bag. I heard the tinkle of coins as the contents were sprinkled across the coffee table.

The thugs seemed satisfied with the amount and, after counting it, the leader scooped it up, and put it in a purse which disappeared into the folds of his tunic. Shortly afterwards the young thugs stood up and left the coffee shop.

Within a few minutes Burger finished his coffee and left too.

I sat there for some time, toying with my coffee, shocked and concerned by what I had discovered. Then I paid for my meal, and hurried back to the Gideons' with my bad news.

'Planning to murder Paul?' said Joe Barnabas, a tone of shocked disbelief in his voice.

They were all gathered in the living room of the house—David and Miriam Gideon, Ananias, Nicolaus, George, Barnabas, and Paul himself.

'I'm certain of it,' I replied.

'But why?' asked Ananias.

'Paul as a follower of Jesus is more dangerous than

any of us,' I suggested, 'and a bigger embarrassment to the authorities.'

'Yes, that's true,' said George, nodding his huge head. 'That makes sense.'

'So what do we do?' asked Miriam.

'Paul must escape,' said David firmly.

'But the gates!' protested Ananias. 'If they have assassins posted at all the gates to the city wall—both day and night—escape is impossible.'

'Nevertheless,' said Joe earnestly, 'a way must be found.'

Everyone put their heads together to come up with a solution to the threat facing Paul. As the sun started to set, and the shadows lengthen, we were still talking and debating the possibilities.

Miriam made a large pot of coffee, and David phoned out for pizzas. Then the planning and discussion continued well into the night. The oil lamps were flickering, and the room was littered with cardboard pizzas boxes and leftover pizza when George finally said: 'Why not go *over* the wall!'

'What was that?' asked Ananias, startled.

'If all the gates are guarded,' said George slowly, 'and assassins are stalking Paul in the city. Why not get him out *over* the city wall!'

'Is that possible?'

'Can it be done?'

'Surely not!' came the clamour of voices, all speaking at once.

'Hang on,' I said, waving everyone to silence, 'tell us more George.'

'Well, as you know, I am a member of the city guard.'

'Yes, that's right,' said Barnabas, light beginning

to dawn for him. 'You patrol the gates and the city wall.'

'Correct,' continued George. 'You probably know that there is a walkway around the top of the wall.'

'How wide is it?' I asked.

'About a metre,' replied George, 'anyhow, I was thinking, what if we got Paul up to that walkway, and then let him down on the other side of the wall?'

'They wouldn't be expecting that!' said David, sounding delighted.

Paul was also smiling and nodding at the plan.

'But would it be safe?' asked Miriam.

'Safer than Paul staying in Damascus,' said Ananias.

'Yes . . . I guess that's true,' agreed Miriam.

'What do we need, then?' asked Joe, ever practical.

'Well, the first thing is rope,' I suggested.

'Correct,' said George. 'A lot of rope, in fact. It's a long way down that wall—a long way!'

'That's not a problem,' said David quickly. 'There's a lot of rope on my building sites. I can get that for you anytime.'

'Fine,' said George. 'Now, Paul, how fit are you feeling.'

Paul explained that he was still recovering from his experience on the road to Damascus, and wasn't sure he could manage the long climb down the rope.

'You won't have to,' George assured him, 'I have a plan.'

CHAPTER 36

George's plan involved finding a large, sturdy basket.

'Down at the fruit markets they'll have something like that,' I said.

'The wife of one of the fruit merchants is a friend of mine,' said Miriam. 'I'm sure that if I pop around to her place now she'll be able to lend us something like that.'

'I'll come with you,' said David, 'and help you carry it.'

They both leapt up, eager to get started. As the door closed behind them George said, 'The next question is: when should we do this? Late, I would think. Probably after the midnight shift has started.'

One o'clock the next morning found George, Barnabas, Paul and I, all heavily cloaked, making our way up the winding stone stairs that led to the parapet on top of the city wall.

George, who knew the way, was leading. When he reached the top he turned and said, 'You three wait there, in the shadow of the stairs, while I scout around a bit.'

That was all right for George, he was the only one not staggering under the weight of a huge, heavy fruit merchant's basket.

'See if we can lower this thing,' grunted Barnabas, 'and rest it on the stairs for a while.'

With some grunting, and a bit of awkward shifting around on the narrow staircase we managed this, and it was a great relief to have the weight off our shoulders for a while.

We stood there in the dark, the only sound the desert wind, whistling through the turrets and over the rooftops of Damascus. The wind seemed, to my imagination at least, to carry with it the scents and aromas of date palms from some distant oasis, and the mingled smells of the marketplace in faraway Baghdad.

Thick clouds scudded across the sky, turning the buttery yellow light of the moon on and off like a flickering flashlight. Then a darker shadow loomed up in the darkness at the top of the stairs.

'All clear,' came George's whispered voice. 'The guard has just passed on his round. Come on.'

The three of us shouldered the basket again, and followed George's broad back up the rest of the stairs and onto the narrow walkway that ran around the top of the wall. Only a yard wide, and boarded on either side by low, stone parapets, it was no place for a man with vertigo.

After we had walked about a hundred yards George said, 'Here will do.'

We lowered the basket and George took the loops of rope off his shoulders. Barnabas tied the rope to the handles of the basket with an expert fisherman's knot.

'Now,' said George, 'Paul, climb into the basket.'

Paul did as he was told.

'You two grab the other side, I'll take this,' grunted George as he bent forward and began to take the load.

Side by side Barnabas and I lifted our end of the

basket and, with George taking most of the weight in his massive, muscled arms, raised the basket and its precious human cargo until it balanced precariously on the stone parapet.

'Farewell, dear brother,' said Barnabas to Paul. 'We shall meet again.'

Then with a mighty heave we got the basket over the edge and hanging from the end of the rope. Slowly, hand over hand we let the rope out. Barnabas and I were straining and doing our best, but it was the mighty George who was taking most of the weight.

The minutes ticked, as the rope inched through our fingers, and our back and shoulder muscles began to scream out their complaints.

Finally the rope went slack, and a distant call from far below told us that Paul was safely on the ground. Paul's instructions were to set out for Arabia, at once, on foot. He had been supplied with money and provisions for the journey, and the believers had prayed for him before he left.

George, Barnabas and I leant out over the wall, and stared blindly into the impenetrable darkness. We could catch no glimpse of Paul.

'Quick,' urged George, 'the guard will return soon. We have to pull the basket back up.'

It was lighter now, but our muscles still protested at the effort. A few minutes later, rope and basket were lying beside us on the top of the wall, and George was packing the rope inside the basket. Putting the basket on his shoulders, he urged Barnabas and I to get a move on.

As we reached the top of the stairs we heard the distant footfalls of the approaching guard—completing his circuit along the top of the city wall.

'Hurry!' whispered George.

We didn't need any encouragement, and scurried down the narrow, winding staircase as quickly as we could.

We arrived back at the Gideons' half an hour later.

'How did it go?' asked Miriam anxiously.

'Like a charm,' said George, his face beaming.

Then and there David called for an impromptu prayer meeting to thank God for Paul's escape to safety.

Later, Barnabas and I returned to the subject that was haunting me.

'Tonight is just another example,' I said.

'Example of what?' asked Barnabas.

'Of suffering. Or, at least, on this occasion, of suffering and persecution that has been avoided. But only just avoided.'

'Yes—that's true.'

'What are we supposed to *do* about suffering, Barnabas?' I asked.

'Well, in the end, Ben,' he replied, 'there is only one thing we can do that will actually *deal* with suffering.'

'And what is that?'

'Repentance,' he said firmly. 'When people talked to Jesus about suffering he didn't hesitate. He simply said, "Unless you repent you too will all perish." That's how we handle suffering—by repenting.'

'How will feeling sorry fix suffering?'

'Repenting doesn't mean feeling sorry. Far from it. No, repentance means changing direction. It means turning from my way to God's way. Of course, we don't have the inner strength or ability to make such a big change ourselves, so we have to talk to God in prayer and ask Him to change us—to make that big change in our life's direction.'

'To change from the kingdom of Me to the kingdom of God?'

'Exactly. Have you got time for me to tell you a story that will explain what I mean? Or are you too tired?'

'No, I'm wide awake. Let's hear your story.'

'Well,' began Barnabas, 'Pilgrim and his friend were travelling down the long and winding road of this life's journey when they came to a fork in the road. Branching off to the left was the main road. A signpost labelled it "The Human Highway". Branching off to the right was a narrower road. The signpost indicated that this was called "God's Way".

'Pilgrim and his friend asked passers-by the difference between the two ways. Everyone they asked said that both roads ended at the same place—the river of death. However, there *was* a difference about what would be found on the riverbank.

'Those choosing God's Way all said that this way ended at the ferry that would carry them across the river to the fair city on the far side.

'But those choosing the Human Highway were divided in their opinions. Some thought the road just ended, and that was it. Others thought they *might* find a ferry waiting for them at the end, but then again they might not—they weren't too sure. And if there was a ferry, they were not at all sure where it might take them.

'Then Pilgrim asked if either road was any easier to travel than the other.

'At first there was complete agreement that both were the same. The way was hard and the travelling rough and dangerous, no matter which way you went.

But then one of the travellers turning into God's Way said, "There *is* a difference. Those of us who choose this path are committed to caring for each other. And on top of that, the king of the great city towards which we are headed sends us his help. He helps us, and helps us to help each other."

'Pilgrim knew that there was only one place for him, only one right road. So he turned off the highway, and turned down the narrow road, walking God's Way.'

Having reached the end of his story Barnabas paused.

'I understand now what you mean by repentance: turning our life around. But how does that deal with suffering?' I said.

'In the first place,' replied Barnabas, 'it means that an end—a definite end—has been put to our suffering. At the moment when a believer, a member of God's family, of God's kingdom, dies, all suffering ends for that person. On the basis of the death of Jesus on the cross, God lets them into his heaven forever. Of course, the opposite is true for the unbeliever. That is what Jesus calls "perishing". I sometimes think of it like this: the Christian only has to *endure* this world, this is as bad as it gets for us. But non-Christians have to *enjoy* this world, this is as good as it gets for them!'

'I see,' I said thoughtfully.

'Of course there's more to it than that. There is the fact, for example, that we understand why there is suffering, and what is really going on in this world. And there is the fact that we have the spirit of the Living God within us, to help us cope and to give us inner strength. And we have each other. Jesus has taught us to stand by each other, to support each other, and to carry each other's burdens. And it is in all of these things—but starting with repentance—that the suffering of this world is actually dealt with!'

CHAPTER 37

It must have been four o'clock by the time I got to bed, and I slept badly. Dreams came and went. They all involved defending someone charged with murder, but I could never quite see who it was. I was unprepared and didn't have my arguments or my evidence organised. And every time I tried to stop and think through my case, everything around me seemed to start running faster.

I woke up in a cold sweat at about six in the morning and decided to get out of bed and take a walk in the courtyard. I thought a little cool morning air might clear my head.

The sky was reflected in the water of the fountain. The clouds had fled and the courtyard was filled with a warm, watery early-morning light.

As I paced, all the facts of the Malachi Mason case ran through my head—the character of the victim, the way the body was found, the watcher in the apartment block opposite, Tullus's distinctive dagger, the many people who had good reason to hate Mason.

I continued to pace, talking to myself the whole time, and then . . . quite suddenly . . . the pieces began to fall into place for me. 'If that happened then that means that . . . Yes! And, of course that fits in with . . . Ah, yes, I can see it all now!'

The clues had been there in front of me for ages,

but now I found that they were fitting together like the pieces of a jigsaw puzzle.

Later that morning, at exactly ten o'clock, Judge Hezion entered the courtroom.

'The case of the *Empire versus Matthias* on the capital charge of murder,' chanted the clerk of the court. 'This court is now in session, his honour Judge Hezion presiding.'

Then began the tiresome, but important, process of jury selection. Both prosecution and defence had the right to challenge a set number of potential jurors. I reserved my challenges for individuals who might possibly be biased against Tullus.

Some potential jurors slowed down the process by asking to be excused from jury service, and coming up with a range of colourful and inventive excuses to get out of doing their civic duty.

It was almost lunchtime before we had completed the process of empanelling 'twelve good men and true' to hear the case against Tullus. The judge decided to rise for an early lunch, and commence the hearing proper immediately after lunch.

When the court resumed, Burger and I made our opening addresses to the jury. Burger stressed what a horrible crime had been committed, playing on the idea of Tullus violating his sacred duty as a doctor to preserve life, and argued that any doctor who murdered deserved nothing less than the hangman's noose. He went on to claim that he could show, beyond a shadow of a doubt, that the physical evidence proved that Tullus, and no-one else, could be the killer.

I responded by agreeing that this was indeed a horrible crime, and that it did, indeed, involve an appalling violation of trust. However, I insisted that the evidence as to motive, means, and opportunity would fail entirely to prove my client guilty. There would not just be the shadow of a doubt, I promised, but absolute certainty, when the case was over, that my client was completely innocent. Then I caused a sensation by promising that before the trial was over I would also reveal the identity of the real murderer.

The public gallery erupted and there was so much chatter that Judge Hezion had to bang his gavel several times to restore order. A couple of reporters dashed out of the court to file late stories with their papers.

Then Burger began calling witnesses and building the prosecution's case.

This he did with great care, revealing his evidence step by step, leaving no gaps as he went. He began by calling evidence on the finding of the body, using both the first City Watch officer to arrive on the scene, and then Captain Tragg.

Tragg's testimony took most of the afternoon as he repeated his account of the scene of the crime, the identity of the murder weapon, and the arrest of Tullus.

At the completion of each examination by the District Attorney, Burger turned to me and said, 'Your witness, counsellor.'

And each time I replied, 'No questions.'

By the end of the day Burger was giving me odd looks, and Judge Hezion was starting to look worried at how I was conducting my case.

'Are you certain you have no questions, Mr Bartholomew?' he asked, more than once.

'The defence has no questions of this witness, your honour,' I replied on each occasion.

Just before the court rose for the day, Burger called

Dr Galen to repeat his evidence as to the cause of death. Then Tullus was led back to the cells for the night. By then even my friends were looking concerned.

'You haven't given up hope have you, Ben?' asked Joe Barnabas. 'I didn't keep you up too late?'

'No, Joe, so don't worry.'

'Then . . . what . . .?'

'What game am I playing? A very careful game, dear friend. These are the tactics I decided on in the early hours of this morning, and they are the tactics that, in the end, will see both Tullus and Tabitha released without a stain on their characters,' I insisted.

'Well, if you say so, Ben,' said Barnabas, still looking doubtful.

That evening I was plagued by doubts as well. I needed to talk over my plan with someone who would listen, and critically evaluate what I said, but not try and talk me out of it. So I telephoned Rachel in Caesarea.

It was wonderful to hear her voice again and, ignoring the potential size of my phone bill, I explained to her all the facts I now had, and how they fitted together. Rachel agreed that I had solved the case, and there was no gap in my reasoning. Then I told her my tactics. She asked me why, and made me explain and defend my approach. But in the end she agreed it was the best way to go. We spent the last few minutes of the call being intimate.

Having talked the whole thing over, I was clearer in my own mind, and certain that I was on the right track. I decided to try and get a good night's rest.

The next morning in court I stuck to my strategy,

despite the concerned looks I was getting from my friends in the public gallery, and from Tullus in the dock!

Burger called many of the servants from the Mason villa to establish the movements of everyone who visited the household on the day of the murder. After each witness I responded to his offer of, 'your witness, counsellor,' with the reply, 'I have no questions for this witness.'

Burger built up his picture of a room containing a helpless, sick man that could be entered only through one door, and that door under constant observation at all times. Again and again he made his point, 'So the only person who entered—or left—the victim's room was the accused, Dr Tullus Matthias?'

And again and again the answer was the same, 'Yes, sir.' The answer was either given reluctantly, by those servants who were loyal to Tabitha, or eagerly, by those who liked to make mischief. Either way, it was always the same.

By lunch Burger had re-established that, although the two small windows in the victim's room were half open to let in fresh air, they were both heavily barred, and the physical evidence showed that the bars had not been tampered with in any way.

When the court rose for lunch Judge Hezion summoned Burger and myself to his chambers for a private conference.

'What game are you playing at, Mr Bartholomew?' demanded the judge, taking off his wig, and slumping down into the huge leather chair behind his desk. 'You were not like this at the committal hearing! But now you appear not to be trying to put a case for the defence at all. Are you sure that you know what you're doing?'

'Quite sure, your honour,' I replied.

'You're not trying to set up some sort of mistrial on the grounds that all the evidence was not put to the jury, are you? Because if that's so I'd rather abort and start again when you're ready to proceed properly.'

'I have no such plan in mind, your honour,' I assured him.

'Then why aren't you doing your job!' interrupted Burger, irritably.

'I am,' I insisted.

'But you're making no attempt—no attempt whatsoever—to challenge the prosecution's case!' he whined.

'That's because most of the prosecution's case is identical to the defence's case,' I explained, 'except in one small particular—the identity of the murderer.'

'Explain yourself!' demanded Burger.

'To do that, would be to show my hand,' I said.

'But . . . but . . . but . . .' spluttered Burger.

'You can hardly expect your opponent to reveal his tactics to you, Mr Burger,' said the judge quietly, then continued: 'Well, Mr Bartholomew, I cannot pretend that I understand your strategy, but I am satisfied that you have one, and that you are acting in what you conceive to be the best interests of your client.'

'Thank you, your honour.'

'This conference is at an end,' Judge Hezion dismissed us curtly.

CHAPTER 38

That afternoon the parade of prosecution witnesses continued. I let all of them pass without cross-examination.

Finally, Burger felt he had built up a watertight case and announced, 'The prosecution rests, your honour.'

'Is the defence ready to proceed, Mr Bartholomew?' asked Judge Hezion.

'The defence is ready, your honour,' I replied.

'Are you planning to call many witnesses, Mr Bartholomew?' the judge asked.

'Just three, your honour.'

'In that case, we will adjourn now, and sit again tomorrow morning at ten o'clock.'

I sat up late that night going over and over my notes, making sure I was ready to put my case, and that I could lead my key witness—my one vital witness— exactly where I wanted to lead him. I also telephoned the person I wanted to have in the courtroom the next day. I promised her that she would not have to give evidence, simply attend. She promised that she would.

In the end I was satisfied that everything was ready, and slept soundly.

The court sat promptly at ten the next morning.

'Do you have any opening remarks to address to the jury, Mr Bartholomew?' began the judge.

'Only this,' I said, turning towards the jury box. 'You have heard the prosecution build up a careful case on three grounds. These are the usual grounds in a murder trial, namely, motive, means and opportunity. Everything you have heard so far from the prosecution witnesses is quite true. What is false is the conclusion that has been drawn from this evidence. In each area—motive, means, and opportunity—if we push what we already know just a little bit further, we will find that the evidence points clearly, and unequivocally, to another person entirely.

'When you have heard this additional evidence, ladies and gentlemen of the jury, you will be able to safely acquit my client, confident not only that he is innocent, but that you know the identity of the true killer. To this end I intend calling only three witness—one dealing with means, one with motive, and the third with opportunity. In the end, the prosecution's case depends almost entirely on the evidence with respect to opportunity. That evidence will have collapsed before today is over.'

I finished my address and again the court erupted.

'Call your first witness, Mr Bartholomew,' said the judge as soon as the court was settled.

'Call Shem Danielson,' I said.

'Call Shem Danielson,' echoed the clerk of the court.

'Shem Danielson,' came the voice of the sheriff's officer from the corridor outside the court.

Once again the senior steward in Tullus's house took the oath. Once again I slowly took him through the evidence he had given at the committal hearing.

Again, I established that while the weapon used to kill Malachi Mason, the silver dagger, was Tullus's property it had not been seen for a while, and could have been stolen at any time. Burger tried to demolish the significance of this in cross-examination, but failed. By the time Shem Danielson left the stand, it was clear that the means for committing the murder—the silver dagger—was not just available to Tullus, but to almost anyone.

As old Shem shuffled out of the courtroom I said, 'Call Mrs Tabitha Matthias.'

A murmur of anticipation ran around the court as the call was passed on, and Tabitha was produced from the holding cells beneath the court, in accordance with the subpoena I had issued earlier.

I took Tabitha back through her committal hearing evidence, slowly building up, step by step, her relationship with Tullus. By clearly establishing that Tullus and Tabitha were married, I demolished the vague and shadowy motive of passion that the prosecution had hinted at.

Burger was smart enough not to cross-examine Tabitha. He realised that if he gave the pale, frightened-looking young woman a hard time, he would lose the sympathy of the jury.

Still looking nervously over her shoulder, Tabitha was led out of the witness box and back to the cells.

Having shown that the prosecution had failed to establish both motive and means in their case against Tullus, it was time to turn to the big, thorny issue of opportunity. And that meant it was time to pull my rabbit out of the hat, and call my surprise witness. I looked around the faces in the public gallery. The person I wanted was there, as she had promised she would be.

'As its next witness, the defence calls the District Attorney of Damascus, Mr Aaron Burger,' I announced in a clear ringing voice.

The newspaper summed up the reaction the next day with a three-word headline: 'Sensation in court'.

'Objection, your honour!' yelled Burger, when he'd recovered sufficiently from the surprise, to leap to his feet and protest.

'On what grounds, Mr Burger?' inquired the judge.

'On the grounds that it is improper, incompetent and immaterial so to do. On the further grounds that this is a stunt by the defence to grab publicity and draw the jury's attention away from the real issues in this case. And on the further grounds that . . . that . . . well, I'll think of more in just a moment.'

'Both of you will approach the bench,' growled Judge Hezion, ominously, 'and I'll hear your arguments on this motion.'

Burger and I left our respective bar tables and walked up to the judge's bench.

For a moment he stared at the two of us, then he said, 'Well, Mr Bartholomew, you must admit that this looks like a stunt, rather than a proper proceeding in a criminal trial?'

'It may look like that, your honour,' I said, 'but I assure the court that my intention is entirely serious. I am certain that, as a witness for the defence, Mr Burger can reveal relevant matters of fact, and progress this trial rapidly towards a conclusion.'

'Mr Burger?' said the judge, raising one eyebrow.

'Your honour,' Burger's voice had risen a full octave and a half in outrage, 'if I knew anything of relevance to this case I would have volunteered it to the City Watch detectives, or to this court, long ago. If I did not do so, it can only be because I know nothing of relevance. Speaking as an officer of the court, I solemnly assure the court that I have no relevant evidence to give.'

'Mr Bartholomew, since Mr Burger is, as he rightly says, an officer of the court and the District Attorney of this city, I am inclined to take his word on this matter. Do you have anything further to say?'

'Yes, your honour. It may be that Mr Burger does not realise the significance of the information that he has. That possibility cancels his assurances, and explains why he has not come forward. I believe that once he is on the stand and under oath, I can show relevance fairly quickly and elicit information useful to serving the ends of justice in this case.'

'Sounds fair enough. Why not take the stand?' suggested the judge. 'I will protect you in your capacity as a witness, and prevent Mr Bartholomew from straying into areas that he should not stray into.'

'I still protest, your honour,' persisted Burger. 'I am not an unintelligent man, and I do not believe I have anything to offer. I insist that I would have seen the relevance of any information I have, probably sooner than Mr Bartholomew. However, I have seen no such relevance, because I know nothing of relevance in this case. I am not a witness to any of the events that are currently before the court. How can my testimony be of any relevance?'

'I think I can settle this matter,' I said quickly, 'by asking Mr Burger a few questions here, now, not under oath.'

'Do you have any objections to that, Mr Burger?' asked Judge Hezion.

'This questions and answers will not be part of the court record, will they?' said Burger suspiciously.

'Certainly not,' replied the judge.

'In that case,' said Burger, turning to me, 'ask me what you wish.'

'Is it true, Mr Burger,' I asked, 'that you knew the victim of this murder, Mr Malachi Mason, socially?'

'Of course that's true!' snapped Burger. 'Everyone knows that!'

'And that you have known him in a social capacity for many years?'

'Yes! Yes! So what?'

'And that you were a frequent visitor at his house?'

'Sure I was! Again, so what?'

'And that you visited him only one day before his murder?'

'Yes, I did. But so did many other people.'

'And that you, at least once, and perhaps more often, proposed marriage to his daughter Tabitha?'

'Oh, come now!' sneered Burger. 'This can't be relevant! Your honour, will you please put a stop to this charade?'

'I would be interested to know just how well you knew the family, Mr Burger,' the judge said quietly.

'All right! All right! I proposed once. I was rejected! So what?'

'Your honour,' I said, 'I believe I have established that the District Attorney had a sufficiently close personal relationship with the Mason family to justify calling him as a witness.'

'I believe you have, Mr Bartholomew. Mr Burger, your objection is overruled. You will enter the witness box and take the oath.'

With a sour look on his face, Burger reluctantly climbed into the witness box. The clerk of the court administered the oath.

'Do you swear that the evidence you shall give

this court shall be the truth, the whole truth, and nothing but the truth?'

'Yes!' replied Burger, loud and angry.

'Please state your full name and occupation?'

'Aaron Hamilton Burger, District Attorney of the City of Damascus.'

Slowly I rose to my feet and approached the witness box. This was the part that I was going to enjoy.

CHAPTER 39

'Mr Burger, please tell the court about your relationship with the deceased, Mr Malachi Mason.'

'He was a friend,' replied Burger, speaking in a flat monotone, looking as bored as he could manage.

'A little louder please,' I said. 'It's important that the jury hear every word.'

'He was a friend!'

'Thank you. How long had you known him?'

'For the better part of ten years.'

'Would you describe him as a good friend?'

'Yes—yes, I would.'

'Did you visit him often?'

'It varied.'

'Would you like to explain to the court just what you mean by that, Mr Burger.'

'There were periods when Malachi and I visited each other often, and times when we were busy and preoccupied and saw little of each other.'

'Take the last 12 months as an example—was that a time when you saw quite a lot of each other?'

'Yes, in general terms it was.'

'You dined with the Mason family often this past year?'

'Yes, I did.'

'That means that as well as Malachi Mason, you must have seen a lot of his daughter, Tabitha. Is that so?'

'Yes, of course it's so!' snorted Burger impatiently.

'So, you knew her well?'

'Yes.'

'And liked her?'

'Yes.'

'Well enough to propose marriage to her?'

There a long pause before Burger replied, 'Yes.'

'But she refused you?'

'Yes! Yes!'

'And now she is married to the accused in this case. Does that make you jealous of the accused?'

'Your honour!' complained Burger, turning to the judge.

'I have given you a lot of scope, Mr Bartholomew,' said the judge, 'but I think you have now explored this line as far as it is fruitful to go. Please move on.'

'If your honour pleases,' I said politely, it never does to get the judge off side. I then checked through my notes, and turned back to the witness box.

'Since you knew the deceased so well, Mr Burger, can you tell the court something of his character?'

'In his home I always found him to be very friendly. Jovial even.'

'And out of his home?'

'Well, out of his home he was a businessman.'

'A tough businessman?'

'I don't know, I never did business with him.'

'But in his conversations with you, did he give you to understand that he was shrewd?'

'Yes.'

'And tough?'

'Yes.'

'And often got the upper hand in business deals?'

'Yes.'

'Did that make him unpopular?'

'I wouldn't know. I don't mix in the business world very much.'

'Did he ever say to you that he had enemies?'

'Yes, he did say that.'

'People who hated him?'

'Yes.'

'Hated him enough to kill him?'

'I wouldn't know.'

'Did he ever tell you that he feared for his life?'

'Well . . . '

'Well, what?'

'He was careful about security.'

'So, leaving aside the accused, there were many people with a motive to murder Malachi Mason, weren't there?'

'I wouldn't know about that.'

'I put it to you that you would, Mr Burger. And that you know from your conversations with Malachi Mason that the list of people who wanted to kill him was almost as long as the Damascus Telephone Directory!'

'You've made your point, Mr Bartholomew,' intervened the judge. 'Move on.'

'Yes, your honour,' I said. 'Now, Mr Burger, when was the last time you visited the Mason villa before the murder.'

'It was the day before he was murdered.'

'Did you express concern to Tabitha about her father's illness on that occasion?'

'I'm sure I would have.'

'And did you suggest to her that she call in the accused—Dr Tullus Matthias—to treat Mr Mason?'

'I can't remember.'

'You can't remember. If you wish I can recall Tabitha to the witness box to refresh your memory.'

'Well, I may have done. But if I did, I was being sarcastic, not serious.'

'Sarcastic, not serious. Nevertheless, it was you who planted the idea in Tabitha's head of calling in Tullus?'

'I wouldn't know. Perhaps she thought of it herself.'

'Perhaps. And then again perhaps she didn't,' I said loudly enough for the jury to hear, while I rummaged through my notes.

I let the silence hang on for as long as I dared, and then said, 'Now, Mr Burger, will you describe the physical location of the Mason villa to the court?'

'Your honour!' exclaimed Burger from the witness box. 'I protest. The jury already knows everything that is relevant about the geography of the scene of the crime. And in asking me this question, defence counsel is merely on a fishing expedition.'

'Mr Bartholomew?' queried the judge, raising one eyebrow.

'Your honour,' I explained, 'the internal layout of the Mason villa has been explained, but not its location and setting. Since that villa is the scene of the crime, its location and setting are relevant—as I will show shortly. And who better to give expert testimony on the location of the villa than a frequent visitor?'

'Very well, Mr Bartholomew, I will permit the question. But I want you to link this up very soon. Mr Burger, you will answer the question.'

'What exactly do you want to know?' asked Burger, his voice dripping with heavy sarcasm.

'Describe the surroundings of the Mason villa—all four sides please.'

'Well on one side it fronts onto a main street, on another it directly abuts the next villa down the street, on the remaining side, and along the back, are narrow alleyways.'

'Thank you. Please tell the jury what building is directly opposite the front of the villa?'

'It's an apartment block, I think.'

'You think?'

'Yes.'

'But you're not sure?'

'Yes . . . yes, I'm sure it's an apartment block.'

'In fact, Mr Burger, aren't you very sure. Haven't you, in fact, rented an apartment in that block?'

'What would I want to do that for?'

'Just answer the question, Mr Burger. Did you or did you not rent a top-floor apartment in the building directly opposite the Mason villa?'

Burger hesitated, looked uncomfortable, and licked his lips nervously. I turned to the public gallery and signalled to the woman I had asked to attend to stand up. She did so.

'Mr Burger,' I said, firmly and briskly, 'do you recognise the woman now standing in the public gallery?'

'I . . . I . . .'

'She is the concierge of the apartment block opposite the Mason villa, isn't she?'

Silence.

'Isn't she, Mr Burger? Would you like me to put her on the stand to testify that she recognises you as the man who rented her front top-floor apartment?'

'That's not necessary,' said Burger quietly. 'Yes, I did rent the apartment.'

'Louder please, so all the members of the jury can hear.'

'Yes! I did rent the apartment!'

'For what purpose, Mr Burger?'

'Because I . . . I . . .' again his voice faded into inaudibility, 'I guess I'd become obsessed with Tabitha.'

'You were obsessed,' I said loudly and clearly, 'with Tabitha Mason, as she was then, or Tabitha Matthias as she is now.'

Burger scowled at me when I reminded him that Tabitha was now married, but he nodded his head in agreement.

'So you rented the apartment opposite to keep an eye on the villa, is that right?'

'Yes,' he said, again very quietly.

'To spy on the villa?'

'Yes!'

'And that's why you kept a powerful telescope in that apartment?'

'Yes! If you like! That's why!'

'Were you there on the day of the murder? At the time of the murder?'

'Was I where?' demanded Burger, spitting out the words, fighting back angrily.

'Mr Burger,' I said patiently, 'were you in that apartment, spying on the villa, at the time when the murder was occurring?'

'No I wasn't!' he snapped back.

'No, of course you weren't,' I agreed, 'because you were at the Mason villa committing the murder!'

A huge commotion broke out in the court. Reporters rushed out to call their editors to hold the late editions.

'Mr Bartholomew,' said the judge sternly. 'Take

great care in what you say. It is irresponsible of you to cast accusations if you cannot back them up.'

'I believe I can, your honour,' I replied.

'But Mr Bartholomew,' said Judge Hezion, looking puzzled, 'the evidence we have heard in this court thus far has made it clear that no-one approached the victim's room except the accused, and certainly not the District Attorney.'

Burger stood in the witness box trying hard to look like the injured party as the judge was saying this.

'That is certainly what the evidence has shown so far, your honour.'

'Then how can you . . .?' the judge's voice trailed off, and he looked more puzzled than ever.

'If your honour will permit me to continue, I believe I can explain.'

'I certainly look forward to hearing your explanation, Mr Bartholomew,' said the judge, frank disbelief in his voice.

CHAPTER 40

'When I last picked up the murder weapon, the silver dagger,' I said, 'it was during the committal hearing. As I grasped its handle a splinter of wood entered my thumb.'

'Your honour!' shouted Burger from the witness box, 'Of all the incompetent, irrelevant, immaterial farragoes of rubbish that I have ever heard in a courtroom . . .'

'I do hope that we are going to hear about more than minor personal injuries,' said the judge.

'You are, your honour,' I assured him. 'Because of that incident, on the first day of this trial, I filed a private request for a second forensic examination of the dagger.'

'Why wasn't I told?' snapped Burger, forgetting, for a moment, he was in the witness box.

'Mr Burger,' reprimanded the judge, 'no more outbursts please. This situation is difficult enough as it is, without you adding to it. Continue, Mr Bartholomew.'

'This time I asked the forensic experts to look not at the blade—which certainly has traces of the victim's blood—but the handle. I have the resulting report here and submit it as "defence exhibit B". I can, if necessary, call the forensic scientist himself at a later time to substantiate this report.'

At that point I handed the report up to the judge, and distributed copies to the members of the jury.

'As you can see,' I continued, 'minute amounts of a soft timber were found caught in the intricate carvings in the silver handle of the dagger. Undoubtedly the source of the splinter I encountered. Furthermore, the forensic tests identified the type of timber. It is acacia, a soft timber common in North Africa but rare in the Damascus district.'

I paused for a moment to allow this information to sink in. Then I turned back to the witness box.

'Mr Burger, your brother served in North Africa with the Imperial Roman Army, did he not?'

'So what? How did you know, anyway?'

'Oh, you told me, Mr Burger, when I visited you in your office. In fact, on that occasion I seem to recall seeing some souvenirs that your brother brought back for you from North Africa. Is that right?'

'I suppose so.'

'Some native shields and spears.'

'Your honour, I object. This is of no relevance whatsoever to the murder trial currently before this court!'

'Just answer the questions, Mr Burger,' the judge responded, 'I want to see where this line of inquiry is leading. Continue Mr Bartholomew.'

'Thank you, your honour. Now, Mr Burger, when I was in your office I rearranged the display of spears on your office wall because they looked off-centre to me. But they weren't off-centre at all, were they? That appearance was caused by the fact that one of the spears was missing, wasn't it! Namely, the one you used to kill Malachi Mason!'

The judge banged his gavel to hush the murmur of voices in the court.

'But, Mr Bartholomew,' Judge Hezion protested, 'the evidence has shown, you yourself have admitted, that the murder was committed by the dagger that had been the property of the accused.'

'Quite correct, your honour,' I replied, 'but the dagger was fitted to the end of the spear. I imagine,' I continued, turning back to the witness box, 'that you removed the primitive native spear head, since that would leave a distinctive lacerated wound that might be traced back to you. And in its place fitted the silver dagger that you had stolen months earlier from the home of Dr Tullus Matthias.

'On the day of the murder you were watching from your rented apartment. You saw my client visit Malachi Mason alone, and when you saw a guard placed on the door of the room you seized your opportunity. With your combination spear and dagger weapon concealed under your long, dark-blue cloak you entered the alley that runs beside the Mason villa. There you could stand outside Malachi's room, and look in through the iron bars and see the victim lying there, sound asleep. The bars were many inches apart, so there was plenty of room for you to slip the spear between the bars and in through the window. With the victim sleeping so deeply you were able to move the point of the weapon around on his chest until you found the perfect entry point. Then you pushed it home, and killed him!'

A stunned silence filled the courtroom.

'That groping around with the point of the weapon,' I continued, 'caused the strange scratches on the victim's chest mentioned by Dr Galen at the committal hearing. Have you anything to say, Mr Burger?'

He was silent.

'Nothing? Then I'll continue. You had fitted the dagger to the end of the spear handle in such a way that it could be released. Was it tied in place with a slip knot? Something of that sort I imagine, wasn't it? When the deed was done, you simply pulled the end of the cord in your hand, and you were able to withdraw the spear handle while leaving the dagger embedded firmly in Malachi Mason's heart. There it was doing the job it was meant to do—implicating Dr Tullus Matthias.'

I left the bar table and paced slowly and deliberately towards the witness box.

'That's what happened, isn't it, Mr Burger?'

'Why?' squeaked Burger, suddenly finding his voice. 'Why would I do that? Malachi was a friend of mine, a good friend.'

'But not even good friends are allowed to stand in the way of your ambitions, are they, Mr Burger? You wanted Tabitha Mason, and you wanted her for two reasons. One was that for years you had been obsessed with her, as you have today confessed to this court. But more than that, you wanted her money. With her father dead, and her beloved Tullus executed for his murder, you imagined that she would fall into your arms and marry you, and that all that lovely Mason money would be yours. That's right, isn't it Mr Burger?'

'I have no need to do that!' Burger protested angrily. 'I am a highly paid officer of the state.'

'True,' I agreed, 'very true. Highly paid, but not highly enough. Not enough to support your gambling habits. You ran up massive debts, didn't you? Debts that even favours done for criminals couldn't repay. Winning this case, and therefore, you believed, winning Tabitha, was so important that you 'borrowed' the services of a thug, Otto Strong, from one of your gangster friends to try to frighten me out of town. And your gangster friend, Joel Tree, agreed to help because it was the only way he could see that he'd get the massive gambling debts you owed to him. Isn't that true, Mr Burger?'

Burger remained in stunned and sullen silence.

'The demand that you repay your debts was so heavy that when Tabitha proved to be out of your reach, you set fire to your own penthouse apartment to collect the insurance money to pay the debt. That's what happened, isn't it Mr Burger? Remember, you're under oath, and you are, as you're so fond of telling us, an officer of the court!'

There was a long silence, and then Burger said quietly, 'I refuse to answer on the grounds that to do so may tend to incriminate me.'

That was the moment when I won the case!

The jury retired for less than five minutes, and came back with a unanimous verdict of 'not guilty'. There was wild cheering in the court, Tullus rushed into the arms of his friends. He hugged them. He hugged me. They hugged me. And tears of joy were streaming down many faces.

Amidst the pandemonium I approached the bench.

'Your honour,' I shouted over the noise, 'I ask you to use your judicial power to dismiss the warrant issued against Mrs Tabitha Matthias, on the grounds that it charges her with taking part in a conspiracy which has now been found not to exist.'

'Granted,' said the judge, banging his gavel. He then left the bench to sign the necessary papers.

Tabitha was freed from the cells and within ten minutes had joined us, still milling in the courtroom.

'You're a marvel, Mr Bartholomew,' she said, giving me a hug.

'Yes, I know,' I said modestly. 'And please call me Ben.'

'Well, Barnabas,' I said as he helped me carry my bags to the station the next morning, 'the suffering is over for this group of believers. At least for the time being.'

'For which we are all immensely grateful to you for all you have done, and to our loving and gracious God who has given you the skills that you used so well in this case.'

'Last night,' I said, 'was the happiest prayer meeting I have ever attended.'

'That sort of joy is a glimpse of heaven,' said Barnabas.

I gave my bag to the porter to be packed on the baggage camel, and then said in a quieter voice, 'But the suffering will return, won't it? I mean, in this world, suffering is simply . . . well . . . inevitable . . . isn't it? So it will return?'

'Yes,' said Barnabas, 'but so will our Lord. One day we shall see him face to face, and he shall wipe away every tear. And then suffering will end for his people, and end forever.'

'And until then?'

'We are soldiers under his command. We obey him, and we endure the worst that this world can do to us, knowing that, ultimately, he has conquered this world, and the final victory is his. When we are persecuted we endure it; when we are slandered we answer kindly. We may be treated like the scum of

the earth, the refuse of the world, but we will perse-
vere and patiently endure. Our Master will never
allow our troubles to crush us. His way is fair and
just, and he uses our sufferings to make us ready for
his kingdom, while at the same time he is preparing
judgment and punishment for those who hurt their
fellow human beings.'

FROM MYSTERY TO HISTORY

The character in this book I call Paul Benson is a real historical person of great importance.

He was born—the exact year is not recorded—in the city of Tarsus in ancient Cilicia, now part of modern Turkey. At birth he was given the Hebrew name 'Saul', which was changed to 'Paul' when he became a Christian. For the sake of consistency I have called him 'Paul' throughout this book. By race and religion he was Jewish, but his citizenship was Roman, because Tarsus was a Roman colony.

Like all Jews in the first century Paul belonged to a tribal grouping. In his case, the tribe of Benjamin. This is why I have used Benson as his surname in this book—'son' of 'Ben'.

Tarsus was, as Paul himself later said, 'no mean city'. It was a centre of learning, and scholars generally have assumed that Paul became acquainted with various Greek philosophies and religious cults during his youth there. Later he was educated in Jerusalem under Gamaliel, a great rabbi. The word 'rabbi' means 'teacher'.

In the light of Paul's education and early prominence it is safe to assume that his family was of some means and prominence. He was brought up as part of a very strict Jewish group called the Pharisees. As such he was highly trained in Jewish law and traditions.

It was this highly religious, well-educated, wealthy, aristocratic young man who was given official authority to persecute the early Christians. And he did.

Paul persecuted the believers with great energy and enthusiasm. Firstly in the city of Jerusalem, and then, carrying letters of authority, he set out for the city of Damascus.

It was on the road to Damascus that Paul was confronted by a blinding vision of the risen, living Jesus. He continued to Damascus and there regained his sight and was baptised. He immediately devoted his considerable intellectual skills and energy to telling the story of Jesus, the Lord, in the Jewish synagogues of Damascus. As a result, Paul himself became the object of persecution.

He spent some time preaching in Arabia, then returned to Damascus for three years, before returning to Jerusalem, and later his home town of Tarsus. He was eventually recruited by Barnabas, the same Joseph Barnabas we meet in this book, to help in the growing multiracial church at Antioch, in Syria.

After this Paul went on a number of dangerous missions as a travelling preacher, sometimes accompanied by Barnabas, and sometimes by Silas. His footsteps were often dogged by persecution, assault, and imprisonment.

The last that the New Testament records of Paul he was in Rome, the capital city of the great Empire, in chains and under constant guard—imprisoned for his faith. By this time, Paul had played a crucial role in the growth and spread of Christianity—a role that was to have an effect on human history.

Historians believe that Paul was probably set free after his trial in Rome and may have preached in

Spain. After another arrest he was executed in Rome by Nero about AD 67.

The Bible calls Paul an 'apostle'. That word means 'one who is sent with authority to act on behalf of another'. In other words, an ambassador representing a great ruler. The apostles were those people chosen by Jesus to be eyewitnesses to the events of his life, to see him after his resurrection, and then to tell the world what they knew. Paul was the last person to be recruited as an apostle—and he was personally recruited by Jesus!

You can read Paul's story for yourself in 'The Book of Acts' (in the New Testament part of the Bible). I suggest an easy-to-read modern translation of the Bible such as the *New International Version* or the *Good News Bible*.

If you would like to know more about Paul's story, read *Paul: Apostle of the Free Spirit* by F.F. Bruce, or *The Apostle* by John Pollock. The history of the New Testament, including Paul's role, is retold in an excellent book called *From Bethlehem to Patmos* by Paul Barnett. If you want to examine the historical reliability of the New Testament documents, read *Is the New Testament History?*, also by Paul Barnett.

The Apostle Paul himself wrote a number of important letters, which, together, make up about a third of the New Testament. Perhaps the most important of these is the one called *Romans*. If you would like to study what it means, you can do this with the aid of a book called *How to be a Christian without being Religious* by Fritz Ridenour.

Paul is a man who towers over the pages of human history. He took Christianity to Europe, left the priceless legacy of his writings to the church for all time, and kept his faith to the end.

Who Moved the Stone?

Frank Morison

'. . . The third day he rose again from the dead . . .'

This famous book is addressed to the momentous question: What really happened between the arrest of Jesus in the garden of Gethsemane and the discovery of the empty tomb?

'Fascinating in its lucid, its almost incontrovertible, appeal to the reason.'
– J.D. Beresford

'It is as though a skilled advocate, entirely convinced of the truth of his case, were unravelling the threads of some mystery . . . It has the supreme merit of frankness and sincerity.'
– The Sunday Times

ISBN 0-903843-75-7

OM publishing
CARLISLE, UK

Christianity is Ridiculous
Eighty Big Objections to Believing a Word of It

John Allan

'If God knew we would make a mess of this planet, it was irresponsible of him to create it.'

'Jesus and his earliest followers may have been clever frauds.'

'Some books of the Bible disagree with others.'

'All religions lead to God: the church has no monopoly.'

This is a new edition of *Express Checkout*, the classic which came out of John Allan and Guy Eyre's 'Express Checkout' programme at Greenbelt, designed to help people understand Christian basics.

Comprehensive and user-friendly, the book is made up of eight sections: questions about God, about Jesus, about the Bible, about the church, about conversion, about life and death, about world problems and tragedies, and about being a Christian.

ISBN 1-85078-136-2

publishing
CARLISLE, UK